In 1988 Betty Rowlands won the *Sunday Express*/Veuve Clicquot Crime Short Story of the Year Competition. Her success continued with the publication of eight acclaimed Melissa Craig mysteries. She is an active member of the Crime Writers' Association and regularly gives talks and readings, runs workshops and serves on panels at crime writing conventions.

Betty Rowlands lives in the heart of the Cotswolds where her Melissa Craig mysteries are set and has three grown-up children and four grandchildren.

THE MAN AT THE WINDOW

Graham Shipley has come to the Cotswolds to take up a new teaching appointment and to make a fresh start after the break-up of his marriage. But shortly after his arrival, a young girl is found drowned. Foul play is suspected and Graham's past threatens to catch up with him. In desperation, he turns for help to his new neighbour in Upper Benbury, the crime writer Melissa Craig. She soon discovers that this is not a simple case of murder — there are other more complex and sinister influences at work in the village.

Books by Betty Rowlands
Published by The House of Ulverscroft:

BETTY ROWLANDS

THE MAN AT THE WINDOW

Complete and Unabridged

ULVERSCROFT
Leicester

First published in Great Britain in 2000 by
Hodder and Stoughton
a division of Hodder Headline
London

First Large Print Edition
published 2001
by arrangement with
Hodder and Stoughton Limited
a division of Hodder Headline Plc
London

British Library CIP Data

Rowlands, Betty
    The man at the window.—Large print ed.—
    Ulverscroft large print series: mystery
    1. Craig, Melissa (Fictitious character)—Fiction
    2. Cotswold Hills (England)—Fiction
    3. Detective and mystery stories 4. Large type books
    I. Title
    823.9'14 [F]

    ISBN 0–7089–4395–0

Published by
F. A. Thorpe (Publishing)
Anstey, Leicestershire
Set by Words & Graphics Ltd.
Anstey, Leicestershire
Printed and bound in Great Britain by
T. J. International Ltd., Padstow, Cornwall

This book is printed on acid-free paper

For Len, with love

Prologue

'Well, Mr Shipley, that all seems satisfactory so far.' A momentary smile softened the angular features of the head teacher of St Monica's Preparatory School.

Graham Shipley returned the smile with a feeling of relief; for the first time since the start of the interview he felt an easing of the tension that, despite the diazepam tablet he had swallowed before leaving home, had kept him sitting bolt upright on the uncomfortable chair with his hands gripping his knees.

'Your references are excellent and I am impressed with your enthusiasm for your subject,' Miss Monroe continued as she reassembled the sheets of his CV and slipped them back into the acetate folder in which he had submitted them. 'I am particularly interested in your outline project, 'History on the Hoof' — although I have to confess I find the title somewhat bizarre. I imagine it has some significance that the children will understand?'

Graham smiled again and nodded. 'Oh, I've no doubt they will,' he assured her. Really, he thought, this old bird was almost an anachronism, with her iron-grey hair drawn into a bun, her rimless spectacles, her tailored blouse buttoned up to the neck. He remembered noticing when she entered the room that her skirt fell to a decorous calf-length over her stockinged legs — they were surely stockings, he could not imagine her wearing tights — and that she wore black lace-up shoes. She would not have appeared out of place in a Victorian schoolroom.

Aloud, he explained, 'In its modern colloquial sense 'on the hoof' implies doing something — eating, for example — while on the move.'

Miss Monroe frowned. 'That is something I could not approve,' she declared. 'At St Monica's we insist on correct behaviour at meal-times.'

'Oh quite,' Graham agreed. 'I've used the expression figuratively, simply to imply a sense of activity and personal involvement. History shouldn't be seen as something dry as dust and shut up in books and it isn't only about kings and politics and wars. It's about the way those things affected ordinary people — their work, their homes, their problems and especially their children — and the way what happened in the past influences what goes on today.' He felt himself warming to his theme. 'I plan to open the project by asking the children what they think is meant by the title,' he continued, 'and I expect to generate — '

'Yes, Mr Shipley, you have made your point.' Once again the head allowed herself the ghost of a smile. There was a brief silence before she spoke again. 'I think we have covered everything concerning the appointment itself. There now remains the question of your health . . . '

'I assure you, I'm perfectly fit now.'

' . . . and also of your marital status,' she went on as if she had not heard the interruption. 'As to the first point, your doctor appears confident that you are well enough to take up full-time employment again. May I ask if you are still taking any medication?'

'Only a mild tranquilliser for occasional use, to relieve stress . . . I don't need it very often.' Graham felt the tension rising again, threatening to turn to panic. Why had she found it necessary to touch on his private life? How deeply would she probe? He realised at that moment how badly he wanted the opportunity to work in a small, independent school such as this, tucked away in its peaceful rural setting, far removed from the rough and tumble of a state comprehensive. It held the promise of relief from the hideous chain of circumstances that had brought him to the brink of disaster, in the process destroying his marriage and threatening to end his teaching career.

Miss Monroe was nodding as if she approved of his response. 'Generally speaking,' she said, 'stress levels among my staff are, I believe, fairly low. Naturally, problems do arise from time to time, but it is our policy to tackle them as a team and we give one another mutual support — as Christians should.' She paused, as if to give him the opportunity to comment, but he merely nodded and waited for her to continue.

'As you are no doubt aware,' she went on, 'this school is an Anglican foundation and we try to uphold the beliefs and moral principles which many people nowadays unfortunately find inconvenient. You mentioned earlier that you are a committed Christian, and yet you are divorced.' Her tone challenged him to explain this apparent contradiction.

For a moment, he wished he had put 'Single' or even 'Widower' on his application form. He had been tempted, but had on reflection decided that it was better to be honest. The former response would have made him a potential target for any lone woman in search of a partner, a prospect that in his present state of mind filled him with

4

horror. The latter would not merely have invited sympathy, but also created the need to invent a background to support it. The truth gave him a valid and understandable reason for being reserved about his private life.

'I was the innocent party, but I'm not prepared to go into details,' he said quietly. 'And I am not involved with another woman — nor do I intend to be,' he added, reading an implied question in the hint of a raised eyebrow.

'I admire your discretion. Had you attempted to justify your situation by vilifying your wife, I would have hesitated to believe your story . . . or to offer you an appointment on my staff. May I take it that you are still interested in joining us in September?'

It took a moment for Graham to grasp the fact that the interview — it had been almost an inquisition — was over, that his time in the wilderness was at an end, that he was on the verge of regaining his status as a man with a profession and a regular job who could look the world in the eye without fear or shame.

'Yes, I most certainly am,' he assured her.

'Good. Then let us consider the practical details.'

1

It was with a feeling of thankfulness that Melissa Craig, bestselling writer of crime fiction, turned off the main road and drove slowly in third gear on the final stage of her journey from London to the Cotswold village where, a few years ago, she had made her home. She was returning after a short stay with friends; for a few days she had enjoyed the change of scene and the lively pace of life in the capital, but despite having spent the greater part of her fifty-odd years there, nowadays it was only in the unpolluted air and comparative tranquillity of the Gloucestershire countryside that she felt entirely at ease.

Ahead, the lane wound its leisurely way downhill for a short distance and crossed a stone bridge spanning a stream before tackling the steep half-mile climb the other side. Melissa lowered the window, delighting in the sound of birdsong that drove the roar of motorway traffic from her head and the caress of the gentle breeze that cleared its fumes from her lungs. Soon, she would be back in Hawthorn Cottage, enjoying the stunning view across the secluded valley with its quietly flowing brook, cattle grazing on the sloping pasture and the patch of woodland rising to the skyline.

Rounding a bend she caught sight of the single-decker bus which twice a week ran a shuttle service between Stowbridge and the outlying villages. It was just pulling away after dropping off a handful of passengers — four teenage youngsters, three middle-aged women and one elderly man — at the bottom of the hill. She slowed to a crawl to allow it to get well ahead on its slow grind in first gear to Upper Benbury and idly watched as the four adults set off towards the turning to its twin village of Lower Benbury. The women walked ahead in a gossiping group while trudging slowly along behind them, clutching a plastic supermarket carrier, was the unmistakable figure of Tommy Judd, a local character who lived in a tumbledown cottage in the woods and went around winter and summer in the same tattered overcoat and down-at-heel boots.

The youngsters doubled back to the bridge, where they leaned their elbows on the parapet, apparently deep in conversation. As she drew nearer Melissa recognised the pony-tail of Billy Daniels, the elf-locks of Dave Potter and the cropped head of Gary

Tanner, all students at the local comprehensive. Slightly apart from the group of lads was Gary's younger sister Becky, a pert, pretty fourteen-year-old with a swinging mane of glossy chestnut hair. Melissa tooted gently on her horn and waved and they gave brief nods of recognition as she passed. 'Don't forget your French lesson this afternoon, Becky,' she called, and the girl gave a cheeky grin as she waved back.

'I'll be there, Mrs Craig,' she promised.

Melissa completed her journey, put the car in the garage, dumped her suitcase in the porch and spent a few minutes leaning on the field gate opposite her front door. Yes, it was all there, just as she had left it. Other things might change, but the glacial valley had a timeless quality that never failed to soothe. There followed a twinge of nostalgia as she thought how good it would have been if her friend Iris Ash, the owner — and until almost a year ago the occupant — of the adjoining Elder Cottage, had been there to welcome her back with a cup of herbal tea and home-made nut cookies, and put her through a series of yoga exercises to help her unwind after the trip. But last October, Iris had married Jack Hammond and gone to live with him in the South of France. Their departure shortly after former Detective Chief Inspector

Kenneth Harris went off to begin his new career in America had left a huge gap in Melissa's life. On reflection, it seemed that she had missed Iris more than Ken. Her relationship with her ex-lover had been on the turbulent side, particularly towards the end; that with her eccentric artistic neighbour had over the years developed into an enduring, undemanding and mutually supportive friendship.

She heard a car approaching behind her. The gravel crunched beneath its wheels as it bumped slowly along the uneven track leading to the cottages and pulled up a short distance away. There was a creaking of hinges, an increased revving of the engine that faded and died as the car was driven into the garage, the muffled sound of the door being closed followed by a gentle thud of wood against wood and the scrape of a key in the lock. The new tenants, presumably, returning from their day's excursion. There had been a succession of them throughout the summer, for the most part city folk escaping from the hurly-burly of urban life, some quietly enjoying the peace of the countryside, others shattering it with their noisy comings and goings. At least, Melissa reflected as she turned her head with a smile and a polite 'Good afternoon', these latest arrivals didn't over-rev their engines or slam doors.

She was expecting a couple, but it was a man on his own. He was fortyish, on the tall side, thin, clean-shaven and bespectacled. His eyes were clear and candid and his manner pleasant enough, but his smile as he returned her greeting held a hint of reserve.

'I'm Mel Craig,' she said. 'I live here.' She nodded in the direction of Hawthorn Cottage.

'How do you do, Mrs Craig. My name's Graham Shipley.' He hesitated for a moment before saying. 'I've rented Elder Cottage until next March.'

His voice was a light tenor; the hand that took hers and held it briefly in a firm clasp had long, tapering fingers. She wondered if he was an artist, or possibly a musician. At the same time he had a bookish look about him, although the fact that he showed no reaction to her name suggested that crime fiction — or at least, her particular contribution to the genre — was not on his reading list.

'Iris — Mrs Hammond — mentioned that someone had taken Elder Cottage on a six-month lease, but I hadn't realised you were moving in so soon,' she remarked. 'Up to now it's just been let by the week to holiday-makers.'

'It's an idyllic spot for a holiday,' he remarked, with a glance across the valley as it lay soaking up the late August sunshine. 'I know this part of the country, I used to — ' He broke off and a shadow flickered across his face.

She waited for him to finish, but he had switched his attention to the bunch of keys in his hand as if trying to decide which one would open the front door. He spoke with a trace of a Midlands accent and she was about to ask where he came from, but although the shadow had faded she had the impression that a shutter had come down in its place. Her writer's curiosity was immediately aroused, but she sensed that he would stonewall any attempt on her part to enquire into his background and it was clear that he had no interest in learning more about herself.

'I hope you'll enjoy your stay here,' she said. 'Upper Benbury's a lively little village and the people are very friendly. Mrs Foster's shop is quite well stocked, by the way,' she added, briefly eyeing the bulging supermarket carrier he held in one hand. 'I do hope you'll give it a try. We're very lucky to have it — so many small shops are going out of business nowadays.'

He nodded absently without replying.

Having found the right key, he turned away and entered Elder Cottage, closing the door behind him without a further glance in her direction.

'Well, that put you in your place,' Melissa said to herself with a shrug. If he didn't want to be sociable that was his lookout. She glanced at her wristwatch; it would soon be time for Becky's lesson and she had unpacking to do. Humming a tune, she went indoors.

She would have felt a little less light-hearted had she known what was occupying the minds of the four youngsters back at the bridge.

2

A pair of mallards glided out from under the bridge and Billy Daniels picked up a stone and threw it at them. They took off with startled squawks and a noisy flapping of wings. All three lads broke into foolish, braying laughter, but Becky rounded on them.

'Why d'you do that?' she demanded. 'They wasn't doin' you no harm.'

'Fun,' sniggered Billy.

'You're stupid!' she shouted, bunching her fists. 'All of you, stupid!'

'Shut up Becky Tanner or I'll clout you one,' threatened Dave Potter, a mean look in his hard, pale eyes.

Becky flinched, even though she knew he would not dare touch her in front of her brother. 'Don't let him hit me, Gary,' she whined, sidling up to him.

'Leave her be, Dave. She likes to think she's grown up, but she's only a kid.' Becky put out her tongue at him, then lapsed into a sulky silence.

'She's too bloody cheeky,' muttered Billy as he resumed his study of the water.

14

'She's right, though, we are stupid,' said Dave. The others started at him, dumb-founded.

'You gone soft in the head or somethin', stickin' up for a girl?' said Billy.

'Not stickin' up for nobody, just statin' a fact. We came here to think how to get ticket money for Friday evening, not chuck stones at bloody ducks.'

'All right, clever dick, since you're so smart, you got any ideas?'

'I just had one.' Dave jerked his tousled head in the direction taken by their elderly fellow passenger. 'Tommy Judd.'

'What about him?'

'My Dad reckons he's a miser. He draws his pension every week, but he never goes to the pub or buys tobacco or new clothes nor nothin'. So what's he do with his money?' The other two lads turned to look at him, the same idea already half-formed in their minds, while Becky stood scornfully aloof and Dave answered his own question by saying, 'My Dad reckons he hides it somewhere indoors.'

Now their attention was really caught. 'Maybe under the floor in front of the fire,' suggested Gary. 'Like that old git in the book.'

'Yeah, you could be right,' said Billy eagerly. The boys were reading *Silas Marner* at school and Becky had heard them talking about it, but it had never entered their heads that old Tommy might be hoarding treasure like George Eliot's solitary weaver.

'Maybe he gets it out and counts it every day,' said Dave, his pale eyes glistening at the thought. 'I vote we go and look.'

'I think that's a daft idea,' said Becky. 'You won't find no money hidden there.'

The lads stared at her; for the moment they had forgotten she was with them. 'How would you know?' Gary jeered. 'You been there first and nicked it yourself?' The others joined in his scornful laughter.

''Course not.' Becky flushed under their mockery, but she stood her ground. 'If you're thinkin' of breakin' into Tommy's cottage, forget it.'

'What's it to you?'

She scowled at her brother like an angry kitten. 'Use yer brains, Gary Tanner. If you get caught our Dad'll leather you, and then you'll never get to the rounders match, leave alone the barbie 'n' disco after.'

'We won't get there anyway if we don't have the money.'

'That's your problem,' said Becky with a smug smile. 'I got my ticket.'

'You what?' Gary eyed her suspiciously. 'Where d'you get the cash?'

'Dad gives me pocket-money, same as you. You spend yours, I've bin savin' mine.'

'So what did you use this afternoon? You bin shoppin', ain't you? What you got in there?' He made a sudden grab at the bright pink plastic bag she had been concealing under the denim jacket she carried over her arm.

'Give that here!' Becky shrieked, but he yanked it away from her and pulled out its contents. The other two lads whistled in derision at the sight of the scarlet mini-skirt and the scanty knitted top, but Gary looked at his sister aghast.

'You're never goin' to wear these!' he exclaimed. 'You're too young.'

'That's what you keep saying, but I'm nearly grown up, I'd have you know.' Becky tilted her head at a provocative angle, pouted and waggled her hips. Under the close-fitting T-shirt her young breasts made two soft mounds. Billy and Dave looked at her with new eyes. Ever since she was a toddler they had thought of her as merely Gary's kid sister who insisted on tagging along and making a nuisance of herself when they wanted to be alone to do boys' things. All of a sudden she had developed a strange new quality that found echoes in their own adolescent sexuality.

'You're still too young to wear this kind of stuff,' Gary repeated.

'Who says?' Becky reclaimed the garments and stuffed them back into the bag. 'I'm tall for my age — I could pass for sixteen with a bit of make-up.'

'You reckon our Dad'll let you wear make-up?'

'Oh, leave it!' said Dave impatiently. 'We got more important things to talk about, remember?'

'You're right.' Gary glanced at his wrist-watch and gave his sister a shove. 'It's time you went home and got ready for your lesson with Mrs Craig.'

Reluctantly, Becky went up the lane, dragging her feet, while the three lads settled down to some serious plotting.

* * *

'I see you're wearing the French *tricolore*,' Melissa teased as Becky, her good humour completely restored, came bouncing into the kitchen, dumped her bag of books on the table and settled on a chair. 'Did you buy that gear in Paris?'

'Nah, got it in Stowbridge this afternoon. Cool, innit?' Becky got to her feet again and did a little pirouette to show off her outfit

18

before sitting down again with her long, slim legs stretched out in front of her. The scarlet mini-skirt just managed to cover her crotch before stretching itself sensuously over her things; above it a skinny top in royal blue ended a few inches short of the waistband and revealed a strip of tender white flesh and the girl's navel coyly nestling in the gap between the two garments.

'Very cool,' Melissa agreed. 'What does your Dad think of it?'

Becky chuckled. 'He ain't seen it yet. He'll carry on a bit, I guess, but I can get round him.'

'So, how was Paris?' Melissa asked the question in French, but Becky, after a few stumbling phrases and finding her command of the language inadequate to cope with her enthusiasm, quickly lapsed into English. 'One of the French teachers was, like, really *cool* . . . he had this *dreamy* little black beard and black eyes and he spoke English with this *fabulous* accent — '

'I thought everyone was supposed to speak French all the time,' Melissa interposed.

'Yeah, well, we were, but now and again, when we went on the metro and things, like, to make sure we all understood . . . anyway, his name's Marcel and I asked him for his address so's I could write to him and I gave him mine so's he could write back, like, to correct my mistakes — '

'Then I expect to see a great improvement in your French,' Melissa declared in her best schoolmarmish manner.

This made no impression whatsoever on Becky, who assumed a knowing look and wiggled her body suggestively as she insisted that her French was *loads* better. 'I think older men are *loads* more interesting than boys,' she confided. Her brown eyes sparkled roguishly and her prettily curved mouth twitched so engagingly that Melissa could only smile in response. 'That reminds me,' Becky went on. 'Who's the guy in the cottage next door?'

'That's Mr Shipley. He's rented it for six months. Why do you ask?'

'He was up at the window when I got here, looking out. I caught his eye and he gave me ever such a funny look — '

'What do you mean, funny?'

Becky considered, her head tilted to one side. 'Sort of *mysterious*,' she said after a moment. 'I think he looks really cool. What's he do?'

'I've no idea. I've hardly spoken to him, I'm afraid.'

'Oh well, I expect I'll see him around.'

'Never mind him now,' Melissa said and

added in French, 'Let's get on with our lesson, shall we?'

'Okay.'

'In French, please.'

'French people say okay,' Becky pointed out, but all she got in reply to that was, '*Okay, explique-moi ça en Français,*' and from then on the lesson proceeded smoothly.

At the end of it Melissa was pleased to be able to compliment the girl on her improvement. 'I hope you'll keep it up,' she said. 'If you need any help with your letters to Marcel — you'll be writing in French, of course — don't be afraid to ask.'

Becky giggled. 'Not sure I'd want you to see what I write,' she said archly.

'I hope neither of you will write anything your Dad wouldn't approve of,' Melissa said severely. 'He's sure to ask to see the letters.'

'Won't understand them, will he?' Becky glanced at her wristwatch. 'Is that the time? Dad'll be cross if I'm late for tea. What d'you want me to do for next week?'

They agreed on a topic to be discussed at the next lesson and Becky departed. Melissa saw her to the door and stood there for a moment, watching her strutting along the track on her platform soles, swinging her bag of books and flicking back the glossy hair that tumbled round her shoulders. As she passed

Elder Cottage she glanced up. Evidently Graham Shipley was at one of the windows, for she gave a dazzling smile and a jaunty wave of her hand as she passed.

Melissa went indoors with a sense of disquiet. She had never met the girl's mother, but she had heard from those who had known the family for years that Becky had inherited both her looks and her personality. She had also heard it said that the consensus in the village, when Jake Tanner brought home his bride, was that the daughter of a wealthy landowner accustomed to a glittering social life would never settle down to being a farmer's wife — a judgement that was confirmed when she abandoned her husband and children, then aged five and seven, and eloped with a South American polo player. Her family had offered to adopt Becky and Gary, but Jake Tanner had steadfastly refused to give them up or accept any form of help other than that provided by the State. He was hard-working, his farm was well run and moderately successful, and it was generally acknowledged that he had done a good job of bringing up the youngsters. All the same, his neighbours found it curious that he should be particularly strict with his son, a steady lad who took after his father, while being over-indulgent towards his pretty, precocious daughter. Melissa suspected that, rather than blame the wife he had by all accounts idolised, he had held the foreign interloper entirely responsible for the break-up of his marriage and now persuaded himself that the girl was as innocent and virtuous as he had believed her mother to be.

She went back indoors and sat down to write to Iris and Jack. Having responded to a few questions and commented on the news in Iris's latest letter, she brought her friends up to date with recent events in the village.

Mr Shipley moved in while I was up in town for a few days. I met him for the first time this afternoon and from the way he froze me out when I began telling him what a jolly nice lot we Benburyites are, I don't think we're going to develop much of a relationship. He seems civilised and he's certainly quiet, which is a blessing after the last lot. There were times when I really thought they must be throwing the furniture at each other — Gloria and I expected the place to be wrecked after they left, but apart from enough empties to fill a bottle bank everything was surprisingly normal.

The weather has been hot and sunny for several days now after a week of heavy rain and the farmers are at last getting on well with the harvest. The barbecue and rounders match that had to be cancelled because the field was a quagmire has been rescheduled for next Friday. I wonder if I'll be able to coax Mr Shipley to join in the fun — I think it's unlikely but I'll give it a try.

Becky Tanner has learned a lot of French during her school trip — not all of it the sort of thing her teacher would approve, I'm afraid! She's fallen in love with one of the French teachers and the little monkey has persuaded him to write to her — to help with her French, of course! I doubt if that will last long — I've never found written work to be her strong point.

She says she thinks older men are 'cool' and she soon spotted my new neighbour, said he was at the window when she arrived and gave her a 'mysterious' (her description) look. Needless to say, he's cool as well! I'm afraid that girl is her mother's daughter — poor old Jake is going to have trouble with her before long, but as we all know, he won't hear a word against her.

Do you remember the formidable duo at Benbury Manor, Mrs Waghorne and Miss Lane? They have suddenly produced a brother, Gideon, who has retired early, on

the grounds of ill-health they say, and come to live with them. He was in the shop with them the other day and they introduced me. He seems very charming and I can't say he looks particularly delicate — on the contrary, he's quite chubby, with rosy cheeks and an angelic smile, rather like an elderly choirboy. He also has a mischievous twinkle in his eye which makes me wonder whether he has an interesting past. Perhaps his sisters have decided they have to keep an eye on him.
Watch this space!

Melissa closed her letter with the usual messages, sealed it and strolled into the village to catch the evening post. On her return, she happened to glance at the upstairs windows of Elder Cottage. For a second, she thought she saw a faint movement, then told herself that it must have been her imagination. Nevertheless, she had an uncanny feeling that Graham Shipley was up there, watching.

3

Feeling the need for fresh air, Graham set off
for a walk along the valley. The woman who
had introduced herself as Mel Craig was
working in the garden of Hawthorn Cottage
as he passed; she smiled and waved and he
forced himself to nod and smile in return. He
wanted to ask her about the girl, who she
was, whether she would be coming again and
when and how often, but felt it unwise. He
hurried by without a word.

The air was still and the late afternoon sun
had a warm, comforting glow. The footpath
ran for a while beside a brook that reflected
the cloud-dappled blue of the sky and gurgled
softly as it tumbled over loose stones. A male
pheasant startled him by rising from the
ground almost under his feet with a harsh
cackle and a violent whirring of wings. From
the woods on either side came other, less
familiar calls and tantalising glimpses of
smaller birds darting to and fro. He felt
frustrated by being unable to identify them;
tomorrow he would buy the bird book he had
promised himself.

He returned to the cottage, refreshed and

ready for his supper. He put some potatoes on to cook and was just starting to fry the sausages and bacon he had brought home from the supermarket when the telephone rang. He felt uneasy; so far as he knew, the only person who had his number was Miss Monroe and he could not imagine her calling him at this time of day. But it was a man's voice that greeted him.

'Graham Shipley? My name's Sam Rogers — I'm the Deputy Head of St Monica's. Milly Monroe gave me your number and I thought I'd call to say, 'Welcome aboard'!'

The voice had a warm, cheerful quality and Graham was conscious that his somewhat hesitant response of, 'That's very kind of you,' must have sounded stiff and formal. This did not, however, appear to offend the caller, who continued in the same breezy manner, 'When I'm not doing the paperwork, I take PE and sport. I believe your subject's history?'

'It's my special interest, but I take general subjects as well.'

'Oh, understood, we're all into them. What about games?'

'Not really.'

'Pity. I was hoping I could rope you in to help me with this rounders match next Friday.'

27

'Rounders match — before the start of term?'

'Oh, nothing to do with the school, dear boy. It's a fund-raiser for the village hall — there's to be a barbecue and a disco later on. Haven't you seen the posters?'

'Yes of course, but I wasn't planning to — ' Graham began, but Sam broke in. 'But you must come,' he insisted. 'It'll be a great opportunity for you to get to know people. I'm trying to persuade a few of our parents to bring their little darlings along, although most of the kids in the village go to the local primary or Stowbridge Comprehensive. Besides, I'm relying on you to captain one of the teams. Boys against girls . . . which would you prefer? Grown-ups as well, no age limit so long as they can stand up and hold a bat.'

'But I haven't played rounders since I was a kid, I can't even remember the rules — '

'There aren't that many and I'll be explaining them on the night. Just come along and join in the fun.'

Graham longed to decline to have anything to do with the event. The last thing he wanted was 'to get to know' anyone in the village, but apart from having a persuasive manner, Sam Rogers was a senior member of staff at St Monica's and he sensed that, despite his 'hail-fellow-well-met' telephone manner, he would not take kindly to being crossed. There was no way out; he heard himself agreeing to captain the boys' team, acknowledged the warm words of thanks, entered the details in his diary and went back to cooking his supper. As he sat down to eat it, he found himself wondering whether the girl whose name he did not know, but who had waved so provocatively as she passed beneath his window, would also be 'joining in the fun' on Friday evening.

★ ★ ★

'Mum, I've told everyone I'm going and I've paid for my ticket. It's my own money and you can't stop me.'

Jean Wilcox felt her hold over her daughter draining away as she faced the challenge from the other side of the breakfast table. She told herself that it had been a mistake to let Cissie take on that Saturday job in Mrs Foster's shop in Upper Benbury. She was getting too big for her boots altogether, picking up fancy ideas from people she hardly knew and — what in Jean's eyes was even worse — getting to know lads from the comprehensive who sometimes hung around waiting for her outside the shop. Jean was convinced that her daughter had learned from them things

29

no decently-brought-up fifteen-year-old girl should know, much less speak about. She believed this because of something Cissie had asked her the other day — and she had roundly ticked her off for indulging in 'dirty talk'.

Jean had good cause to know what hob-nobbing with boys that age could lead to. As it happened, most of the kids here in Lower Benbury were too young to be a danger, although you read some terrible things in the paper nowadays about even twelve-year-olds having it off with little girls barely out of nappies. At least Cissie had so far been safe during term-time, having won an assisted place at one of the few girls only schools left in the county. But the holidays had become an increasing cause of anxiety . . . and soon she would be going on to sixth form college and who knew what undesirable types were lying in wait for her there?

'I mean it, Mum.' Cissie's voice was steely; she was holding her ground in a way that filled Jean with dread. 'All the other kids in the village are going, and a lot of their parents too. Come with me, why don't you?'

'Pay five pounds for a bit of burnt sausage and a half-cooked chicken leg that'll give me guts-ache as like as not? No thanks. And I don't want you going neither.'

'You don't have to worry about the food. Mrs Foster's in charge of the barbecue and I know she'll make sure everything's cooked proper. You ought to see how fussy she is in the shop, checking nothing's past its sell-by —'

'Just the same, five pounds is still a rip-off.'

'It's to raise funds for the village hall. It needs a new kitchen.'

Recognising that she had lost that argument, Jean changed tactics. 'And what's all this about a disco? If you think you're staying out till midnight —'

'Oh Mum, it won't go on that late. Anyway, you'd enjoy the disco, wouldn't you? You said the other day how you used to go to clubs and dances —'

'Yes, and look where it got me. In the family way when I wasn't much older than you are now.' A wave of bitterness swept over Jean as she recalled the night when Cissie was conceived, against her will although she had fought and screamed and done her best to struggle free. She had been too ashamed to tell her own mother about it at the time and when she found herself pregnant and they went to the police she was told she had left it too late for them to be able to do anything. She knew hardly anything about the young man except that he'd told her his mother was

31

English and his father Chinese. She met him at a night-club and found the faintly oriental look that gave him an air of mystery so devastatingly attractive that she stayed with him for the entire evening, completely forgetting her promise to her mother that she would stick with her friends and come home with them. He had offered to walk her to the bus station and on the way dragged her into a dark alley. She was reminded of him every time she looked at Cissie's almond-shaped eyes and saw the slight upward twist to the corner of her mouth which gave her the appearance of smiling at some highly pleasurable secret.

'Mum, I'll be all right, honest.' Cissie dropped the defiant attitude and became sweetly reasonable. 'There's lots of people going that you know . . . Mrs Waghorne and Miss Lane and their brother . . . and Mr Rogers who teaches at that fancy private school near Carston. He's really nice, not a bit stuck-up. I've promised him I'll go and play rounders and I'm not going to back out now.'

Cissie had very craftily given her mother a reason to capitulate without losing face. This was a watershed and Jean knew it. For years she had cherished and protected her daughter, directing her, making every decision for her, closing her mind to the thought that this could not go on for ever, that one day she would slip the leash for the first time.

'Well, if they're all going to be there, I suppose it'll be all right,' she said reluctantly and the battle — for it had been a battle, although no tempers had been lost or voices raised — was over.

★ ★ ★

'I'm not at all convinced that it's wise of us to allow Gideon to attend this barbecue affair on Friday,' said Esther Lane to her widowed sister Judith Waghorne as they cleared away the supper things. Their brother had disappeared into the sitting-room and turned on the television to watch a football match so there was no risk of their conversation being overheard. Just the same, Esther made sure the kitchen door was properly closed before adding in a lower voice, 'Some of the village girls are very, well, forward — ' Her colourless mouth pursed in disapproval.

'I don't see how we can prevent him, short of locking him in his room and we can't very well do that,' Judith said mildly. 'He was telling everyone after church on Sunday that we're all going to be there. He's even promised Mr Rogers to join in the rounders match if he can be allowed a runner.'

'He's sure to pick on some pretty girl to do the running and — '

'I'm sure Mr Rogers won't allow *that* — the match is going to be boys against girls, he said. Try not to worry, dear — it's only a bit of harmless amusement. It's in a good cause and we'll be there to keep an eye on him.'

'Yes, I suppose so. Anyway, it's too late to do anything about it now.' Esther gave a resigned shake of the head. She opened the dishwasher and began loading the plates and cutlery as Judith passed them to her. 'I must say, though, I'm beginning to wonder whether we did the right thing, inviting him to live with us. A house of retreat might have been more suitable, out of the reach of temptation — '

'We talked it over very carefully at the time,' Judith reminded her. 'And he assured us that he's learned his lesson. He made us a solemn promise — '

Esther frowned. 'That's as may be,' she interrupted. 'I was in the shop with him last Saturday and the way he was looking at that Tanner girl — '

'Young Becky? Well, it's no wonder is it, the way she goes around in skirts that barely cover her knickers. It's enough to make anyone stare. I'm surprised her father allows it, especially after the way her mother carried on.'

'Well, you know what Jake Tanner's like,' Esther pointed out. 'Becky's the apple of his eye and he won't hear a word against her. Not that anyone would dare say such a word, with that temper of his — '

'Yes, and you can imagine what he'd do to anyone who laid a finger on her. Gideon knows that as well as any of us.'

'But Becky Tanner isn't the only girl in the village and we know that Gideon has this terrible weakness — '

' — and it's our duty, as his sisters, to help him overcome that weakness,' said Judith earnestly. 'That's why we're going to this affair next Friday, isn't it? We won't let him out of our sight.'

'We can't control his thoughts. There's temptation everywhere.'

Judith laid a hand on her sister's arm. 'I know dear, but we must give him the chance of proving himself strong enough to resist it. We must watch over him and pray for him. Why don't we offer a prayer for him now?' Without waiting for a response, she folded her hands and closed her eyes and Esther, after a moment's hesitation, did the same. 'Dear Lord,' said Judith softly, 'Watch over

our brother and lead him not into temptation, Amen.'

'Amen,' Esther repeated in a harsh whisper.

'Come now,' said Judith in her normal
voice. 'Let's make some coffee and take a cup
in to him. Perhaps we should stay and watch
the football. You never know, it might be
entertaining.' She reached for the kettle,
affecting not to notice the slightly contemptuous expression that flitted across her sister's
thin features.

4

'That Mr Shipley's a strange one,' Mrs Foster remarked as with a large two-pronged fork she prodded and turned the sausages, burgers and chicken portions sizzling on the barbecue set up outside the village hall in Upper Benbury. From a nearby field, lent for the occasion by farmer Jake Tanner, came the occasional thwack of stick against ball, shouted instructions, cries of encouragement or derision, the odd protest — promptly settled by Sam Rogers, whose authoritative baritone rang out above the clamour — and the occasional round of applause.

Melissa Craig, who had volunteered to help with the food and was struggling in the mild but lively breeze with a large roll of white paper with which she was covering a pair of wooden trestle-tables, acknowledged that Graham Shipley did seem to be a bit of a loner. 'I thought about suggesting he came along to the barbecue this evening, but I never got around to it,' she continued, when she at last managed to secure the paper with drawing pins. She began setting out paper plates, napkins, baskets of bread rolls, bowls of salad and squashy containers of mustard, mayonnaise and tomato sauce. 'I was surprised when I heard he'd agreed to help with the rounders match.'

'Ah, that was Mr Rogers' doing,' said Mrs Foster. 'Mr Shipley starts at his school in September.'

'Really? Is he a teacher?'

'Been living next door to you for a week and you never knew that!' Mrs Foster's plump features, pink from the heat of the barbecue, registered mild astonishment. The minutiae of other people's lives were meat and drink to her and it was difficult for her to accept that there were those who found them less than enthralling.

'I've only set eyes on him a couple of times,' Melissa explained. 'I was away when he moved in and since I got back I've been too busy with a new book to take much notice of him.'

'Ah, well — ' Mrs Foster gave a little toss of her snowy head as if to imply that such eccentricities had to be accepted, if not fully understood, by ordinary folk. As proprietress of the only shop serving Upper and Lower Benbury, and having a talent worthy of a gossip columnist for extracting information, she acted as a clearing-house for the dissemination of news about the inhabitants of the twin villages: their state of health, where they were going for their holidays, whose varicose veins were currently being treated, which house was being extended, who was getting married, baptised or buried and even — although such nuggets were shared 'in the strictest confidence, mind you' with only the favoured few — who was 'carrying on' with whom. From the mechanics at the garage who regularly popped into the shop to buy snacks and drinks she knew whose car had failed its MoT and who might shortly be expected to appear in the village in a new one. So it came as no surprise to Melissa that she had already picked up a few titbits about the new tenant of Elder Cottage. The temptation to try to extract more was irresistible.

'I don't think he's a local man — ' she said tentatively and Mrs Foster took the bait with glee.

'Comes from somewhere near Birmingham,' she said. 'Used to teach in a comprehensive, so Mr Rogers told me. Tough lot up there,' she went on, implying by intonation that the city was in a far-off, barbaric land instead of a neighbouring county. 'Too much of a strain for him, perhaps — he looks a sensitive sort of gentleman. He'll find it quieter down here.'

A rousing cheer and prolonged clapping put an end to further speculation and Mrs Foster began wielding her fork with renewed energy. 'Sounds like they've done playing,' she remarked as she shifted the cooked items to one side to make room for a further batch. 'They'll be as hungry as bears.'

'And thirsty,' commented the rector, the Reverend John Hamley, who had hurried away from the field of play in advance of the rest to take charge of the drinks table.

'So who won, then?' asked Mrs Foster.

'It was a draw.' He began pouring beer and fruit juice into plastic tumblers. 'Sam Rogers is talking about a play-off after supper, but I doubt if it'll happen. The youngsters will be keen to get the disco started and I don't suppose the older ones will feel inclined to do any more running around — and anyway, it'll soon be too dark. Ah, here come the five thousand.'

A cheerful crowd came surging up the lane in waves, making a bee-line for the food and drink. For a while, Melissa's attention was focused entirely on doling out helpings of salad before the chattering queue moved on to receive their allocation from the barbecue.

'Only one of each to start with,' said Mrs Foster firmly when Gary Tanner and his friends pleaded for extra sausages. 'Come back later for seconds when everyone else has been served.'

'You can give Gary my sausage,' called Becky Tanner, who was a couple of places behind her brother in the queue. 'I have to watch my figure,' she explained, flipping her hair back from her face and shooting a pert glance up at Graham Shipley, at whom the remark was apparently directed. She was standing immediately in front of him and it seemed to Melissa that she kept unnecessarily close to him as the queue shuffled along. He paid no attention to her, but kept his eyes focused on Alice Hamley, who had been next in line to him until Becky, with a cheeky ''Scuse me!' slithered in between them. Alice was praising his performance as captain of the boys' team and he was listening politely enough, but it seemed to Melissa that he was far from comfortable.

'Was it a good match?' asked Mrs Foster as she served him with a chicken leg and invited him to help himself to bread and seasonings.

'I think so. Everyone seemed to enjoy it,' he replied woodenly and Melissa mentally added, *Everyone but you, by the look of it*, as he took a glass of fruit juice from the drinks table. Becky, evidently piqued at being ignored, accepted her food without a word and glared after him before flouncing off to join her brother and his friends.

After a moment's hesitation, Graham wandered over to where a few of the younger children were sitting on rugs to eat their supper. He squatted down beside them and Melissa noticed with interest how eagerly they greeted him; one freckle-faced lad whom she recognised as Wayne, the ten-year-old son of her cleaning lady Gloria Parkin, moved up and urged him to 'Sit down 'ere, sir,' while his elder brother Darren offered a sausage — politely declined — from his own plate. It was the first time she had seen him smile, and the effect was heart-warming.

'He's well at home with kids of that age,' said a voice at her elbow. 'Handles them just right. I reckon he's going to be a real asset at St Monica's.' Sam Rogers, tucking into a burger generously laced with mustard, nodded towards the little group.

'It's the first time I've seen him looking relaxed,' she replied. 'I've tried the usual neighbourly approaches, but he gives the impression he just wants to be left alone. I didn't even know he was a teacher until Mrs Foster told me.'

Sam took another bite from his burger before replying. When he was free to speak again he said with a chuckle, 'I think he's scared of women. Young Becky Tanner was trying to chat him up during the match and he froze like a rabbit caught in a searchlight.'

'I know what you mean. She was giving him the come-hither while they were queuing for their food a few moments ago and he tried to pretend she wasn't there.'

'He'll have to watch his step.' Sam's round, good-humoured face became serious. 'Girls that age can be a real menace and that one looks a natural trouble-maker. Is it true the mother took off with some playboy or other?'

'A wealthy polo player, so I'm told. I don't know the full story — it all happened before I came to the village. I once heard Mrs Foster say she was a 'poor little rich girl' who got tired of playing at being a farmer's wife. Jake never speaks about it, but I can imagine he was pretty cut up at the time.'

'Understandable. And from the look of her, the girl is her mother's daughter. He should keep an eye on her.'

'That's part of the trouble — he idolises her and in his eyes she can do no wrong, yet he's really strict where young Gary's concerned.' Melissa was about to float her theory on the reasons for the apparent inconsistency, but at this point Sam was buttonholed by a couple with a young child who, Melissa gathered, was a pupil at his school. She glanced around; everyone seemed to have been served and had either settled in the chairs set out for them on the little patch of lawn beside the hall or, feeling the chill of the evening breeze, taken their food and drink inside.

'Time we had a bite ourselves,' said Mrs Foster. 'Help yourself, Mrs Craig. Rector, what can I give you?'

'Oh, a little of everything please. I'm just looking for Alice and the children — ah, there they are.' He located his little family, already seated a short distance away, and waved to them. 'Do come and join us, ladies.'

Mrs Foster declined the invitation on the grounds that she had to keep an eye on the barbecue, but Melissa accepted and sat down beside Alice. For a while the grown-ups ate in a companionable silence while the children, happily free from the restrictions of family meals at table, ran around kicking a ball while munching their sausages and chicken legs. In the adjoining field, Jake Tanner's tractor clattered up and down ploughing up the cut stubble, followed by screaming flocks of gulls and rooks. Overhead, swallows and martins rushed past in their endless pursuit of insects. On the western horizon, the sun was sinking into banks of fluffy golden clouds.

'Been lucky with the weather, haven't we?' John Hamley remarked and there were murmurs of agreement. Alice expressed the hope that the evening would prove a financial success and the conversation drifted thence to other parish matters. Melissa found her attention wandering; presently she became aware of another set of voices, younger ones this time. She glanced round and saw Becky Tanner with her brother Gary and his friends Dave and Billy tucking into their food a short distance away.

'You still ain't told me where you got the money for the tickets,' Becky was saying.

'None of your business,' her brother retorted.

'You was all skint a couple of days ago.'

'What's it to you?' snapped Billy. 'We ain't askin' where you got yours.'

'I told yer, I saved me pocket-money.'

'Oh yeah, we believe yer.'

'It's true.'

'Okay, have it your way. Who cares anyhow?'

There was a pause, then Becky remarked, 'Good turn-out, innit? Bet the rector's pleased — looks like everyone in the village is here.'

'All except Tommy Judd,' said Dave. The three lads sniggered and exchanged knowing glances.

'What's so funny?' Becky demanded. No

one answered. Melissa, who by this time was giving her full attention to these exchanges, saw the girl's expression alter. She gave a little gasp and clapped a hand to her mouth. 'Gray,' she said, 'You never — ?'

'Shut yer face!' Gary snapped. He leaned forward, grabbed his sister by the arm and gave it a shake. 'Just forget it, will you?'

'Don't you bully me or I'll tell our Dad,' Becky threatened. She jerked her arm away, scowling, but held her tongue. The lads paid no further heed to her and began talking about football.

'Might as well pack this lot up and take it indoors,' Mrs Foster called from behind the barbecue, indicating the remaining food and bringing Melissa's attention back to the job in hand. Around them, people were beginning to drift away. 'Getting too chilly to sit out here,' Mrs Foster continued. 'Anyway, the music'll be starting soon — if that's what they call it,' she added sourly as the disc jockey hired for the occasion began testing his equipment with a track from the latest Oasis album. 'Can't think what anyone sees in that noise, it's enough to wake the dead.'

'It's all to do with what's known as the generation gap, I believe,' Gideon Lane remarked as he placed three paper plates, three crumpled paper napkins and a little heap of plastic cutlery carefully on the table. 'Thank you very much, Mrs Foster, that was delicious.' He glanced round for confirmation from his sisters, standing just behind him.

'Excellent,' said Judith Waghorne as she handed over three plastic cups.

'A most successful evening all round,' Esther Lane agreed. 'We'll just say good night to the rector and then we'll be going home.'

'My dear, we can't go yet,' Gideon protested. 'The dancing has only just begun, and I'm so looking forward to watching the young people enjoying themselves. Besides,' he added, nodding in the direction of Jean and Cissie Wilcox who were hovering behind them, 'I know these two young ladies would like to stay on for a while and I've promised we'll see them safely home. It's on our way.'

'If it's too much trouble — ' Jean began, but Gideon waved her anticipated objection aside.

'No trouble at all, it'll be a pleasure,' he said firmly and turned back to his sisters. 'If you girls don't want to stay, I'll drive you home and come back for . . . Cissie, isn't it, and Jean . . . later on. About ten o'clock, shall we say? Or shall we make it half past?'

The two older women exchanged glances, then Esther said, 'There's no need for you to make two trips, Gideon. Judith and I will help

Mrs Foster and Mrs Craig clear up, then we'll watch the dancing for a while and all go home together.'

'Splendid!' Gideon beamed at them all. Bright lights and loud pop music were streaming from the open doors of the hall and he took Jean and Cissie each by an arm and led them in, leaving his sisters outside. They exchanged a brief, uneasy glance before Judith began stacking chairs while Esther accepted a black plastic bag from Mrs Foster and began gathering up the evening's debris. It was clear to Melissa, who was piling the remaining food on to dishes and covering them with aluminium foil, that they were far from happy about the arrangement.

* * *

'Mr Lane's a nice gentleman, isn't he?' remarked Jean Wilcox as she and Cissie were drinking a cup of tea in their kitchen after the disco. Gideon had insisted on allowing them to stay almost until the end, despite the obvious disapproval of Judith and Esther.

Cissie shrugged. 'You reckon? Bit of a dirty old man, if you ask me.'

'Cissie! Whatever makes you say that?'

'Dunno. Just think he is.' It might have been her imagination, Cissie told herself; after all, there had been three of them in the back of the car, but he had seemed to be sitting closer to her than was strictly necessary with his leg pressed against her thigh. And why, having earlier offered to take his sisters home and then come back for Cissie and her mother, had he later insisted that Judith drive while he sat in the back between the two of them? It was true he'd said something about being 'perhaps a teeny bit over the odds', but she could have sworn he'd been drinking orange juice most of the time.

'I can't believe that of him, he's never been anything but a perfect gentleman to me,' her mother declared. Although there was some criticism of the sisters in the village from time to time, principally on account of their autocratic ways, she always leapt to their defence, saying that they were real ladies, she should know, she'd been doing a regular cleaning job for them ever since Cissie was a baby and they'd always been very good to them both. When Gideon moved in with them a few weeks ago, she had automatically extended her loyalty to him.

'It was really kind of them all to put themselves out for us like that,' she went on. 'I wouldn't have had you coming home on your own, or with any of those boys you were dancing with. Wouldn't trust any one of them as far as I could spit.'

'You reckon?' Cissie repeated. She rinsed her cup and yawned. 'I'm going to bed, I have to be at the shop by eight o'clock tomorrow.'

5

It was gone eleven o'clock when Melissa reached home. It had been an enjoyable evening, during which she had taken particular pleasure at seeing Graham Shipley take part in his first village event. It had been encouraging to see how well he responded to the younger children and how relaxed he appeared in their company. Although he was a complete stranger he was after all a neighbour, someone with whom she hoped to be on good — although certainly not intimate — terms during his tenancy of Elder Cottage. That should, she told herself, have been the extent of her interest, yet there was something about him that puzzled and at the same time intrigued her. She sensed an underlying unease and sadness in his demeanour, and as she drove the short distance home her imagination set to work, devising possible causes.

Elder Cottage was in darkness when she turned out of the lane; thinking that he was probably asleep she left the car outside rather than cause a disturbance by opening and closing the garage doors. Although it was

51

getting late, her brain was still active and before going to bed she made a pot of tea and spent some time reading over what she had written earlier in the day. She quickly became absorbed and it was nearly two o'clock before she turned in.

It was gone ten when she awoke to a typical late August day of glowing sunshine that, despite its warmth, held hints of autumn in the ripening berries in the hedgerow and the dew-drenched grass under the laden apple tree in her garden. She got dressed, prepared a light breakfast, carried it outside on a tray and settled in a secluded corner, conveniently screened by tall rose bushes from observation by a neighbour who seemed to spend quite a lot of time looking out of the window. It was Iris who had suggested planting this little arbour, not so much for its privacy — there had been no need at the time for such considerations — but for its protection from the chilly breezes that even on a fine day had a habit of sneaking up the valley from the north. In her early months at Hawthorn Cottage Melissa's knowledge of gardening had been zero; it was Iris who had taken charge, practically ordering her to plant vegetables, helping her to plan her little plot and insisting that she establish a compost heap and cultivate it on strictly organic lines.

It had all seemed a chore at first, but gradually she had taken to the task and in the end found it not only satisfying but therapeutic. She reflected, as she sipped her coffee and nibbled her toast, on some of the knotty problems faced by her fictitious detective, Nathan Latimer, that had been resolved over an afternoon's pruning or digging.

The click of the front door of Elder Cottage brought her back to the present. She caught a glimpse of Graham Shipley's car as it reversed out of his garage and listened idly to the familiar sounds of the double wooden doors closing. His footsteps crunched on the gravel, the car door slammed and the engine revved as he drove off, leaving a tiny curl of exhaust hanging for a few moments in the air outside her own gate. She glanced at her watch; it was gone eleven and she had promised herself a shopping trip to Cheltenham. With some reluctance, for it had been so pleasant sitting in the sunshine, she went indoors.

On her way out she stopped at the village shop to collect her morning paper. Cissie Wilcox was there, bright as a button in a knitted top that hugged her softly rounded figure and appeared, from his twinkling glance as she weighted out tomatoes for him, to meet with Gideon Lane's unqualified approval. He offered her a five-pound note in payment; she took it and counted the change into his hand without meeting his eye, merely saying 'Thank you, sir,' in a cool voice before turning to greet Melissa with a warm smile and a friendly 'Good Morning, Mrs Craig'. Lane appeared faintly embarrassed as he turned to leave, acknowledging Melissa with an old-fashioned little bow as he went.

'Good morning, Cissie, did you enjoy yourself last night?' Melissa said as she received her copy of *The Times*.

'Oh, yes thank you Mrs Craig, it was lovely.'

'And we were so lucky with the weather, weren't we?' Melissa went on. She was studying Cissie curiously as she spoke; there was something different about the girl and she suddenly realised what it was. 'Cissie, am I dreaming or have you grown six inches overnight?'

Cissie giggled. 'Four, actually. It's me new platforms.' Ignoring Mrs Foster's disapproving eye, she skipped out from behind the counter and showed off what seemed to Melissa the ultimate in ungainly footwear. 'I wanted to wear 'em last night, but they weren't right for rounders so I was going to change for the disco, but I forgot and left 'em at home. D'you like 'em?'

'They're very, er, trendy, and that yellow's a lovely bright colour,' Melissa said tactfully. 'Are they comfortable?'

Cissie looked vaguely surprised, as if comfort had not been a consideration in her choice. 'Oh, sure,' she said dismissively.

'They say wearing shoes like that can damage your back after a while,' said Mrs Foster. 'If you don't fall off them and break your neck, that is,' she added darkly. Her eye fell on a small cardboard carton lying on the counter and she tutted in annoyance. 'There, Mr Judd's gone without his eggs.'

'That's all right, I'll drop them in to him on the way home,' said Cissie. She retreated behind the counter and put the carton on a shelf.

'Well, bye-bye, mind you don't scuff your lovely shoes going through the wood,' said Melissa, and Cissie gave her a bright smile and a wave as she turned to serve the next customer.

★   ★   ★

At one o'clock Mrs Foster locked up the shop, turned the cardboard notice hanging on a string behind the glass door from 'Open' to 'Closed' and drew down the blind. She took some cash from the till and put it into an envelope, which she placed in Cissie's eagerly outstretched hand.

'Now put that safely in your bag and mind no one sees it,' she admonished as Cissie attempted to stuff the envelope into a jeans pocket barely deep enough to hold a bus ticket.

'Yes Mrs Foster,' the girl said meekly. 'Thank you, see you next Saturday.'

She made for the door, only to be called back with the reminder, 'What about Mr Judd's eggs then?'

'Oh yes, sorry.' Cissie scuttled back and retrieved the carton. Mrs Foster unlocked the door and held it open just far enough for her to slip through before relocking and bolting it behind her.

Normally Cissie walked home along the lane to Lower Benbury, which for half a mile or so followed the route taken by the twice-weekly bus before branching off to the left a little way before it reached the main road. Today, however, she took a short cut through a patch of woodland which brought her to the path leading from the lane to Tommy Judd's cottage. It ran along the top of a steep bank above the brook which flowed under the bridge where, a day or two earlier, Becky Tanner had rounded on Billy Daniels for throwing stones at ducks and been in turn scolded by her brother Gary. Cissie knew nothing of that little altercation, but Gary was in her thoughts just the same although for different reasons. Last night, at the disco that followed the barbecue, he had asked her to dance and later if he could walk her home, but of course she had to say no and be driven instead with that horrid old man in the back of the car. Gary had offered to take her to the pictures one Saturday. 'Not tomorrow, I'm playing in a football match, maybe next week,' he had said and she had answered, 'Yeah, maybe,' knowing full well that her mother would never allow it, but unwilling to admit how restricted she was compared to Becky and the other girls of her age, who seemed to do pretty much as they liked. Still, she wouldn't be sixteen for ever.

Remembering Mrs Craig's remark about not scuffing her shoes, she picked her way carefully, avoiding the stones protruding through the layer of beech masts and leaf compost built up over countless seasons and tamped down by numberless feet. It had rained within the last week; the ground was still soft without being muddy and the brook was running full, gurgling quietly over its rocky bed. The air was fresh and full of birdsong, but Cissie hardly noticed either.

Part of her mind was reliving the disco; the other part told her she was hungry. Her main thought now was to complete her errand and go home.

The cottage stood in a clearing behind a tangle of old elder trees. It was reached by a brick path, laid generations ago and now, like the stone tiles on the roof, covered with moss. Cissie trod carefully to avoid slipping on the damp surface. There was no knocker on the ancient wooden door and she tapped with her knuckles and called, 'Mr Judd, I've brought your eggs, you forgot them.'

There was no response and she tapped again; still receiving no reply she lifted the rusty latch and pushed. The door swung open and she found herself in a dimly-lit, stale-smelling room with dingy net curtains drawn over the windows. Hearing a faint moaning sound as if someone was in pain she stepped inside in alarm and called, 'Mr Judd, are you there? Are you ill or — '

At that moment, as her eyes became used to the poor light, she caught sight of him. He was kneeling by the empty fireplace; his eyes had a glazed expression and he was gazing at the floor. His face was flushed, his mouth hung slackly open and he was breathing heavily; the moaning noises were getting louder and more frequent. For a second,

Cissie stood there bewildered and uncertain, wondering whether he was having some sort of fit, whether she should run for help. Then she caught sight of what lay between his splayed knees while the gnarled fingers manipulated something she had only heard about in biology lessons. At the sound of her involuntary scream of disgust the old man started and turned his head towards the door, his eyes bulging at the sight of her. The moans ceased abruptly and he began to fumble with his clothing, muttering something incoherent. For a second Cissie stood there petrified; then, as he began getting awkwardly to his feet, she dropped the box of eggs on a nearby chair and fled. Twice she lost her footing on the slippery path and fell on her hands and knees, then scrambled to her feet and ran blindly on, heedless of the mud and scratches on her new shoes, half-choking on the bile that rose in her throat at the thought of what she had seen. She barely heard the old man's distant shout of, 'I meant no 'arm, don' ee tell no one,' heard only the memory of those hideous moans. All her life, ever since she was old enough to distinguish between the sexes, her mother had been warning her against boys and young men, hinting darkly at 'horrible things' that, given half a chance, they would do to girls. In her own limited experience boys had posed no threat; it was old men one had to guard against. First there was Gideon Lane, slimily rubbing himself against her in the car last night and ogling her in the shop this morning, and now Tommy Judd, whom she had known all her life and never had cause to fear, caught doing something unspeakable, something that he wanted no one to know about, might do anything, go to any length to keep secret.

She ran till her chest hurt, then paused for breath and glanced fearfully over her shoulder. Through the trees that lined the winding track she caught a glimpse of him a short distance away, still pursuing her but at a slow, shambling trot. She could easily outrun him to the lane where she would be safe, where cars would be passing, other people walking; he wouldn't dare touch her where someone might see. She ran on again, then stopped abruptly as, rounding a bend, she caught sight of another figure approaching, a figure which, in her shock and confusion, appeared to have huge, blank, gleaming eyes like an alien from a science fiction film. The realisation that the oversized 'eyes' were merely dark glasses reflecting the sun did little to reassure her because the wearer was also a man, potentially as dangerous as the filthy animal panting at her heels. She was trapped between the two of them, there was no escape that way. In a fresh wave of terror she left the track and plunged into the wood.

6

Melissa was in a contented, relaxed frame of mind as she drove home from her shopping trip to Cheltenham. She had met a friend for lunch and together they had wandered round the shops, tried on some clothes, made a few purchases and had tea in the Everyman Theatre café before going their separate ways, agreeing that they had spent a thoroughly enjoyable afternoon and would repeat it in the not too far distant future. The weather had been fine and mild, but as she turned off the main road and headed for Upper Benbury she noticed heavy clouds piling up in the south-west, threatening rain.

She caught up with the bus bringing its load of Saturday shoppers back from Stowbridge and was forced to crawl behind it as it trundled tortoise-like along the lane, scattering a cluster of young pheasants pecking at the roadside, before stopping at the bottom of the hill. While she was waiting, Alice Hamley approached from the opposite direction in her elderly Cavalier and crept past the bus with inches to spare; when she saw Melissa she pulled up alongside and wound down her window to chat about the previous evening's event and tell her that it had raised a substantial sum for the village hall kitchen. Meanwhile, half a dozen or so people left the bus, among them Jean Wilcox who waved, smiled and informed them triumphantly that she had 'managed to get some fresh herrings for Cissie's tea, they're her favourite'.

Alice said goodbye and went on her way as the bus moved off. Melissa was about to follow it, then decided to wait a few more minutes to give it time to drag itself to the top of the final steep climb into Upper Benbury. As she idly watched its ponderous progress, her attention was attracted by a disturbance in the woodland to her left, not far from the track leading to Tommy Judd's cottage. The next minute a man came crashing through the undergrowth as if pursued by a bull. He scrambled up the bank, reaching the track close to the point where it joined the road, ran forward a few paces and then stopped, looking wildly from left to right as if uncertain which direction to take. It was Graham Shipley and it was clear, even from a distance, that he was extremely agitated. Thinking that he might be ill, Melissa pulled off the road, got out of the car and hurried towards him, calling his name.

The sound of her voice seemed to disturb him even further; he swung round and broke into a stumbling run back the way he had come. She called again and he stopped short, hesitated and then slowly turned towards her. His features were contorted and his eyes wide with terror; he stared at her like a half-wild creature uncertain whether to stand its ground or flee. She went slowly up to him and put a hand on his arm; he was trembling violently and appeared to be trying to speak, but only incoherent mumblings came from his mouth.

Keeping her voice as quiet and soothing as possible, she said, 'Mr Shipley . . . Graham . . . are you ill?' He did not answer and she said, 'Is something wrong?'

His reaction alarmed her. He grabbed at her arm, swaying slightly. For a second she wondered if he might be drunk or even drugged, but he took a deep breath and gasped, 'By the water . . . a girl . . . I think she's dead!'

'Good heavens! Where? Show me!'

'That way.' He pointed and together they hurried towards the brook, scrambling as fast as possible down the steep, overgrown bank. Even before she reached the bottom and found herself gazing down in horror at the girl's face with the muddied strands of blond hair half concealing the ugly bruise on the forehead, the one bright yellow shoe still clinging to the left foot had caught Melissa's eye and identified the victim. She dropped to her knees beside Cissie's body, mechanically feeling for a pulse, knowing there would be none, yet praying for a miracle. She had encountered a case of drowning once before; the cold clammy feel of the flesh under her fingers and the froth of bubbles round the mouth, still curved in the same mysterious suggestion of a smile that it had worn in life, put an end to all hope. For an instant she could neither move nor speak; her throat tightened at the thought of Jean at home, at this very moment happily preparing her daughter's favourite meal, and she was temporarily blinded by a gush of tears.

'What do we do?' Graham Shipley's voice, little better than a croak, prodded her into action.

'We must get help. Have you got a mobile phone?' He shook his head and she stood up saying, 'I'll get mine.' Without stopping to see whether he was following she scrambled back up the bank as fast as she could, slithering on mud, stumbling over stones, dodging brambles and ducking under low branches. At the top, she broke into a run, urged on by the faint possibility that if only expert help could reach Cissie soon enough she could somehow be revived, yet knowing in her heart that there was no hope for her.

She reached the car, made her call, sank into the driver's seat and closed her eyes. When she opened them again, Graham was standing a few feet away, staring into space. She leaned across, opened the passenger door and called his name. 'We have to wait here until the police arrive,' she said and without a word, like a man hypnotised, he got in and sat down.

It seemed an eternity before the first police car arrived and when it did it was Melissa who guided the two uniformed officers to the spot where Cissie's body lay. Graham appeared to have fallen into a trance; when they got back to the car he was still sitting motionless, his breathing harsh and ragged, his eyes closed. 'This gentleman actually found the body,' she explained, 'but he seems to be in deep shock. I think perhaps he should see a doctor.'

One of the officers nodded and said, 'I'll mention it. Do you mind staying with him until CID get here?' He opened the driver's door, waited while she got in and closed it behind her. At the sound, Graham started and opened his eyes.

'What happens now?' he asked in a weak, unsteady voice.

'We have to wait here for a little while. You found the body so I'm afraid the police will want to ask you a few questions.'

'Questions?' The word seemed to frighten him. 'What questions?'

'About how you came to find her, and what you did after that. Don't worry,' she went on reassuringly, 'I'm pretty sure they won't press you for a full statement until you've calmed down a bit.'

'Statement?' He looked aghast. 'What statement? I found her there . . . I ran to get help . . . I didn't know which way — ' His voice tailed off and he buried his face in his hands. 'I never touched her,' he muttered as if to himself, 'I swear before God I never touched her, never touched her, never — '

His voice had taken on a mechanical note, as if he was reciting something he had learned by heart. Melissa gave his arm a gentle shake. 'What are you saying?' she asked. 'If you didn't touch her, who pulled her out of the water?'

He shook his head and his eyes were full of tears. 'I never touched her,' he repeated. His voice was dull, flat, full of despair.

A siren wailed in the distance, drawing rapidly closer. The next moment, the quiet little backwater was swarming with more police, some in uniform, some in plain clothes. They disappeared into the wood carrying equipment which she knew from experience would include a tent to erect over the body to protect it from the rain which had already begun falling, gently at first but soon drumming on the car roof and blurring the windscreen. An ambulance arrived; the crew jumped out and followed the police.

'What can they do?' Graham mumbled. 'She's dead, isn't she?'

'It's routine. They won't move her until a doctor arrives.' He fell silent again, his head half-turned away as if to conceal his emotion.

Two figures in plain clothes approached. With some relief, Melissa recognised Detective Sergeant Waters and DC Savage. Matt Waters was an old friend; Audrey Savage she had met a couple of times before and knew her to be both sensitive and practical. Matt, too, could be relied on not to put undue pressure on a witness who was obviously traumatised by his gruesome discovery. They climbed into the back of the car and she introduced them to Graham Shipley as 'My new next-door neighbour who's renting Elder Cottage.'

'I understand it was you who found the body, sir,' said Matt.

'I never touched her — ' Graham began,

but the sergeant went on without giving him time to finish.

'If you don't mind coming with me to my car while I ask you a few questions, DC Savage will stay here and talk to Mrs Craig. Don't worry,' he said kindly, 'I can see that you're feeling pretty shocked and this won't take long. You can give us a full statement when you're feeling better.'

Without another word, Graham got out of the car and stood passively, oblivious to the pouring rain, until Matt, after conferring briefly in a low voice with his colleague, took him by the arm and led him away. Audrey climbed into the passenger seat and shut the door.

'So, tell me exactly what happened?'

'I got stuck behind the bus and I decided to wait here a couple of minutes rather than crawl up the hill breathing in its exhaust,' Melissa began. 'I saw Graham come crashing out of the wood as though the Furies were after him.' Briefly, she described what followed; when she came to the point where she recognised Cissie's body her voice cracked as the full implications of the tragedy overwhelmed her. 'She was only just sixteen . . . such a lovely kid . . . and Jean — her mother — simply doted on her. I don't know how she'll cope . . . she's got no other family . . . Cissie was her whole life — '

'Take your time.' Audrey's quiet voice had a calming effect. Melissa brushed a hand across her eyes and breathed deeply for a few moments.

'There isn't much more to tell,' she said when she was composed again. 'I ran back to the car and called the police on my mobile, and we just waited until they arrived.'

'You didn't touch the body, or see Shipley touch it?'

'I felt for a pulse, that's all, while Graham stood watching. I didn't look back while I was running to the car, but he was only seconds behind me and I've no reason to think he interfered with it in any way. In fact, he keeps on repeating, 'I never touched her' — over and over again.'

'Yes, I heard him say that. I take it you waited together in the car?'

'Yes. As you saw for yourself, he's obviously in deep shock.'

'You said he's your new neighbour, so you can't have known him long?'

'Just a few days. He seems a pretty solitary sort of man and he doesn't welcome what one might call 'neighbourly advances'.'

'D'you know what he does for a living?'

'He's a teacher. From what little I've seen of him, I think he gets on better with kids than adults.'

'When he said, 'I never touched her', have you any idea what he meant?'

'I assumed he meant he found her like that — ' Melissa broke off, frowning, casting around for alternative explanations. The obvious one raised potentially ominous questions.

'If that's the case, someone else pulled her out of the water, saw that she was dead and left her there without reporting it,' Audrey said thoughtfully, echoing Melissa's thoughts. 'We'll have to see what Graham's got to say. In the meantime, can you remember seeing anyone else while you were waiting for the bus to go, or after it left?'

'About half a dozen people got off. As far as I know, they all live in Lower Benbury — anyway, they all headed in that direction. And while I was waiting I was chatting to Alice Hamley — our rector's wife — who was driving that way as well.'

Audrey made a note of the name. 'I'll have a word with her, just in case she noticed anyone after she left you. By the way, where does that track go — the one leading to the spot where you saw the body?'

'It's a public right of way that follows the brook for a couple of miles and then links up with other footpaths, one leading to Carston and the other to Stowbridge.'

'It looks quite wide and well used. Does anyone live along there?'

'Old Tommy Judd. He's a widower, an ex-employee of Benbury Park Estates. He's got a cottage about half a mile along the track. It's dreadful old hovel really, but he's lived there so long I don't think he notices it.'

'We'd better have a word with him. He might have seen something.' Audrey wrote in her notebook, closed it and tucked it into her pocket. 'Well, thanks Melissa.' She got out of the car, then popped her head back in and said, 'I see Matt Waters has finished talking to your neighbour. He's heading back this way — I daresay he'd appreciate a lift home.'

Melissa nodded resignedly. 'All right, leave him to me. Look, I'm sure Jean Wilcox has friends and neighbours who'll look after her, but if she needs someone to go with her to identify the body and there's no one else — '

Audrey gave a grateful nod. 'Thanks, I'll tell her.'

7

By the time they got back the rain had almost stopped and a watery sun was breaking through. Melissa parked the Golf outside her garage door and said to Graham, 'You look all in. How about a cup of tea . . . or maybe a drop of brandy?'

'I'd appreciate a cup of tea, thank you.' His voice was still quiet, but it had grown firmer and he had stopped trembling. To her surprise he got out of the car and hurried round to hold open the driver's door. She stepped out, unlocked the boot and began unloading her shopping.

'Let me take those,' he said, reaching out a hand.

'Thank you.' He stood patiently holding the packages while she closed the boot and fished in her handbag for her house keys. He followed her indoors and waited while she slipped off her coat, hung it up in the passage and led the way into the kitchen.

'Just dump it all down there,' she said, indicating a spot behind the door. 'There's nothing breakable; I'll unpack it later. Your jacket's damp,' she went on. 'Why don't you take it off and I'll hang it near the Aga to dry off a bit.' He hesitated for a moment and then complied.

It was a heavy tweed jacket, of good quality but by no means new. His shirt was clean but had plainly not been ironed. 'It's pretty old, but it's still serviceable,' he remarked as he handed over the jacket and smoothed the front of the shirt with his hands, as if he could read her thoughts.

It was a relief to hear him speaking more openly. In their previous encounters he had shown every sign of wanting to keep her at arm's length. She recalled how she had mentally likened him to a timid animal and the comparison still seemed appropriate, only now he was beginning to gain the confidence to allow himself to be approached. Perhaps the dreadful experience they had so recently shared had in some way encouraged him to trust her.

She filled a kettle, put it to boil and took a teapot from a cupboard. 'Do sit down,' she said and for the second time he did as she suggested, this time without hesitation. He watched without speaking as she made the tea and poured it out, following her every move with close attention as if it was something he was seeing for the first time. She put two cups of tea on the table together

74

with a bowl of sugar and an open tin of biscuits, and then sat down opposite him.

The silence was becoming oppressive and she was casting around in her mind for something suitable to say when he suddenly asked, 'Who was she?'

'You mean the dead girl?'

'Yes.'

'Her name's Cissie Wilcox. She lives — lived — in Lower Benbury. I hate to think what her mother's going through,' Melissa went on, biting her lip. 'Jean's a single parent with no other family that I know of.'

'I'm so very sorry. It's a dreadful thing to have happened.'

'Terrible.' She thought for a moment, then asked, 'How did you come to be there?'

The question seemed to trouble him and it was some time before he answered. When he did, he spoke very slowly between mouthfuls of tea as if his memory was uncertain and he was trying to be sure of getting it right. 'I was out for a walk. I'd been into Stowbridge this morning and bought a bird book and the man in the shop was a keen birder. We got talking and when I mentioned where I lived he said that stretch of water was a good place to see kingfishers.' He put his free hand to his brow. 'Oh God, if only I hadn't — ' he began, then broke off, set down his cup, snatched his spectacles from his nose and began furiously polishing them with a handkerchief.

'If only you hadn't what?' Melissa asked cautiously. He shook his head, put the glasses back on, blew his nose and returned the handkerchief to his pocket.

'Nothing,' he said, and then after another long pause, 'I suppose someone had to find her.'

Seeing how much calmer and more rational he seemed, Melissa ventured to raise the question that had been troubling her during the drive home. 'Graham,' she said quietly, 'you said you never touched her, is that right?'

'Yes.'

'So it couldn't have been you who pulled her out of the water, could it?'

He stared down into his empty teacup. 'No, it wasn't. I told the policeman, but I don't know if he believed me.'

'Why shouldn't he?'

'He might think I had something to do with her death.'

'But why? I don't understand — ' she began.

'No, of course you don't.' His mouth compressed and for a moment she thought he was going to break down, but with an effort he steadied himself and said, 'Could I have some more tea, please?'

'Of course, but are you sure you wouldn't like something stronger?'

He shook his head; she poured out the tea and he drained his cup a second time before saying in a voice full of quiet despair, 'I came here to make a fresh start, you see.'

'You've had some trouble?'

'My marriage fell apart and I'm not . . . I don't see my daughter any more. I thought, if I moved somewhere far away, I could forget what happened and start again. And now this — '

'Oh, poor you!' It was, Melissa thought, a pretty feeble expression of sympathy, but it seemed that no words could express the sorrow and indignation she felt on his behalf at such a cruel trick of fate. 'How old is your daughter?'

'Thirteen. She's very clever . . . and tall for her age. You could take her for fourteen or fifteen,' he added, paternal pride and distress struggling for the upper hand.

And Cissie Wilcox was barely sixteen and small for her age, Melissa thought with compassion. Anyone finding her body would have felt a sense of shock, but to someone in Graham's situation it must have been especially poignant. She was casting around for something comforting to say when he stood up and said, 'Thank you very much for the tea, Mrs Craig — '

'Oh please, call me Melissa.'

'Thank you, Melissa. I'll be going now, you must have other things to do.'

'Not especially, if you'd like to stay and chat a little longer.' He shook his head and she took down his jacket and handed it to him, saying, 'It's still a bit damp, but at least it feels warm.' He gave a vague nod, but made no comment as he put it on. 'By the way,' she went on, 'have you ordered a Sunday paper?'

'Yes, *The Independent*. Why do you ask?'

'I'll be going into the village in the morning to pick mine up. I could bring yours if you like.'

'That's kind.'

'We could take it in turns to fetch our daily papers,' she suggested. 'That's what Iris and I used to do.'

Again, he nodded without replying. He was already edging past her on his way to the front door; his manner had become formal and distant, but the unnatural brightness of his eyes betrayed the pain he was suffering. The thought of him going back to an empty house and eating a solitary meal — or possibly, not eating at all — prompted her to say, 'I'll have to think about some supper presently. Would you care to — ?'

'I have plenty of food in the house,' he interposed hurriedly, 'and I'm used to looking after myself. Thank you all the same,' he added as if aware that his response had been less than gracious.

From her own point of view Melissa felt relieved at his refusal. Mention of Iris had brought home to her just how much she missed her friend, how good it would have been to unwind in her company after the stress of the afternoon. There would have been little opportunity for relaxation with Graham; a quiet evening on her own with a book would be far more therapeutic. *He's not your problem, but at least you made the offer*, she told herself as she closed the door behind him and began unpacking her shopping.

She cooked a light supper, but her appetite was poor; haunted by the memory of Cissie's pathetic little drowned body she pushed the food around her plate and ended by throwing half of it away. She took a cup of coffee into the sitting room and tried to settle down with her many times reread copy of *Emma*, but found it impossible to drive the tragedy from her mind. When at about eight o'clock the telephone rang she picked it up with a sense of foreboding.

'Hallo,' she said cautiously.

'Hi Mel, Bruce Ingram here.'

The sound of his cheery voice was like the touch of a soothing hand. 'Bruce, how nice to hear from you! Are you still on duty?' Besides being a friend of several years' standing, Bruce was the *Gloucestershire Gazette*'s ace reporter.

'No, what makes you think that?'

'You mean, you aren't calling about the accident?'

'What accident?'

'You haven't heard?'

'Not a thing. Penny and I have been out all day with Kirsty.' Bruce had recently acquired not only a wife, but an adorable baby step-daughter as well. 'What's happened?'

'A girl from Lower Benbury has been found dead, drowned in the brook.'

'How dreadful. Who found her?'

'My new next-door neighbour came across her body while he was out bird-watching, but I happened along a few moments later which was just as well because he was running around like a headless chicken without a clue what to do. Luckily, I had my mobile with me and was able to contact the police right away.'

'Your *new* next-door neighbour — does that mean Iris has sold Elder Cottage?'

'No, she's rented it for six months to a man called Graham Shipley. He's a teacher from somewhere in the Midlands and he's starting next term at a local school. I imagine he'll look for a permanent home once he's settled. I do feel sorry for him; he's just been through a marriage breakdown and now this — '

'Poor chap.' There was a faintly abstracted note in Bruce's voice, as if his mind had momentarily wandered elsewhere. 'Whereabouts in the Midlands is he from?'

'The Birmingham area, I believe. Why do you ask?'

'No particular reason.'

He sounded evasive, but she knew from experience there was no point in probing. 'You haven't told me yet why you're phoning,' she reminded him.

'Oh sorry, I was forgetting. It's Kirsty's birthday tomorrow and Penny and I wondered if you'd like to come to her tea-party. My mother and father will be there — ' He did not add, *'but as you know, Penny's parents are both dead and she's got no one else'*, but Melissa was quick to grasp the thought that had prompted the invitation.

'I'd simply love to come, thank you for asking me. You haven't given me much time to buy Kirsty a present, though.'

'Give her an autographed copy of your latest book. We'll keep it for her as an investment,' Bruce chuckled. 'About half past three, then?'

'I'll look forward to it. Bruce — '

'Yes?'

'You won't let any of your news-hounds go pestering Graham for an interview, will you? He's pretty upset.'

'We'll have to wait and see how our editor decides to handle the story after the briefing tomorrow. I can't make any promises, I'm afraid.'

'No, of course not. I'll see you tomorrow, then.'

Melissa's feelings as she replaced the receiver were mixed. She would enjoy a game with Kirsty and a chat with the others, but she was troubled on Graham's behalf. It wasn't just the effect on his already shaky morale of having journalists knocking at his door and asking how he felt when he found the girl's body. There had been something in Bruce's tone to suggest that he was interested in her new neighbour for some other reason — one he was not prepared to divulge.

8

When Melissa arrived at the village shop the following morning to collect the Sunday papers she found it crowded with people who had come on a similar errand and stayed to talk over with their neighbours what little was known about the previous day's tragedy. Like a group of journalists chasing a story, they pounced on her as soon as she entered.

'I heard you found the body,' said Mrs Foster. She was plainly distressed; her voice quavered and her face was pink and crumpled. 'That must have been dreadful for you.'

'I heard she'd been attacked and, er, interfered with,' Alice Hamley said hesitantly. 'Is it true?'

'Wherever did you get that idea?' Melissa asked, frowning.

'Mrs Daniels said her Billy was there with his friends and saw the body being taken away and they thought that must have been what happened — '

'I never saw them — they must have turned up after I left. I suppose they saw all the police activity, put two and two together and made five. No one knows yet exactly what happened and it's very naughty of them to go spreading tales like that.'

'So it *was* you who found her,' said Mrs Foster. 'I just can't believe it. She was so happy when she went off yesterday with her pay packet, in those new yellow shoes she was so proud of — ' The postmistress pulled out a handkerchief and wiped reddened eyes. 'Such a lovely girl.'

'It was actually Mr Shipley who found her,' Melissa explained. 'I was at the bottom of the hill by the bridge when he came running out of the woods and told me he'd found a dead girl. I went with him to look — it was an awful shock for both of us.'

'But you don't think she'd been, you know, what the lads suggested?' The speaker was Gideon Lane, who was wedged in a corner behind the door with his copy of the *Observer* and looking as if he would like to get away but was unable to do so without pushing past everyone else.

'Indecently assaulted, you mean? I saw nothing at all to suggest that,' Melissa assured him. 'She certainly had a nasty bruise on her forehead, but my first impression was that she had drowned, perhaps after tumbling into the brook and knocking herself out on a stone.'

'Poor little girl,' said Gideon with a

sorrowful shake of the head.

'We shan't know for certain until after the post mortem. If only someone had come along sooner — ' She broke off, recalling that Graham had begun to say something beginning with 'If only', but had for some reason left the remark unfinished.

'What I don't understand is, what she was doing in the woods in the first place. It's right out of her way,' said Miss Brightwell, a slightly acid-tongued spinster who lived in a cottage behind the church. Her tone held a note of disapproval, as if to suggest that a girl who went wandering into woods on her own might well have been up to no good.

Mrs Foster was quick to refute the unspoken slur. 'She was doing an errand for me,' she said firmly. 'Mr Judd left his eggs behind and she offered to drop them in to him. Oh dear, I shouldn't have let her, but how was I to know?' she faltered and her eyes filled again.

'Maybe old Tommy heard something?' someone suggested. 'I wonder if the police have interviewed him.'

'I can confirm that they did, or intend to,' said Melissa.

'I doubt if he'll have heard anything,' Alice observed. 'He's pretty deaf.'

'That's true, but he might have seen

something,' Melissa pointed out. 'Of course, we don't know yet whether she ever got as far as his cottage. I do hope someone's looking after Jean Wilcox,' she added. 'The poor woman must be in a terrible state.'

'She's staying with a neighbour,' volunteered Mrs Yates, who lived in Lower Benbury. 'She's dreadfully cut up, poor love, but everyone's rallying round with support and the Reverend Hamley's been to see her,' she added, casting an appreciative glance in Alice's direction. 'You know,' she went on, 'it's odd you should mention those boys, Mrs Hamley, because almost the first thing Jean said to me when I popped in to see her was something like, 'I knew I should never have let her spend the whole evening with that Tanner boy'.'

'You aren't suggesting that Gary Tanner had anything to do with her death, surely?' said Melissa in astonishment.

'I'm not suggesting anything, I'm only telling you what Jean said. But if she was on her way home, what was she doing down by the brook? Even if she had been to Mr Judd's cottage, there's no short cut that way. D'you think she might have been running away from someone?'

There was a brief silence while everyone considered the question — one that Melissa had already asked herself a number of times during the previous night's wakeful hours without being able to think of a satisfactory answer. Cissie had been so proud of her new shoes and yet it appeared that she had for some reason left a comparatively firm, even path and gone scrambling down a steep, muddy, overgrown bank where they were almost certain to be damaged. 'Perhaps we should wait until we hear the result of the police enquiry,' she suggested. There were nods and murmurs of agreement, but she knew full well that nothing would stop the speculation, the exchange of theories, the pointing of fingers in this or that direction as the news spread further and further afield, losing nothing in the telling.

Mrs Yates began edging towards the door clutching an armful of papers. 'I must be getting back, everyone'll be waiting for these.' The tinkling of the bell as she opened the door to leave echoed round the shop and triggered a general exodus.

For a moment, Melissa found herself the only customer remaining. 'I'll take Mr Shipley's *Independent* as well,' she said.

A gleam appeared in Mrs Foster's pale, pink-rimmed eyes. 'Funny *he* should be the one to find her, don't you think?' she remarked as she handed over the papers.

'What makes you say that? Someone had to.' For the second time, Melissa found herself repeating Graham's own words.

'Well, we're agreed there's something odd about him, aren't we?' Mrs Foster's manner was almost conspiratorial.

'Are we?'

'Well, he's not very forthcoming about himself, is he? Living next door to you and not even letting on he's a schoolteacher — '

Knowing at least part of the reason for Graham's reticence and having no intention of betraying his confidence, Melissa said, 'It's probably because he's a bit shy.'

'Schoolteachers aren't usually that shy,' said Mrs Foster with a sniff.

'I hope you're not suggesting he had anything to do with Cissie's death — ' Melissa began and the postmistress hastily back-tracked.

'Oh no, I meant nothing like that. I just thought . . . after what we were saying on Friday evening — '

You mean after what *you* were saying, Melissa thought to herself. Aloud, she said, 'I think perhaps we shouldn't mention that to anyone else. A lot of damage can be done to perfectly innocent people — '

'Oh, I'm not one to gossip.' Mrs Foster sounded slightly offended, as if she thought

Melissa was about to accuse her of spreading rumours. 'It's just, well, it seemed funny, after what we were saying. It wouldn't surprise me if other people have noticed it as well.'

'I think we'd better forget all about it,' said Melissa firmly as she paid for the papers. 'No doubt we'll learn exactly what happened once the police have completed their enquiries.' Without waiting for a response, she left the shop and set off for home.

As she was about to push the newspaper through the letter-box of Elder Cottage, Graham opened the door. He was wearing a sweat shirt, rumpled chinos and an old pair of trainers but no socks and she suspected that he had not long been out of bed. His face was pale and unshaven and his manner, though polite, was unsmiling.

'Thank you, Melissa. I'll fetch yours tomorrow,' he said as he took the paper and handed over the money.

'Fine.' She was on the point of asking him how he had slept, but before she had the chance to say a word he stepped back and closed the door. It occurred to her as she let herself into her own house that he must have been at the window, watching for her return.

★ ★ ★

'You took your time,' said Esther as Gideon entered the kitchen where his sisters were preparing breakfast. He gave an apologetic smile as he sat down, unfolded the paper and began scanning the headlines. Judith, busy with coffee-pot and toaster, shot her sister a reproachful glance but said nothing.

'There were a lot of people in the shop,' Gideon explained. 'I was at the back of the queue.'

'All talking about what happened to poor little Cissie, I suppose.' Esther's features, sharp and colourless beneath a carefully arranged mound of iron-grey hair, registered a mixture of sadness and disapproval. 'Anything like that seems to bring out the worst in people,' she complained. 'They rake it all over and make up the wildest stories, and then have the cheek to complain about the lurid things that appear in the papers — ' She gave a little gasp and put a hand to her mouth as she uttered the final words. 'Oh my goodness, we were all too shocked when we got the news to think of anything except looking after poor Jean . . . it never occurred to us . . . all this is sure to be in the papers, there'll be reporters asking questions — '

'There's no reason why they should be interested in talking to us, is there?' said

Gideon, laying the paper aside and helping himself to toast.

'That depends,' said Judith uneasily. 'Giddy, you haven't told us where you went yesterday afternoon. You didn't go anywhere near, you know, where it happened, did you?'

'What are you suggesting?' her brother demanded.

'I'm not suggesting anything.' Judith's soft, rosy features, which contrasted sharply with her sister's, registered acute concern. 'It's just, well, the police are sure to ask anyone who was in the area at the time to come forward — you know how they do — in case they saw anything that could help them with their enquiries. I mean — ' Judith broke off in confusion at the sight of the anger and resentment in Gideon's face.

'Yes, what exactly do you mean?' he asked.

'She means that if you were anywhere near and anyone saw you, your name would quite likely get into the papers.' Esther's expression was stony, her greenish eyes hard and accusatory. 'And we know what that might lead to, don't we?'

Gideon shifted uncomfortably under the combined gaze of his sisters. 'I never saw Cissie, if that's what you're getting at,' he muttered.

'But you were there?' Esther persisted and

he gave a reluctant nod. 'Why?'

'If you must know, I was going to see old Mr Judd.'

'Whatever for?'

'Just for a chat. He gets lonely, living alone, and I thought I'd — '

Esther stared at him in astonishment. 'What in the world have you and he got to chat about? You don't even know him.'

'As it happens, I do. I got talking to him one day in a newsagent in Stowbridge. He'd come in on the bus, but you'd lent me the car that day so I gave him a lift home. And I resent being cross-examined like this,' Gideon went on with a sudden show of indignation. 'I do an act of Christian kindness — '

' — and I'm sure Mr Judd was very appreciative,' said Judith, who had listened to the acrimonious exchanges between her brother and sister with growing distress. 'Don't be hard on him, Essie . . . I think it was very kind of him.' She gave Gideon an encouraging smile and offered him another slice of toast.

Esther appeared unimpressed by her brother's claim to altruistic motives. 'What time was this?' she asked.

'About half past one, I suppose. I was out for my usual stroll after lunch and I thought I'd drop in for a chat with Tommy.' There was a hint of bluster in his voice as he went on, 'Look, what are you accusing me of?'

'No one's accusing you of anything, but we want the truth,' said Esther sternly. 'Don't think we didn't notice the way you were eyeing that poor girl on Friday, or how you managed to sit next to her in the back of the car after making that excuse about having drunk too much so that Judith would have to drive home.'

He dropped his eyes, his face sullen, and took a bite of toast. 'Don't know what you're talking about,' he said with his mouth full.

'Gideon, look at me!' Esther commanded. Reluctantly, he obeyed. 'Will you swear on the Bible that you did nothing that might have given that girl cause to fear you?'

'Esther!' Judith's voice was full of gentle reproach. 'Of course he didn't, how could he? We were all in the car together.' Her brother shot her a grateful glance as she went on, 'But it is important that you remember everything that happened round about the time the police think Cissie died. You say you never saw her, but did you see anyone else as you were walking along?'

Gideon thought for a moment. 'One or two cars passed, but I didn't recognise the drivers — oh, except that fellow who delivers the frozen food. His van passed just as I reached the lane.'

'What was Colin doing there, I wonder?' said Judith. 'He doesn't usually come on a Saturday.'

'He was probably making a special delivery,' said Esther. 'He does, now and again. Did he see you, do you think?'

'I suppose he must have done, but I doubt if he recognised me. He's only called once since I came to live here.'

'Let's hope not,' said Judith fervently.

It seemed to be dawning on Gideon that he could be in serious trouble. He thought again and said, 'I do remember hearing a squeal of brakes just after he drove past, as if he'd had to stop suddenly. He'd gone out of sight round a bend, so I didn't see what happened.'

'He probably met another vehicle. People drive much too fast along that lane,' Judith observed.

'I don't remember seeing another car just then. Perhaps there was an animal in the road.'

'Or another person.'

There was a short silence as the three of them considered the possible implications should it become known that Gideon had at the crucial time been near the spot where the girl met her death. At last Judith said, 'The police told Jean they think Cissie might have been running away from someone and she's got this fixation about Gary Tanner because of all the time he spent dancing with Cissie on Friday night.'

'Well, we know how protective Jean has always been towards Cissie, but I can't believe that of Gary,' said Esther. 'He's a decent lad and I don't think for a moment he'd do anything to frighten her. No, unless I'm very much mistaken, they'll be looking for an older person.' Her expression as she looked her brother full in the face was grim. 'They'll be looking for an older *man*.'

9

It was Melissa's first visit to Bruce and Penny Ingram since they moved into their new house shortly after their marriage, and the first time she had seen either of them for several months. She was immediately struck by a subtle change in Bruce; while losing nothing of his lively personality and boyish charm, the exuberance which had on occasions led her to compare him with an eager terrier had given way to a mature, responsible air which went well with his new position as householder and family man. The change in Penny was even more striking; she had blossomed from a harassed, struggling single mother with neither the time nor the money to spare for herself into a well-groomed and confident young woman. Kirsty, whom Melissa had last seen as a baby not yet able to talk, was now a lively, chattering toddler, plainly doted on by her adoptive grandparents.

'We'd begun to think he'd never settle down,' Bruce's mother confided to Melissa as the four of them sat round the tea-table watching Kirsty, enthroned in a high chair, blowing lustily on the two pink candles on her birthday cake. 'We'd given up hope of ever having grandchildren. Penny's such a sweet girl — it's wonderful to see them so happy.'

When Melissa got up to leave, Bruce escorted her to the door. Once out of earshot of the others he said, 'Any more developments in the enquiry into that girl's death?'

'Not that I know of. Haven't you been in touch with your office?'

'Of course, but all they've got is the initial police report of a body having been found in the woods — no details.'

'All I've heard is a lot of idle speculation,' said Melissa drily. 'You know what people are for making up stories — '

'Almost as bad as journalists, eh?' said Bruce with a grin. 'By the way, seen anything of your new neighbour since we spoke on the phone?'

'Only to hand him his Sunday paper. He was in church this morning, but he didn't speak to me, or to anyone else as far as I could see. What's your interest?'

Bruce's eyebrows lifted at the word 'church', but he made no comment. He picked up a manila envelope that had been tucked out of sight behind a vase of flowers on the hall table and handed it to her. 'Have a look at that when you get home.'

'What is it?'

'Some faxed material I got from a friend who works in Birmingham Central Library. There's a photograph of a man — I'd like you to tell me if you recognise him. Thanks so much for coming, and for Kirsty's present,' he hurried on without giving her a chance to question him. 'I'll give you a call in the morning, if that's all right with you.'

He had switched from his rôle as dedicated family man to that of a professional journalist on the track of a story. It was clear that he had no intention of saying any more for the moment; with a shrug, Melissa slid the envelope into her handbag. 'I suppose so,' she sighed, 'but I hope you aren't going to involve me in another of your off-the-record investigations. I do have a book to finish, you know.'

'Of course, don't you always? And haven't I given you some very useful material in the past?'

★　★　★

There was no sign of life in Elder Cottage when Melissa reached home shortly after six. As soon as she got indoors she opened the envelope Bruce had given her. Inside were faxed copies of a series of extracts from the

Birmingham Post. She read through them with an increasing sense of shock and dismay. The first, dated some eighteen months previously, was a front-page item bearing a photograph of Graham Shipley and reporting his suspension from his post as history teacher at a local comprehensive following allegations by a girl pupil of indecent assault. Subsequent items traced the story as it unfolded: a categorical denial by Shipley; declarations of confidence by some parents; doubts expressed by others that 'there was no smoke without fire'; an eventual statement by the police that there was insufficient evidence to bring charges; an announcement by the chairman of the school governors that they accepted the teacher's version of events and intended to reinstate him; the formation of a pressure group of parents challenging the governors' decision. The final item, dated almost a year ago, appeared to have been tucked away on an inside page and briefly reported that Shipley, described as 'the teacher at the centre of the recent allegations of indecent assault at Woodfield Comprehensive', had resigned on the grounds of ill-health.

Melissa sat for a long time deep in thought. She was torn between conflicting emotions: on the one hand, sympathy for the tortured individual who, in a state of near hysteria following the discovery of Cissie Wilcox's body, had allowed her a brief insight into his personal tragedy; on the other, unease over the unanswered questions that had up till now lain at the back of her mind but which now began to assume an alarming significance. She was mulling them over and speculating on possible answers when there was a ring at the front door. Half expecting it to be Graham Shipley, she hastily returned the papers to the envelope and slid it into a drawer before answering, wondering as she did so what on earth she could say to him in the light of what she had just learned. However, it was not Graham but her old friend Detective Sergeant Matt Waters who was standing in the porch and she greeted him with relief.

'Matt, how nice to see you! Come in.'

'Thanks.' He stepped inside after carefully wiping his shoes. 'I hope this isn't an inconvenient time to call.'

'Not at all. Is it a social visit or official business?' she asked with a glance at the notebook in his hand.

'A little of both, actually. I've been a bit concerned about you after the upset of finding that poor girl's body . . . knowing you haven't got Iris or . . . I mean, after that kind

100

of experience it helps to have a friend to talk things over with — '

He had, she knew, been on the point of blurting out Ken Harris's name. He was one of the few people who knew how close her relationship with his former chief had been and she guessed that he had checked himself for fear of causing hurt or embarrassment. As much to reassure herself that the pain of parting was becoming daily less acute as to put him at his ease, she patted him on the arm and said, 'Matt, that's such a kind thought — and you're right, it would have been a relief to have Iris or Ken around. But I'm okay now,' she went on as she led the way into her cosy sitting-room and invited him to sit down. 'Would you like a drink, or a cup of coffee?'

'No thanks, not for the moment.'

She sat down facing him. 'You said this was partly official business. I expect you know that I called in at the station to sign my formal statement on my way to visit some friends this afternoon. Did I leave anything out?'

'Not that I know of. No, actually I wanted another word with Shipley, but he doesn't seem to be in. I don't suppose you've any idea when he's likely to be back?'

'Sorry, none at all.' She hesitated for a

moment, then asked, 'Would it be indiscreet to ask what it's about?'

'Well, since we're old friends and I know I can rely on you to treat this in the strictest confidence — '

'Of course.'

'And it's off the record as far as I'm concerned too.'

'You mean, this isn't an official interview?'

'Right.'

'Okay, I'm listening.'

'Well, Shipley was so distressed after finding the body that I let him go home after asking him to call at the station to make his formal statement — which he did this morning. Audrey Savage took it and although he was much more coherent it basically contained nothing he hadn't already told me. Audrey and I talked it over and we both feel he's hiding something. You went with him to view the body and Audrey said you brought him home after I'd spoken to him — did he say anything to you that might help us figure out exactly what happened?'

Melissa suppressed a shudder as she mentally relived the chain of events that followed her first sighting of a confused and apparently disorientated Graham Shipley. 'He seemed totally out of it at first,' she said. 'I could tell there was something wrong; I thought he might be ill so I called to him . . . but you already know that.'

'Yes.' Matt flipped open his notebook. 'You mentioned that he kept repeating, 'I never touched her'. What did you think he meant?'

'I assumed he meant that he had found her lying there dead, that someone else must have pulled her out of the water. In fact, he said as much — he also said he'd told you the same thing, but he didn't think you believed him.'

'I wonder why he should think that,' said Matt quietly. He fixed Melissa with the steady, searching gaze that seemed to be part of every policeman's stock-in-trade, designed to convince a witness that he or she would be well-advised to tell the whole truth.

Had the question been put to her an hour previously, Melissa would have replied frankly that she had no idea and probably gone on to admit that it had been troubling her as well. The explosive information in the newspaper extracts that Bruce had given her would, if she handed them over to the police, change the whole course of their investigation. Coming as it did in the wake of Graham's own personal tragedy, the consequent stress might easily cause him to suffer another breakdown, destroying — perhaps for ever — the fresh start of which he had spoken. He had not been found guilty of any offence; the complaint against him could have been entirely without foundation, even malicious. According to those reports, there had been no other evidence against him and he was entitled to be regarded as innocent. And if the story did come out in the course of the investigation into Cissie's death, she preferred not to be the one to break it.

These thoughts flashed through her brain in a nanosecond, yet she was aware from Matt's expression that he was waiting for her answer and had sensed that she had something to tell him. To account for any hesitation, she said, 'He didn't say, but he did talk a bit after I brought him home. It was very personal . . . he didn't actually ask me not to tell anyone, but — '

'If it isn't relevant to our enquiry, it won't go any further,' Matt promised.

'All right, I'll tell you. I think the reason he was so upset is that Cissie reminded him of his own teenage daughter.'

'He told you this?'

'Not in so many words. He told me that he had come to live here to 'make a fresh start' as he put it, after his marriage broke up and that he found 'all this' — presumably meaning the shock of finding Cissie — a terrible setback.'

'Did he talk about his wife?'

'No. He didn't mention her at all, only his daughter, who's a couple of years younger than Cissie, but big for her age. He sounded really proud of the kid and reading between the lines I had the impression that seeing the body of a girl about the same build and apparently the same age as his own daughter had given him a profound shock.'

'That's understandable.' Matt ran his fingers through his iron-grey hair, apparently deep in thought. After a few moments he asked, 'Did Shipley give any indication as to why the marriage broke down?'

'No. He did mention that he doesn't see his daughter any more.'

'Any idea why?'

'No.' That question had been niggling in Melissa's own thoughts as well. 'It could be the ex-wife has moved a long distance away — maybe gone back to live with her parents — and taken the child with her.'

'Possibly.' Matt closed his notebook and put it into his pocket. 'Mel, is the offer of a drink still open?'

'Of course. What shall it be?'

'Coffee will be fine.'

'Right. I'll go and make it. I could do with a cup as well.'

She went into the kitchen and he followed her with the easy familiarity of an old and trusted friend. While waiting for the kettle to boil, she said, 'Matt, you don't really think Graham Shipley had anything to do with Cissie's death, do you?'

'There's nothing at all at this stage to suggest that he had, but there are one or two things that are puzzling us. The obvious one is, if Shipley's story that he wasn't the one who pulled the body from the water is true, why didn't the person who did raise the alarm right away?'

'Yes, I've been thinking about that. And I've been wondering as well how she came to be down by the brook in the first place.'

'All the indications are that something or someone frightened her, that she went charging into the woods to get away and either missed her footing or tripped over something before falling into the water and knocking herself out. Her skirt was torn — we found a shred of cotton caught on a bramble that might have come from it and we've sent that to forensics — and one of her shoes had come off. Everything points to the fact that she was in a great hurry and not looking where she was going.'

Melissa's throat contracted at the mention of the new yellow shoes of which Cissie had been so proud. An image flashed into her mind's eye of a terrified girl fleeing in a blind panic, not looking where she was going in her desperate attempt to escape. Escape from whom? Surely not . . .

Aloud, she said, 'Graham Shipley seems to have a very good rapport with kids, especially the young ones, but I haven't seen him show the slightest interest in teenage girls. On the contrary,' she added, remembering his discomfiture at Becky Tanner's brazen advances.

'Meaning?'

She explained, and for a moment Matt's serious expression relaxed in a smile of amusement. It was not the first time she had entertained him with stories of Becky's antics. 'Of course, I've only known him a very short time,' she admitted, 'but no one could have behaved more properly in that situation. Becky went off in a paddy at being given the brush-off.'

'What we can't be sure of,' said Matt as Melissa put two mugs of coffee on the table and they both sat down, 'is, did that bang on the head — we're pretty sure it was caused by a nasty jagged piece of rock on the bed of the stream — knock Cissie out for long enough for her to drown?'

Melissa stared at the detective in horror as the significance of his words sank in. 'Matt, are you suggesting that someone — '

'Held her down to make sure she did

drown?' Matt said as she broke off, unable to bring herself to voice the thought. 'I'm afraid it's a possibility we have to consider. The pathologist wouldn't commit himself, except to say that drowning in fresh water can occur pretty quickly, but equally that she might have been only momentarily stunned and quite capable of picking herself up again within a couple of seconds.'

'But surely, if someone did that, there'd be marks — on the neck, for instance?'

'The flat of a hand on top of her head would have done the trick, and with that mop of hair no one would be any the wiser.'

'You're suggesting that someone may have threatened her or made sexual advances, that she ran away from him and fell into the brook, that he followed and when he saw what had happened took the opportunity of making sure she wouldn't be able to give him away?' Melissa felt her stomach churning at the picture her own words had conjured up and she covered her eyes in a futile effort to shut it out. 'It's monstrous. How could anyone do that to a lovely girl like Cissie?'

'We don't know that anyone did, but we have to consider all the possibilities,' said Matt gently. 'We know that she'd been dead for approximately three to four hours when her body was found, but she hadn't been in the water for the whole of that time because her clothes had begun to dry out. We also know that she delivered a box of eggs to the old man who lives along that track, presumably ten to fifteen minutes after she left the shop at around one o'clock. We interviewed him, but he wasn't much help. He's very deaf and he said he never heard her call — he said the eggs were on his kitchen table and he didn't even realise he hadn't brought them home himself with his other shopping. He ate one for his lunch and then spent the afternoon working in his vegetable plot behind the cottage and never saw anyone.'

'So she met whoever she was running away from after leaving Tommy's cottage and was presumably on her way home?'

'That's how it looks. Whether or not that person actually killed her, he must have done something that scared her pretty badly and we want to find him before he does it again. Shipley insists he was nowhere near the spot at the time and we've no reason to think he's lying, but — ' Matt stared moodily into his empty mug, plainly frustrated. 'We're appealing for witnesses and so far no one has come forward, but of course, it's early days yet. Look, I think I've taken up enough of your time — I'll be on my way. Thanks for the coffee.'

After he had gone Melissa prepared a light supper, but the possibility, however remote, that Cissie's death might not have been accidental weighed on her mind and destroyed her appetite. The notion that Graham Shipley was a murderer seemed unthinkable, yet there was the evidence, still lying hidden in her kitchen drawer, that he had at least once before been involved in some kind of confrontation with a teenage girl. She began to wonder whether she had done the right thing in withholding the information from Matt, then told herself that it was there in the public domain and if the police felt it necessary to probe into Graham's past they would quickly turn it up for themselves. There remained the possibility that Bruce Ingram might consider it his duty to release it. He had promised to call her in the morning and she resolved to tell him enough of Graham's sad history to persuade him not to do anything precipitate that might jeopardise the fresh start that he so desperately needed.

With that resolve, she went to bed, comforting herself with the thought that it wouldn't be her fault if it all came out.

10

It was Monday afternoon. There were still ten days to go before the start of the new term, but a trip to a special performance of *Romeo and Juliet* had been organised by Mr Jeremy Evans, who taught English and sport at Stowbridge Comprehensive. Gary and Becky Tanner, Billy Daniels and Dave Potter had — encouraged and subsidised by their parents — joined the party. After the bus chartered for the occasion dropped them off the three boys had, by tacit consent, made for the bridge spanning the stream a couple of hundred yards or so from the spot where, only two days before, Cissie Wilcox had met her death. It had long been one of their favourite places; more often than not during term time they would wander over there after getting off the school bus to lean their elbows on the parapet, puff a forbidden cigarette and exchange idle gossip on whatever currently exercised their minds. Favourite topics were sport and the world of pop music, more often than not some spectacular event on the football field or the latest bizarre antics of a group renowned — and admired — as much for their outrageous behaviour as for the quality of their performances. Today, affected as much by the recent tragedy in their own small community as by the fate of Shakespeare's doomed young lovers, they were unusually silent. They stared morosely down at the swiftly flowing water that had taken the life of their pretty young neighbour.

Normally Becky — who had gone along more out of an interest in the handsome, athletic Mr Evans than in Elizabethan drama — would have been hanging around with them. Today, however, she had said a perfunctory 'See you later,' to her brother and set off to walk the short distance home, calling 'Things to do!' over her shoulder when he demanded to know why she was in such a hurry. 'What things?' he had shouted at her retreating back, but received no answer.

After a while, Billy said thoughtfully, 'That Cissie, she were about the same age as Juliet, weren't she? Funny, that,' he added, half to himself as the others made no comment. 'Wonder if she were in love too?'

'Dunno 'bout that, but I reckon this lad here fancied her,' said Dave, indicating Gary with a jerk of his head. 'What about it, Romeo?' Receiving no reaction, he dug Billy in the ribs and whispered audibly behind his hand, 'No wonder her Mum reckoned it were

112

him what were chasing her.'

'Shut up!' Gary shouted. His face worked and tears oozed from his eyes despite his desperate efforts to control them.

'Leave it!' said Billy. 'Can't you see he's upset?' He put a hand on his friend's shoulder and gave it a squeeze, but Gary pulled away from him with a convulsive jerk. Billy withdrew his hand and looked at his feet in embarrassment.

'I asked her out, but she kept putting me off,' Gary said. 'Okay, I did like her, but not . . . I mean, I never . . . I knew how strict her Mum was . . . I was going to offer to walk her home on Saturday after she finished work, but I didn't think she'd let me so I — ' He covered his eyes with his hands; his chest heaved with the sobs that he fought to choke back. 'If I'd gone with her it might never have happened,' he finished brokenly.

'Not your fault,' said Billy. 'You wasn't to know.'

'D'you reckon old Tommy Judd did something to scare her?' said Dave after another long silence. 'I mean, suppose she saw what we saw — he wouldn't want her to run home and tell her Mum, would he?' He seemed taken with the notion of Tommy Judd as the villain of the piece. 'I can't see Cissie doin' deals with him like we did,' he added with a leer.

'I heard me Dad say the police reckon she were runnin' away from someone,' said Billy. 'It could have been Tommy — what d'you think Gary?' Gary shook his head. He was plainly finding the conversation distressing.

'I dunno,' he muttered.

There was a silence while they pondered the imaginary scenario. Then Billy said, 'D'you reckon we ought to tell?'

'What's the point of that?' Dave demanded. 'An' who're you thinkin' of tellin'?'

'The police, I suppose.'

'No, we can't do that!' This time it was Gary speaking. His voice was no longer shaky and he sounded alarmed at the suggestion. The others looked at him in surprise.

'Why not?' demanded Billy.

Gary hesitated for a moment as if casting around for reasons for his outburst. Then he said, 'They'll want to know how we found out.'

'That's a thought,' said Billy. The probable consequences of admitting to authority what they had been up to a week or so ago made the idea suddenly less attractive. 'We could say we was just peerin' through the window,' he suggested. 'We don't have to tell about, you know — '

'Tommy might grass on us,' Gary pointed

out, 'to get his own back, don't you see, and then we'd be in big trouble. Besides,' he continued as another thought occurred to him, 'he ought to be good for another supply before long.'

'You got a point there,' agreed Dave with a snigger. 'I vote we keep quiet.'

'I reckon so too,' said Gary. 'You agree, Billy?'

'I dunno.' Billy looked troubled.

'You listen to me!' Gary took him by the arm and swung him round. 'You don't say nothin' to no one, d'you hear?' he hissed. He was the taller of the two by several inches and more heavily built. His face was flushed and his jaw thrust out as he glared down at Billy.

'Okay, okay.' Billy pulled away and rubbed his arm, glancing at his watch as he did so. 'Let's forget it — I'm goin' home for me tea.'

'Me too,' said Dave and the two of them trudged off in the direction of Lower Benbury. Gary remained there for several minutes, deep in thought, before he too set off for home.

★ ★ ★

When Becky reached Oak Tree Farm she found her father in the kitchen. Whenever the work about the farm allowed, he made a point of being there to welcome his children home and his normally morose expression lightened as she entered.

'How's my girl then?' he asked, giving her a hug. 'Enjoy the play, did she?'

'It were okay.' She kissed him briefly on his prematurely lined, weather-beaten cheek and perched on a corner of the scrubbed deal table on which Jake had lined up three blue and white striped pottery mugs, a bowl of sugar and a bottle of milk. A kettle was singing on the stove and a white teapot stood on the draining board next to a red and black tea-caddy patterned with oriental figures and peacocks picked out in silver and gold.

'Where's Gary?' he asked.

'Stayed behind talkin' to Billy and Dave.' Becky studied her slim brown legs with satisfaction as she swung them to and fro.

Jake frowned. 'I don't trust that Dave Potter, he's a bad influence. His Dad's a dodgy character as well.'

'Oh, Dave's a bit of a prat, but he's okay,' she said carelessly.

Her father gave her a sharp look. 'That's not a nice word for a lady,' he chided.

'Sorry.' She gave a disarming smile and his frown of disapproval faded. 'Dad, you know Cissie Wilcox's Mum does for the ladies at Benbury Manor?'

'What of it?'

'She's too upset to work at the moment.'

Jake gave a sympathetic nod. 'Only natural, poor woman. I know how I'd feel.' He brushed his daughter's soft cheek with toil-worn fingers and she grabbed his hand and held it for a moment against her face.

'Dad,' she said, looking up at him with an earnest expression in her chestnut-brown eyes, 'I've been thinking — suppose I offer to help out until she's ready to start again?'

'You mean, charring?' Jake's face darkened and he pulled his hand away. 'You'll do no such thing, my girl. I'm not having you scrubbing floors for those toffee-nosed old biddies.'

'Oh Dad, it won't be scrubbing floors, just a bit of ironing and dusting, that sort of thing. It's only to keep Mrs Wilcox's job open for her till she feels better.'

'Let Gloria Parkin help out. She's used to that kind of work.'

'She's doing for some of Cissie's Mum's ladies, but she hasn't time for all of them. Please, Dad,' Becky slid off the table and snuggled up to her father. 'She can't afford to lose the job and it'll only be for a little while. I'd like to do something to help.'

Jake put an arm round her and gazed fondly down at the young, unusually serious face turned up to his. 'You're a good, kind girl, Becky,' he said, dropping a kiss on her forehead.

'So it's okay, then?'

He did not answer, but gave her a squeeze before releasing her and attending to the kettle, now coming to the boil. He poured hot water into the teapot, swilled it round, poured it down the sink and reached for the tea-caddy. He was whistling softly, the way he always did when considering a question. Becky watched his every move. She had learned long ago how to handle him, when to plead her case and when to remain silent. She was confident that she had said enough in this instance to persuade him to let her have her own way.

He made the tea, stirred it, put the lid on the pot and said, as he did every time, 'I'll just let that draw for a minute or two.'

'What d'you say, then?'

'All right,' he said at last. 'Only for a couple of weeks, mind, and as long as it doesn't interfere with your school work.'

She was careful not to appear triumphant. 'Thanks Dad, I'll go and see them right away.'

She made for the door into the hall, but he called her back. 'Aren't you having a cup of tea with me first?'

''Course I am. I'll have it when I've changed.'

In her bedroom she rummaged through her wardrobe, pulling out one garment after another, considering, rejecting, impatiently running her fingers through her glossy mane while trying to decide on the most suitable outfit. She longed to wear the new mini-skirt and figure-hugging top, but reluctantly put them aside as being inappropriate for today's purpose. She finally settled for jeans with a loose-fitting sweat shirt and trainers. She brushed her hair, tied it neatly back from her face and considered her reflection in the full-length mirror that had belonged to her mother.

'Yeah, that'll do,' she said aloud. 'For a start anyway,' she added with a giggle. She reached for a perfume spray, then changed her mind and put it back. 'First things first,' she told herself and went downstairs to have tea with her father.

★   ★   ★

At about the same time as Becky set off on her mission to Benbury Manor, Melissa received the expected telephone call from Bruce Ingram.

'Sorry I couldn't make it earlier,' he said.

119

'Seen anything of your reclusive neighbour today?'

'He put my morning paper through the letter-box, but I didn't actually see him. He must have gone up to the shop as soon as it opened.'

'And no sign of him since?'

'I've not been keeping him under observation, you know. I've been working my socks off most of the day.'

'I take it you've had time to look at the stuff I gave you yesterday?'

'Of course.'

'And — ?'

'It is the same Graham Shipley, if that's what you want to know. What are you planning to do about it?'

'Nothing for the moment. The police haven't released the name of the person who found Cissie's body and there was nothing in today's briefing to suggest that they're treating the death as anything but accidental.'

'Then why not let sleeping dogs lie?'

'I've had a word with my editor and we've agreed to do just that for the time being, unless there are further developments.'

'That's good.' Somewhat to her own surprise, Melissa found herself even more anxious than before to protect Graham from press intrusion based on hearsay and unproven circumstantial evidence. The image of his ravaged face, as he spoke of his broken marriage and separation from the daughter he obviously adored, was still vivid in her memory. Hard common sense told her that she should distance herself from any emotional judgement, but her instinct, based on the ability to judge character on which she prided herself, insisted that he had been a victim of circumstances and deserved to be left in peace to rebuild his life.

'Of course,' Bruce went on, 'there's no guarantee that some other paper won't get hold of the story and use it.'

'What about your Birmingham friend — the one who sent you the faxes? Is she likely to pass it on?'

'I doubt it. It's part of her job to hunt through back numbers in response to requests from people like me. She won't be the least bit interested in the story for its own sake.'

'You'll keep me posted, won't you?'

'Sure — and you'll do the same if you unearth any more details?'

'I don't plan to do any digging, if that's what you mean.'

But before long, Melissa was to find herself doing just that.

11

After a long, tiring but fruitful day spent toiling over her novel, Melissa took a hot shower, ate her supper in her dressing-gown and was in bed soon after nine o'clock. She snuggled down among the pillows with *Emma*, intending to read for an hour or so, but the events in Jane Austen's elegant imaginary world were powerless to prevent her mind reverting to the brutal reality of Cissie Wilcox's death, Matt Waters' disturbing remarks about its possible cause and — despite her wish to believe in his innocence — the doubts raised in her mind by the reports of Graham Shipley's encounter with a nameless, faceless adolescent girl. His life had been devastated, he had admitted to having a breakdown, and who could tell what long-term damage his mind had suffered as a result? A picture flashed into Melissa's head of Becky Tanner sidling into the queue in front of him at the barbecue and looking up at him with a provocative smile that was almost an invitation. He had shown no reaction, had appeared to ignore the girl's presence completely, yet there had been something in his set, expressionless face that, on reflection, she found disturbing. Then the picture changed and she saw him sitting on the ground with the Parkin boys and their friends, talking and laughing with them, the epitome of the kindly schoolmaster. Surely, a man who showed such a natural rapport with children, such spontaneous pleasure in their company, was incapable of violence? Clinging determinedly to this thought, Melissa eventually fell asleep.

It was gone nine o'clock when she awoke to a wet and blustery day that would, she decided, be most profitably spent in reading over and editing the chapter she had drafted the previous day. She got dressed and went downstairs; her copy of *The Times* lay on the mat and she remembered with a pang of guilt that Tuesday was her day for fetching the papers. Graham must have got tired of waiting, she thought, as she took it into the kitchen and settled down to do the crossword over her breakfast coffee and toast. As she unfolded it, an envelope with her name pencilled on it fell out. It contained a brief, unsigned note which read, *Can you spare me a little of your time? I badly need to talk to someone.*

As if he had been sitting beside the phone awaiting her call, he answered straight away and was at the door a couple of minutes later in response to her invitation. His face was drawn and his eyes red-rimmed; it was plain that he had not slept. He accepted a mug of coffee and, after a slight hesitation, a slice of toast. He ate and drank without speaking; his hands were shaking, his whole body seemed tense and there was a nervous, watchful quality in his manner, as if he feared something dire might happen at any moment.

At last he said, 'You must think me presumptuous — I mean, you hardly know me, but I — '

'It's all right,' she said as he appeared to be at a loss how to continue. 'Neighbours should help one another if they can.' It sounded banal, but it was difficult to think of anything more constructive without betraying that she had a shrewd notion of what the problem was. He was plainly on a knife-edge and the most important thing at the moment seemed to be to help him calm down and talk when he was ready.

His next words took her by surprise. 'That policeman who called on me on Sunday — is he a friend of yours?'

'You saw him? He said you weren't in.'

'I saw him, yes. I was looking out of the window, but it was getting dark and I had no lights on so he didn't see me.'

'So you pretended to be out?'

'Yes. I suppose you're wondering why.'

'If you want to tell me.'

'I was afraid he was going to ask me questions about . . . what happened to me last year.'

'When you had your breakdown?'

'Yes.' Graham began fiddling with his coffee mug, avoiding her eye. 'I never told you how it all started, did I?'

'You don't have to tell me now if you don't want to.'

'But I do want to, if you don't mind listening. You'll probably hear about it soon enough, now your policeman friend knows — '

'Not necessarily,' Melissa interrupted. 'I'm not privy to everything that goes on during a police enquiry.'

'Oh.'

He seemed nonplussed and she said, 'Look, if you want to change your mind — '

'No, no, I want to talk about it.' He covered his face with his hands for a moment and swallowed hard before continuing. 'Sergeant Waters called again yesterday morning and this time he saw me through the window so I couldn't avoid him.'

'And — ?'

'He said he'd been 'making a few enquiries

about me'. He'd found out,' — here Graham closed his eyes for a moment and drew a deep, shuddering breath as if summoning the strength to continue — 'that in my last job a girl called Jasmine Dixon accused me of indecent assault. That's why I had to leave, why my marriage collapsed and my wife refuses to let me see my daughter — ' Suddenly, his control snapped under a wave of pent-up fury and bitterness. 'That bitch . . . that little tart . . . she'd been practically throwing herself at me for weeks. I never said anything . . . I know now I should have spoken to the Head, I knew how tricky this sort of thing could be but I was so careful not to give her the slightest encouragement . . . and then . . . she came to me one afternoon in the classroom when all the other kids had gone and broke down in tears . . . she seemed genuinely distressed and I put an arm round her to comfort her . . . it was the stupidest thing I'd ever done . . . and then one of her friends came in and immediately she . . . Jazzie . . . began shrieking that I'd touched her, put my hand up her clothes, if the other girl hadn't come in I'd have . . . raped her.' He lowered his head and his voice dropped to a hoarse whisper on the final words.

Anxious not to betray the fact that she

126

already had some knowledge of the affair, Melissa said, 'I assume there was a police enquiry?'

'Of course, and I wasn't allowed anywhere near the school, or to talk to any of the students while it was on. Eventually the police said that the evidence wasn't strong enough to bring charges. Privately, one of them admitted that they suspected the girls had set me up — out of spite, because I'd rejected Jazzie's advances. The head teacher and the school governors accepted my version and I was reinstated, but the damage was done. Some of the parents stood by me, but others began a campaign to get me out, saying they were afraid for their daughters. It was damaging the school's reputation and the only thing I could do was agree to resign. The whole thing had put a terrible strain on my marriage and that was the last straw. Sheila left me the next day and took Patsy with her.'

He was calm now, unnaturally, unhealthily calm, speaking in a dead, toneless voice, his eyes fixed on infinity. Melissa had the impression that he was no longer aware of her presence and the notion set a prickling sensation running up her spine. To bring him back to reality, she stood up and reached for the empty cafétière. 'Shall I make some fresh coffee?'

The suggestion had the desired effect and he shook his head and stood up. 'No, thank you. I must go home now, I've got some work to do — you know, preparing for next term.'

'I do hope you'll be happy in your new job,' she said.

'Thank you. And thank you for listening to me. I — ' He broke off in apparent embarrassment and fiddled with his latchkey. 'You're the only person here who knows — '

'And that's how it will stay so far as I'm concerned,' she assured him and he gave a grateful smile that chased some of the weariness from his face.

As she was seeing him out, a small white van bumped along the track and pulled up opposite her front door. A burly young man in a white jacket got out and sprinted through the rain to greet her with a cheery smile. 'Glad I caught you in, Mrs Craig,' he said in a soft Scottish accent. 'I've some really tempting goodies for you today.'

'Right, come in and tell me about them.' As she stood aside for the newcomer to enter, she said, 'Graham, meet Colin. Give him half a chance and he'll sell you a couple of hundredweight of frozen kippers.'

'*Excellent quality* frozen kippers,' corrected Colin. 'And plenty of other things besides.' From his pocket he produced a slightly crumpled leaflet which he thrust into Graham's reluctant hand. 'Here's our complete list. Would you like me to give you a call?'

'Maybe some other time,' said Graham over his shoulder as he hurried across to his own front door.

'He'll not survive to 'another time' if he doesn't look where he's going,' Colin remarked. 'He nearly ran under my wheels last Saturday — dashed out in front of me as if Rob Roy and all his Highlanders were after him.'

'Where was that?' Melissa asked in surprise.

'Just outside the village, by the bus stop at the bottom of the hill. I was on my way to make a special delivery to your village shop; I'd promised to be there before one o'clock and I was running a bit late — '

Melissa frowned. 'What time would that be, then?' she asked uneasily.

'About half past one, at a guess.'

'You're sure it was the same man?'

'Positive. We ended up practically eyeball to eyeball. Mind, I don't think he'd recognise me — he had a sort of glazed expression, but of course that could have been shock. Now, what can I interest you in today?' He reeled off a list of special offers before dashing back to his van and returning with a stack of boxes. 'There's something new I'd really like you to try — we're doing a special introductory price — '

It was evident that he had heard nothing of the tragedy and Melissa decided not to mention it for the time being until she had a chance to organise her thoughts following this new and startling piece of information. She allowed him to talk her into buying boxes of individually frozen portions of marinaded chicken and salmon-en-croûte, responded to his enquiry about the progress of her current novel and offered him a cup of coffee, which he politely refused. When he had gone she went up to her study, but found it impossible to settle down to work.

Her thoughts were in turmoil. Nothing Graham had told her — or, presumably, included in his statement to the police — suggested that he had been at the scene of Cissie's death around the time it was presumed to have occurred. Matt Waters had guessed that he was hiding something and it was clear, from Graham's own account, that he now knew of the Jazzie Dixon episode, doubtless via the Police National Computer. If he had also known of this latest revelation, Graham would almost certainly at this very moment be at the police station, 'helping with enquiries'.

Despite her instinctive sympathy with the man, she could not shut her eyes to the fact that aspects of his account disturbed her. He had shown no further sign of the latent fury he had betrayed as he began to tell his story, but it was surely still there, seething like steam in a pressure vessel, threatening to erupt whenever provocation became too great to bear. A precocious, sexually active teenager had ruined his life; the experience must have left terrible psychological wounds. For the second time her mind flew back to Becky Tanner and the blatantly coquettish efforts she had made to attract his attention. She asked herself what might have been going through his mind as he stood there, stony-faced and unresponsive. Had it been anger at memories the girl's behaviour aroused? And then a more horrifying thought thrust itself forward: was it possible for a corrosive, uncontrollable rage at such memories to express itself in physical violence against anyone who reminded him of the girl who had brought about his downfall? What might his reaction have been, had there been no one else present?

Melissa's thoughts raced uncontrollably on. Could the sight of any nubile young girl, however innocent, trigger such a reaction?

Cissie had undoubtedly been dead for some time when she saw her body moments after Graham claimed to have found it, but in the light of Colin's evidence, he could have already known it was there *because he himself had killed the girl and was waiting for someone to come along and witness his supposed 'discovery'*. Yet what could quiet, modest little Cissie, innocently making her way home after delivering Tommy Judd's eggs, have done to remind Graham of the scheming, vindictive Jazzie Dixon? Now if it had been that little hussy Becky Tanner . . .

'Stop it!' Melissa said aloud. 'This is ridiculous — you're letting your imagination go berserk. Go and see the man — give him a chance to explain.' Resignedly abandoning all thought of getting any work done that morning, she went next door and rang the bell.

It was several moments before he answered; for once, it seemed, he had not been watching out of the window. 'I need to speak to you,' she said and without a word he stood aside for her to enter. He ushered her into the sitting-room — the same room where she and Iris had spent many an evening cosily chatting after a delicious vegetarian supper — and invited her to sit down, but she declined with an impatient shake of the head and without preamble began, 'You never told me you were near the brook a couple of hours before I saw you there.'

He winced as though she had struck him in the face. 'That Scottish fellow who brings the frozen food . . . was it his van that I nearly ran into?' She nodded and he hammered his forehead with clenched fists. 'God, what a fool I've been! I should have said . . . but it was so hard to explain, I felt sure no one would believe me . . . you won't believe me — '

'Try me.'

'I . . . I was telling the truth when I said I was out bird-watching. I'd just started walking along that path when I saw this girl running towards me. I didn't recognise her, but I could tell she was upset . . . distressed . . . and she was coming straight at me. I thought, if I wait for her . . . if she's in some sort of trouble and I try to help her . . . and anyone comes along — '

'So you turned and ran, and nearly got yourself run over,' Melissa finished as he broke off with a gesture of despair. 'Did you see anyone else — anyone she might have been running away from?' He shook his head. 'Or which way she went after that?'

'No, of course not, how could I?'

'You're sure you never did anything, before

you ran away, to make her frightened of you?'

'Of course I'm sure. What are you suggesting?'

'I'm just wondering why she should have changed course — as she apparently did — and gone charging into the woods and down that steep bank.'

'I've no idea, I really haven't.' He moved restlessly to and fro in the small, low-ceilinged room. 'It's something I've asked myself a dozen times. I keep thinking, if only I hadn't panicked and made off like that, maybe she'd still be alive.'

'Is that why you came back later — to make sure she hadn't come to any harm?'

'Not really. I'd forgotten about it by then, told myself not to be so stupid. I just wanted to see if I could spot a kingfisher.' He gave a harsh laugh. 'Can you believe that? A girl was lying there dead and all I could think of was some wretched dicky-bird — '

'You weren't to know,' Melissa said, moved almost to tears by his look of utter, hopeless misery. 'You mustn't blame yourself — '

'I swear I never touched her, but in a way I feel responsible for her death. What should I do?' he asked, looking Melissa full in the face, his mouth working. 'Must I tell the police?'

'That's up to you, but it's obvious they aren't completely satisfied about the cause of death, which means they're still ferreting around. Sooner or later they'll find out you've not been telling them everything you know — '

' — and they'll think the worst,' he finished with a touch of bitterness in his voice. 'You're probably right, but . . . I must have time to think.'

'Of course. I'll leave you for now.'

He had stopped pacing about and was standing at the window, staring out at the rain. He seemed to have forgotten her presence and she went home without another word, closing the door behind her as quietly as if there was a sleeper in the house.

12

On returning home, Melissa made a determined effort to work, telling herself for the umpteenth time that Graham Shipley's problems were no concern of hers. Two hours later she sat back in her chair with a sigh of relief, having reread yesterday's output and found no serious fault with it. She made a few necessary corrections, set up the printer, spent a few minutes stretching and exercising cramped muscles, realised that she was hungry and went down to the kitchen in search of lunch.

By the time she had consumed a bowl of soup and a cheese sandwich, checked the newly printed pages and filed them away, it was gone two o'clock. For the first time since hurrying back from Elder Cottage in the rain she looked out and saw to her surprise and pleasure that the sky had cleared, the rain had stopped and drifts of steam were rising from the stone paths, already drying in the steadily rising temperature. She opened the window and the sweet trill of a robin floated into the room on a breath of warm, moisture-laden air. Thankful for the opportunity to get out of doors, she went downstairs and into the garden.

A movement on the other side of the low fence that separated her plot from that of her neighbour caught her eye. He was there, standing with his back to her, drinking beer from a glass tankard held in one hand while idly fingering the blooms on a scarlet rose bush with the other. He appeared to be deep in thought and she was trying to decide whether to speak to him or to move away, pretending she had not noticed him, when he turned and saw her. Unexpectedly, he smiled and came over to the fence.

'Lovely to see the sun, isn't it?' he said conversationally. 'And aren't they just beautiful!' His face was flushed and it crossed her mind that the drink in his hand might not be his first. Her suspicions were confirmed when he swayed slightly as he made a sweeping gesture towards the roses he had just been admiring.

'Yes, they are,' she agreed. 'Iris loved her flowers, she spent every spare moment out here. She grew all her own vegetables too, but her kitchen garden's been grassed over. She had it all replanted when she left to make it easy to maintain and arranged for one of the village lads to look after it.'

'Yes, that was all explained to me when I

signed the lease.' Graham took another swig from his glass, suppressed a belch and leaned an elbow on the fence. 'Me, I don't know a thing about gardening,' he confided. 'Sheila — my wife — used to do everything. Knew her stuff, too. Lady Greenfingers, I used to call her. Here's to the disbelieving cow!' He raised the glass in mock salute before draining it. 'How about you? You like gardening?'

'I didn't know a thing about it until I moved here. Iris taught me all I know.'

'You miss her, don't you?'

'Yes, I do. We became very close friends.'

'Must be nice to have a close friend.' His face took on a self-pitying expression and Melissa, feeling she had given him enough sympathy for one day, was trying to think of a polite way of breaking off the conversation when a voice called, 'Excuse me!' and they both looked round to see where it was coming from.

Unobserved by either of them, a young man in jeans and a denim jacket had entered the garden of Elder Cottage through the side gate and was walking up the path towards them. Melissa noticed with a twinge of suspicion that he held a notebook in one hand. 'Sorry to barge in,' he said. 'I tried the bell, but got no answer, and then I heard voices so I took the liberty — '

Graham's flush deepened and he glared at the newcomer. 'Who are you and what do you want?' he demanded.

'My name's Peter Blake and I'm doing a course in Media Studies at Stowbridge College. Are you Mr Graham Shipley?'

'What if I am?'

If Blake noticed the hostility in Graham's tone, he gave no sign of it. 'I've been given this practice assignment,' he explained. 'I wonder if I could ask you a few questions?'

Graham scowled. 'Why should I waste my time answering your questions?'

'I'm on a couple of weeks' work experience on the *Gloucester Gazette* — '

'You're a journalist?' Graham blushed again and he took a step forward, his grip tightening on the empty tankard.

Melissa half-expected the young student to back down, but either he had not read the signals or had cast himself in the rôle of the hard-nosed newshound, determined not to be put off by a difficult interviewee. His manner became ingratiating. 'I hope to be, sir, one day, and I'd really appreciate your help. I understand that it was you who found the body of — '

He glanced briefly in his notebook to check the name of the victim, but before he could utter another word, Graham snatched it from his hand and flung it into the rose-bed with a snarl of 'Get out!'

Blake looked startled, but stood his ground. 'I assure you, I meant no offence, sir,' he said in a conciliatory tone. 'This is only a practice interview, none of it will get published — '

'GET . . . OUT!' Graham bellowed, his face contorted with fury. Without warning he lunged at Blake and took a swing at his head with the heavy tankard, but staggered sideways as he did so, missing his target by several inches and almost losing his balance. Melissa, feeling obliged to intervene before things got completely out of hand, reached over the fence to put a restraining hand on his arm and with the other gestured towards the gate.

'You heard what the gentleman said. Please go,' she said sharply.

Even then, Blake was reluctant to give up. 'And you are — ?' he said hopefully.

'Never mind who I am. I know the editor of the *Gazette* and if you're not off these premises in ten seconds flat I shall report you to her,' she threatened, and the would-be ace reporter hurriedly retrieved his notebook and fled.

'I told him, didn't I?' exulted Graham,

waving his tankard aloft like a sportsman brandishing a trophy. He evidently believed that he had routed his enemy single handed. 'That'll give the cheeky young bugger something to report!' Then a thought appeared to strike him and his air of triumph collapsed like a deflated balloon. 'They're on to me,' he groaned. 'They'll send someone else . . . like they did before . . . my name will be plastered all over the paper and everyone will know what happened to me . . . oh God, what have I done?' He slapped his forehead; his eyes were wild and he sent darting glances around as if he suspected reporters of lurking behind every bush.

Melissa began to be seriously concerned about his state of mind. In an attempt to introduce a note of normality, she said, 'Graham, when did you last have anything to eat?'

'Eat?' He looked bemused, as if the word was unfamiliar.

'Yes, eat. Have you had any lunch?' He shook his head. 'Why not? You said yesterday you had food in the house.'

'Wasn't hungry,' he muttered. 'Didn't fancy anything. Thought I'd have a drink instead.'

'It's bad to drink on an empty stomach.'

'Yes, I know.' He contemplated the bottom

of the tankard with an abstracted air. 'I'll think about it.'

Reluctantly, because she had no wish to become further embroiled in his problems, but fearing that if she left him to his own devices he would probably ignore her advice and drink himself into a stupor, Melissa said, 'Would you like me to make you a snack — a bacon sandwich, or maybe an omelette?'

'You're very kind.'

Fifteen minutes later he was ensconced in her kitchen, wolfing down eggs, bacon and toast. When he had cleared the plate and accepted a second cup of tea, he put down his knife and fork and said, a little humbly, 'I'm afraid I'm being a great nuisance to you.'

'You are a bit,' she admitted, adding with mock severity, 'I hope it's not going to become a habit.'

'I used to have a counsellor and I do miss her.'

'Have you registered with a doctor since moving here?' He shook his head. 'Then I think you should find one. I'll give you the name of mine if you like.'

He brightened at the suggestion. 'I think I'll do that. It would get me off your back, wouldn't it?' he added with a smile.

Melissa smiled back. 'Luckily for you, I had a successful couple of hours' stint on my book after you left this morning and I was taking a breather anyway.'

'You're a writer?'

'You didn't know?'

'I'm afraid not.' He looked embarrassed. 'What do you write?'

'Until recently, crime fiction, but I've been trying my hand at something different lately. My last novel was a bit more serious — 'literary', the critics called it.'

'Do you write under your own name?'

'Meaning you've never heard of me,' she teased him.

'I'm sorry — '

'You don't have to apologise. I think Sam Rogers mentioned that your subject's history,' she went on, hoping to lead him on to talk about his own interests. Unfortunately, the remark had the opposite effect. He clapped his hands to his temples and groaned.

'Rogers . . . and Miss Monroe, his head teacher . . . they're going to find out what I did . . . what I'm supposed to have done . . . they'll see it in the paper and cancel my contract . . . it'll start all over again!' The spark of animation flickered and died; once again, despair overwhelmed him.

'Now, you listen to me!' Melissa adopted the brisk, slightly authoritative, maternal tone that, years ago, she used when reprimanding her son for some teenage folly. 'You heard what that young man said — he's only doing work experience and nothing he writes is going to get published. They probably got fed up with him hanging around the office and getting under their feet — '

'So why did he pick on me? Someone must have given him my name.'

The same thought had occurred to Melissa. She knew — because she had checked with Matt Waters — that the police had not identified either of them in their press release, and the report in the *Gazette* had merely referred to Cissie's body being discovered by a local resident while out for a walk. It would not, however, have been difficult for young Blake to find someone in the village more than willing to talk about the event that was still uppermost in people's minds. Mrs Foster, for example, was always ready to offer her opinion and she had already hinted that she half suspected Graham Shipley of having something to hide. There was a real danger that when Blake returned to the office and reported his hostile reception, someone — Bruce Ingram, for example — would decide there was a story to be followed up.

'I should have changed my name,' Graham said suddenly. 'I thought of it, when I applied for the job at St Monica's, but it would have been difficult with official records and so on, and anyway it seemed unethical . . . it wasn't as if I'd done anything wrong — ' He looked at her with a pathetic, almost hang-dog expression. 'What should I do now?'

'I'm afraid that's something you have to decide.' Melissa did her best not to let him see that she was becoming a little weary of her rôle as mother confessor. 'We spoke this morning about your telling the police that you saw Cissie shortly before she died . . . have you done that?'

'No. I can't make up my mind — '

'Well, think about it. The sooner they have all the facts, the sooner they'll be able to clear up the case.' Melissa stood up and began to clear the table. She glanced out of the window, trying to figure out a polite way of indicating that it was time for him to leave. She found inspiration in the sight of the laden branches of the one small fruit tree in her garden. 'Would you care for some apples?' she said. 'I was thinking earlier, it's time I started picking them.'

'That's very nice of you,' he said dully, and then, as if it struck him that he owed her a gesture of appreciation, 'Shall I give you a hand?'

It was not what she had in mind, but it was

better than being stuck indoors on what had become a brilliant afternoon. As it happened, he quickly tired of the exercise, complained that the sun was giving him a headache and went home half an hour later, thanking her profusely for her kindness and clutching a plastic bag full of apples.

★　★　★

Towards evening the air became still and heavy, with cloud building up from the west. Unsettled weather was forecast and some time in the small hours Melissa was awakened by the sound of the promised rain lashing against her bedroom window. Then came the lightning, swiftly followed by crashes of thunder indicating that the storm was practically overhead. Unable to sleep, she got up, put on a dressing-gown and went downstairs to make a pot of tea. The wind roared around the cottage like a marauding beast, with every so often a momentary, uncanny stillness as if the elements were silently regrouping for the next onslaught. She switched out the kitchen light and sat at the window to watch the jagged rods of lightning tearing apart the blackness of the sky. She tried to find words to describe the awesome spectacle, could think of nothing that did not sound twee and banal, thanked her stars that she did not have to be out in it, finished her tea and went back to bed.

A little over a mile away, Tommy Judd lay in a deep, snoring slumber, oblivious to the howling of the storm. Even had it been a still night and he wide awake, his muffled hearing would not have detected the creak of the kitchen window-frame being stealthily opened, nor the faint sounds of movement as the intruder carried out his search. Not until he came downstairs the following morning and saw the gaping hole in the floor did the old man realise that he had been robbed. His shock and anger were compounded by the knowledge that he dare not report the break-in to anyone, least of all to the police.

13

Wednesday was the day that Gloria Parkin, the blonde and buxom wife of Stanley Parkin, second-hand car dealer, and the proud and devoted mother of Darren, Wayne and Charlene, spent two hours energetically cleaning and polishing Hawthorn Cottage while bringing Melissa up to date with the latest news and gossip from the twin villages of Upper and Lower Benbury.

Today, inevitably, her sole topic was the tragedy that had befallen the little community. She was a warm-hearted, emotional creature, easily moved to both laughter and tears, and her eyes filled as she spoke of the grief of the bereaved mother. 'Can't get the poor love out of my mind,' she declared, brushing moisture from her eyes with the back of her hand. 'I keeps asking myself, what would I do if anything like that happened to my Charlene? And no man to comfort her,' she added with a sniff.

'Have you seen her? How is she coping?' asked Melissa. 'Mrs Yates said she's staying with neighbours.'

'That were just Saturday night. She went

home Sunday morning. They tried to make her stay, but she would go, said she felt nearer to Cissie in her own home.' Gloria's tears flowed more freely and Melissa felt her own eyes pricking as she went on, 'Mrs Yates and the rest of us pops in regular and takes in food and tries to cheer her up, but she spends most of her time in Cissie's room, just sitting there looking at her picture and saying as how she should never have let her go to that disco and dance all evening with Gary Tanner.'

'She seriously thinks Gary had something to do with it?' said Melissa in disbelief. 'But how?'

'Search me.' Gloria's plump face puckered in bewilderment. 'She's got this notion in her head about teenage boys being sent by the devil to get girls like her Cissie into trouble.'

'She told you that?'

'Something like that, a while ago it were, before Cissie began working in the shop of a Saturday. Said she didn't like the idea because of all the lads she might meet. I told her it was the older men she should be watching out for — like that Mr Lane at Benbury Park,' Gloria added, her sorrowful expression giving way to a knowing wink. 'Told her I'd spotted him more than once eyeing up the girls and she got quite shirty, said I must have imagined it.'

Melissa was about to comment that she too had observed what she had described in her recent letter to Iris as 'a mischievous twinkle' in Gideon Lane's eye, but decided that it would be unwise. Gloria did not have a shred of malice in her make-up, but her tongue was inclined to run away with her and the last thing Melissa wanted was to be the source of any further rumours.

Gloria's next remark filled her with dismay. 'They reckons that Mr Shipley next door to you might know something,' she said over her shoulder as, after enveloping her ample frame in a flowered overall, she began taking cleaning materials from a cupboard in the kitchen.

'What do you mean, know something?'

'Someone said they'd seen him out walking near the brook the day Cissie died.'

'That's not surprising. He was the one who found her.'

'I mean, earlier.'

'Oh?' So Colin must have mentioned Graham's near-fatal dash elsewhere — unless there had been yet another witness to his presence. Trying not to betray her concern, Melissa said, 'Who told you this?'

'Mrs Foster. She got it from Miss Brightwell. Tell you something else, she saw that policeman driving this way on Monday and wondered if maybe he were going to ask Mr Shipley more questions.'

'If I were you, I'd be careful about spreading these rumours,' said Melissa. She had spoken a little more sharply than she intended and Gloria looked at her with a hurt expression.

'It were only what Mrs Foster were saying,' she protested.

'I know, but if it got back to Mr Shipley, he might think people suspected him of having something to do with Cissie's death. He's upset enough as it is.'

Gloria's toffee-brown eyes registered a blend of shock and remorse. 'Ooh my, I never thought . . . but no, no one would think that of him, would they? Such a nice gentleman, my kids really took to him at the barbie. We just wish he were going to be their teacher — ' She broke off as she caught sight of the kitchen clock. 'Oh my, just look at the time, I must get on,' she said and bustled out.

Melissa went to her study and tried to settle down with her novel, but found her mind constantly harking back to the tragedy. So far as she knew, the police were still working on the theory that Cissie had met her death while fleeing from a potential attacker. There seemed no doubt that she had tripped and fallen into the brook, knocking herself out as she did so, but — as Matt Waters had told her in confidence — there remained the sickening possibility that whoever was chasing her had made sure that she never recovered consciousness. If Graham Shipley was telling the truth — and she sincerely believed that he was — then someone else, probably but not necessarily the girl's pursuer, had pulled her body from the water but failed to raise the alarm. Why?

Further questions piled up in her mind. She had not set eyes on Graham since yesterday afternoon; had he in the meantime plucked up courage to go to the police and admit that he had seen Cissie shortly before she died? If so, had his explanation been believed? Perhaps by now Colin had heard about the appeal for witnesses and come forward. Could someone else have seen Graham at the crucial time and reported it to the police? And had Peter Blake's abortive interview done anything to cause the *Gazette's* editor to order some serious investigation? Because of his troubled history, Graham Shipley was already under exceptional stress. Who could tell what effect further harassment might have on his state of mind?

On impulse, Melissa picked up the phone and called Bruce Ingram's number. It was a long shot, but there might be something he could do to call off the dogs.

'Hi, I was about to call you,' he said. 'What can you tell me about your neighbour threatening to glass young Peter Blake? It's caused quite a stir in the office.'

'It wasn't quite like that, and the chap was rather objectionable, wouldn't go when he was asked.'

'I'd like to hear your version, then. The editor has asked me to follow it up.'

'I was afraid of this,' Melissa sighed. 'That's why I called — I was hoping you could do something to play it down.'

'No chance, I'm afraid, not with Shipley's history — '

'Bruce! I asked you not to — '

'Don't blame me. I wasn't the one to dish out that assignment — it was just something for young Peter to do. If your friend had answered a few anodyne questions instead of cutting up rough, the kid would have come back and written up a nice little practice piece that would never have seen the light of day. As it is, a lot of questions are being asked.'

At that moment there was an interruption as an excited Gloria banged on the door and burst into the room without waiting for a response. 'Guess what!' she exclaimed. 'That

Mr Shipley's been arrested!'

'What!' Melissa hastily covered the mouth-piece and gasped, 'Are you sure?'

'I were at the window shaking me duster . . . I saw him get in a car with two men . . . policemen, I reckons . . . they all drove off in a hurry.' Her eye fell on the receiver in Melissa's hand and she uttered an apologetic squeak. 'Ooh, sorry, didn't see you was on the phone, just thought you'd like to know. It's nearly eleven,' she went on, clearly oblivious to the shattering effect of her announcement. 'Shall I make the coffee?'

'Yes, please,' said Melissa weakly, 'I'll be down in a minute.' Into the receiver she said, 'I presume you overheard that?'

'I heard the bit about the arrest. Is it true?'

'I can't be certain, but it sounds very much like it.'

'Hmm.' There was a short pause while Bruce considered this new development. 'I'd better nip along to the nick and see what I can pick up,' he said. 'Meanwhile, off the record, exactly what did happen when Peter Blake called on Graham Shipley?'

With an effort, Melissa controlled the urge to scream. 'Just go away Bruce, will you?' she hissed.

* * *

Graham Shipley sat slumped in his chair in the interview room and stared down at the grey plastic surface of the table separating him from the two police officers. He felt a tight band round his head and a hard lump in his stomach; the room was warm to the point of stuffiness, but he felt cold. They had offered him a cup of tea and when a young uniformed officer brought it he clasped the thick pottery mug in both hands in an effort to absorb some of its heat into his shivering body.

The events of the past half hour had brought him to a state of utter confusion. One minute he had been staring out of the window in the upstairs room of Elder Cottage, seeing nothing, conscious of nothing but the need to take some sort of action, yet unable to decide which path to follow. The next, the choice had been taken out of his hands as the car drew up outside and two men — he would have known immediately that they were police officers even if he had not recognised Detective Sergeant Waters — got out and knocked on the door. He barely heard what they said; he only knew it meant they had found out that he had lied to them and that he had to go with them. He could no longer think; his mind was like a vehicle out of control, racing helter-skelter downhill towards an abyss. Nothing lay ahead but darkness and despair.

He had lain awake for hours during the night, trying to summon up the resolve to come clean, to go to the police, admit that he had been lying and do his best to make them understand why, rather than wait for them to find out from other sources. Common sense and his conscience told him that this was the right thing to do — make a clean breast of everything, tell the whole truth and trust that he would be believed. His faith had helped to sustain him during the Jazzie Dixon affair and he clung to it now, praying for guidance. And his prayers had been answered, hadn't they, through the kindly wisdom of a sympathetic neighbour? He felt certain that she believed in his innocence; why had he not acted on her advice while he still had the chance? It was because he lacked the courage. He should have prayed for that as well. Now it was too late, and he had only himself to blame.

Detective Sergeant Waters began the questioning and despite his quiet manner and total lack of any hint of bullying there was a steely edge to his voice. 'According to the statement you made shortly after you reported your discovery of the body of Cissie Wilcox,' he began, 'you had not previously been anywhere in the vicinity on the day of her death. Have you anything to add to that statement?'

With an effort, Graham raised his head to look the detective squarely in the face. His eyes met a penetrating, unblinking gaze that chilled him to the marrow and turned the hot tea in his stomach to ice. He licked his dry lips and faltered, 'Yes.'

'Fine.' Waters settled back in his chair; his manner became almost avuncular as he added, 'Take your time.'

It might have been meant to reassure, but it had the effect of reminding Graham that there was no hurry because they had the power to keep him here all day and all night if necessary. Maybe longer. Maybe for years. Maybe this time he would never be let out. He had heard of what happened in prison to people found guilty of harming children and a wave of panic engulfed him. For a minute or two he could barely speak.

At last, in a series of jerky, ill-constructed sentences, he managed to stammer out the story of how the sight of a distressed Cissie running towards him seemed to threaten a repeat of the moment when Jazzie Dixon had sprung her trap and how the possibility of having to live through a similar nightmare all over again had swept every rational thought aside.

The two detectives listened in silence. When he had finished, Waters leaned forward and said quietly, 'We know, because we have a reliable witness, that at approximately one thirty you rushed out into the road and almost got yourself run over by a white van. Are you claiming that what happened nearly two years ago had the effect of making you so desperate to avoid contact with any other teenage girl that you ignored the possibility that Cissie Wilcox might be in genuine need of help?'

'Yes.' Graham brushed a hand over his eyes as guilt and misery threatened to break his fragile self-control. 'Do you think I haven't thought of that a thousand times since?'

The detective made no direct reply, but took a sheet of paper from a file on the table in front of him. 'I have here a note of a conversation I had with the head teacher of your last school. He said, and I quote, 'My impression of Shipley was of a compassionate and caring teacher who achieved some very good results, sometimes with quite difficult students.' Is that how you see yourself, Mr Shipley?'

'I've always tried to do my best for the kids in my charge. Some of them come from pretty miserable backgrounds . . . they need a lot of help and support — '

'Quite so,' said Waters with a nod. ' 'Compassionate and caring',' he repeated. 'I put it to you, Mr Shipley, that an experienced schoolteacher with those qualities, seeing a sixteen-year-old girl in obvious distress, would be more likely to go to her help than to run away.'

'I've tried to explain that . . . I panicked . . . I wish to God I had stayed to help, she might still be alive — '

'Perhaps you did stay to help,' Waters suggested in a deceptively quiet voice. 'Perhaps you ran towards her, put your arms around her to try and comfort her. And perhaps she mistook your intentions . . . screamed . . . tore herself away and went charging into the woods and down that steep, slippery bank where she lost her footing and fell into the water, knocking herself unconscious. And perhaps you followed, and when you saw her lying there, perhaps' — here the hint of steel returned to Waters' voice — '*that* was the moment when you panicked, when you realised that there was a real chance that when — or should I say *if* — she recovered consciousness, she would give a very different version of the incident to yours.'

'Are you suggesting that I deliberately left that poor child to drown?' Graham exclaimed. 'That's monstrous!'

159

'According to our pathologist's report,' Waters continued implacably, 'there was a fair chance that she was only momentarily stunned, that left alone she might well have come round in time to struggle out of the water by herself. Unless of course, she was prevented from doing so. Would you care to comment on that, Mr Shipley?'

14

'I know you have your reservations, Esther,' said Judith Waghorne as she laid the table for breakfast on Wednesday morning, 'but I sincerely believe that it showed a very nice spirit on Becky Tanner's part, offering to help us out with the housework until poor Jean feels able to start again.'

Her sister, who was placing sliced tomatoes on the grill pan, looked over her shoulder and commented tartly, 'I doubt if she's doing it entirely out of the goodness of her heart.'

'What do you mean by that?'

'I mean,' said Esther as she finished arranging the tomatoes and opened a fresh packet of butter, 'that she's more likely to be doing it for the money. Which is why,' she went on, placing the butter on a white porcelain dish before carefully folding the greaseproof wrapper and disposing of it in the pedal bin under the kitchen sink, 'I made it clear that if we accepted her offer we would pay her at a lower rate than we pay Jean.'

'And she agreed to that without any argument,' Judith pointed out. A slightly reproachful expression clouded her softly

161

rounded features. 'I do feel, Essie, that we should give her the benefit of the doubt. I've heard you say some rather unkind things about Becky — and I agree, she is inclined to be a little forward at times,' she went on as her sister's eyebrows rose at the implied criticism, 'but it must be hard for her, not having a mother. I'm sure there's no real harm in her. Let's be honest, we all have our shortcomings, don't we?'

'You know your trouble.' Esther, who was slicing bread for toast, gestured at her sister with the bread-knife to emphasise her point. 'You're too soft-hearted — and too easily fooled. As for Becky not having a mother, well, we know what kind of woman *she* was, don't we? In my opinion, that girl takes after her. I should never be surprised to hear that she's got herself into trouble.'

'You don't mean . . . pregnant?' Judith's mouth fell open. 'That's a dreadful thing to say! She's still only a child herself.'

'She's fourteen and physically very mature, and she's always hanging around with the boys — you must have noticed.'

'They're her brother's friends,' Judith pointed out. 'I don't think we should hold that against her. And if you feel so strongly about it,' she went on, 'I'm surprised you agreed to let her come.'

'I wouldn't have done had I been here on my own, and certainly not if Gideon had been here. It was you who persuaded me, falling for all that sentimental twaddle she was talking about Cissie Wilcox being a dear friend of hers and how she owed it to her mother to do whatever she could to help — '

'I thought it showed a very kindly, caring attitude. Why do you say it was twaddle?'

'For one thing, she and Cissie went to different schools. As far as I'm aware, they hardly knew one another.'

'Perhaps they met at the youth club.'

'This is all beside the point. I'm not happy about having her in the house.'

'It's only for a couple of hours one morning a week,' Judith pointed out, 'and probably only for a week or two at the most. And we've made it a Wednesday morning, haven't we, knowing it's Giddy's day to go into Stowbridge — '

'*I* was the one who insisted on making it a Wednesday morning,' Esther interposed. 'And I hope you've remembered not to mention it to him.'

'Of course I haven't mentioned it,' said Judith in a hurt voice. 'I'm as concerned about shielding him from temptation as you are.'

'I'm sure you are dear,' said Esther in a

163

softer tone, 'but you must admit, you can be a little forgetful at times.' She laid rashers of bacon alongside the tomatoes, placed the pan under the pre-heated grill and stooped to put plates in the oven to get warm. Glancing at the clock on the wall as she straightened up she said, 'You'd better give him a call and tell him the breakfast will be ready in fifteen minutes. We don't want him missing the bus.'

'Isn't he taking the car?'

'Not today. He asked for it, but I'm driving into Cheltenham immediately after breakfast to have it serviced. I'm sure I mentioned it to you,' she added with a touch of exasperation.

'Oh yes, so you did. Well, I've got plenty to do indoors so I'll be here to keep an eye on Becky.'

'Quite.' The sub-text of the monosyllable was, *That's the way I've planned it and I'm glad there are to be no arguments.*

★   ★   ★

'You're up bright and early,' Jake Tanner observed as he came in from the yard at Oak Tree Farm at half past eight and found his daughter in the kitchen, fully dressed in close-fitting jeans and a figure-hugging knitted top. She was frying bacon in a heavy iron pan and he inhaled in appreciation.

'That smells good, love. Any chance of a bacon sandwich for your old Dad?'

'Sure.' Becky fetched more rashers from the refrigerator. 'Goin' to help out at Benbury Manor this morning,' she explained, adding them to the pan and prodding them with a fork. 'Mustn't be late on the first day, must I? There's tea in the pot, help yourself,' she added.

'I hope those old biddies are paying you for this,' observed Jake. 'I'm not having you do it for nothing — '

'Sure they're paying. Not the full rate, though.'

'Why not?' Jake paused momentarily in the act of filling his cup. 'I'm sure you'll do every bit as good a job as Jean.' He put down the pot, added milk and sugar to his tea and stirred vigorously, then went over to his daughter with the cup in his hand and put his free arm round her shoulders. 'I could tell them how handy you are with a dishcloth and duster — when you're in the mood,' he added teasingly, giving her a squeeze.

She snuggled against him and looked up into his face with a winning smile. 'I hoovered up the other day, and I do the ironing don't I? And I keep my room tidy — '

'Most of the time,' he agreed fondly.

'You only get the iron out when there's

165

something of your own that needs doing,' said a voice behind them. Gary had entered the kitchen unnoticed and was inspecting the teapot. 'What's all this in aid of, then?'

'All what?' Becky demanded.

'You being up so early, cooking breakfast.'

'Oh, tell him, Dad.' Becky's sunny mood evaporated in the face of her brother's surly attitude.

'She's helping out at the Manor until Jean Wilcox feels up to it again, and it's a real kind act she's doing,' said Jake. 'I haven't noticed *you* doing much around the house lately.'

'I give you a hand round the farm, don't I?'

'When you feel like it.'

'Oh stop it, the pair of you. Here, help yourselves.' Becky slammed a plate piled with bacon sandwiches on the table, sat down and grabbed one for herself. Jake did the same, biting into it and masticating with appreciation. Gary ignored the food and sat in silence, his eyes on his sister's face.

'What you looking at me like that for?' she demanded.

'Like what?'

'Glaring at me as if I'd done something wrong.' He made no reply and Becky added slyly, 'It wasn't me that got in late last night.'

Jake gave his son a sharp look. 'You been up to something you shouldn't?'

Gary helped himself to a sandwich and inspected it closely before taking a bite. 'No,' he said defensively, with his mouth full.

'Because if you have — ' Jake's brow knotted menacingly.

'Haven't been up to anything. She's just stirring it.'

Becky finished her sandwich and stood up. 'Take no notice of him Dad, he's just in a mood. I got to go.' She dropped a kiss on the top of his head, picked up the shoulder bag she carried everywhere, gave her brother a mocking salute and went out of the back door.

When she had gone, Gary put the half-eaten sandwich back on the plate, got up and turned to leave the room. Jake called him back. 'Just you finish that up, my lad,' he ordered. 'I'll not have you wasting good food.'

'I'm not hungry.'

'What's up with you then?'

'Nothing,' Gary muttered. 'Just leave me alone, will you?' He was out of the room before his father had a chance to say another word. The sound of his footsteps echoed through the house as he bolted upstairs and slammed his bedroom door.

In mounting anger, Jake finished his breakfast, cleared the table and put the used plates and cutlery in the sink. Then he too went storming upstairs and flung open the door to his son's room. For a moment, it appeared empty. Then the lad's head appeared above the bed; at the sight of his startled, guilty expression, Jake strode round and stood over him as he half-knelt on the floor. 'What the hell are you up to?' he demanded.

'N . . . nothing . . . I was looking for my trainers — ' Gary stammered, his face scarlet.

'You're hiding something.'

'No Dad, honest — '

'Out of the way!' Elbowing his son aside, Jake crouched down, groped under the bed and dragged out an envelope. 'What's this, then?' Without waiting for a reply, he tore it open. For one dreadful moment they stared at one another before the father grabbed his son by the shoulders and dragged him to his feet. 'Where in God's name did you get hold of that?' he demanded, almost choking with fury.

'Please, Dad.' The lad's teeth were chattering and his face was contorted with distress. 'I was going to get rid of it . . . burn it . . . I didn't want you to find out — '

'I'm sure you didn't,' Jake said grimly. 'Now, are you going to tell me where you got it, or do I have to shake it out of you?'

To Jake's consternation his son, whom he

had not seen crying since he was about seven years old, burst into tears. It was several minutes before he was calm enough to be able to tell his father the whole, miserable, sordid story.

★ ★ ★

Blissfully unaware of the drama about to be played out at home, Becky set off for Benbury Manor. She had been instructed to report for work at ten o'clock, but she had deliberately set off early because she wanted to be in the narrow lane linking the Manor with the main road into the village well before the half past nine bus to Stowbridge came along. She was well aware that Mr Gideon Lane often travelled on that bus because he had told her so when, the previous week, she had been on it herself and he had made a point of sitting next to her even though there were plenty of empty seats. Once or twice, as the bus swung round a corner, his hand had fallen — as if by accident, and he had been most apologetic — on to her lap. By the end of the journey she was in no doubt that he fancied her, and she was even more sure on the way back when he moved as close as he could and from time to time rubbed his thigh against hers. She hadn't responded, but she hadn't pulled away either.

She had a shrewd idea — because that sniffy Mrs Waghorne and her soppy sister had been so definite that she could only come on a Wednesday, and then not till ten o'clock — that the idea was to make sure their brother was well out of the way before she appeared. They probably knew what he was like; she giggled gleefully to herself at the thought of how she was on to their little game. At that moment Gideon himself appeared round a bend in the lane. He beamed and raised his cap with a polite little bow that delighted her. He was such a gentleman, just the type she most admired.

'My dear, what a charming surprise! You look very happy — where are you off to on this lovely sunny morning?'

'To your house,' Becky said, flashing him her most alluring smile. 'And you're off into town, so you won't be there — what a shame.'

'You mean you're calling on my sisters?' Gideon looked puzzled.

'Didn't they say?' said Becky innocently, reasonably certain that they had not. 'I'm standing in for Mrs Wilcox, till she feels better. Cissie's mother,' she added as he looked blank. 'The lady who does your housework.'

'Ah yes, you mean Jean,' he said. His smile became an expression of serious concern. 'Such a terrible tragedy. How is the poor lady bearing up?'

'She's taken it pretty hard. I thought someone should step in and hold the fort for her, keep her job open — '

'What a lovely thought! You are a good girl.' By way of expressing his appreciation at such a kindly deed Gideon moved closer, put an arm round Becky's shoulders and gave her a little squeeze. His hand drifted downwards, slid beneath her arm and cupped her breast, his thumb and forefinger seeking — and finding — the erect nipple.

She slapped his hand in mock indignation, but did not pull away. 'Ooh, Mr Lane, you are naughty,' she giggled. 'Suppose someone comes along and sees?'

His hand lingered a moment longer before he released her. 'That would never do, would it?' he murmured. His eyes devoured her and she shivered a little in anticipation; she had a shrewd notion of what was going on in his mind. His next words confirmed that she had read him accurately. 'Suppose I asked you to meet me somewhere a little less public?' he said, lowering his voice to a whisper although there was no living thing within earshot but a black and white cow scratching its chin on the top of the stone wall that bordered the lane.

Becky decided to play it cool, just for fun. She glanced at her wristwatch and said coyly, 'It's almost time for your bus. You don't want to miss it, do you?'

He leaned closer. 'You haven't answered my question,' he said. He was breathing heavily and the flush had deepened in his already rosy face. 'What do you say?'

'I might,' she said, with a toss of the head that sent a few strands of her hair brushing across his cheek. 'Now, I really got to go. Ta-ta!'

She did not turn back to look as she continued on her way, but she was confident that he was watching her. She hoped he was enjoying the slinky, Marilyn Monroe wiggle that she had been practising lately.

15

Thoroughly unsettled by the latest developments, Melissa found it impossible to tackle
any further work that morning. After Gloria
had left she ate a light lunch and at one
o'clock switched on the radio to listen to the
local news. The first item confirmed her fears:
'A man is being questioned in connection
with the death of sixteen-year-old Cissie
Wilcox, who was found drowned last
Saturday in a stream running through a
lonely patch of woodland near her home.'

Barely two hours had passed since Gloria
had come bursting into her study with the
news. They haven't wasted any time in
releasing the information, she thought gloom-
ily as she switched off the radio. She
wondered how Graham was standing up to
this new ordeal. From what she had seen of
him he was in a highly volatile mental state
and to be subjected to more police
questioning could push him dangerously
close to another breakdown. He should be
seen by a doctor. She hoped Matt Waters was
handling the interview; he had the experience
to spot the danger signals, but — in company

no doubt with every other officer involved with the case — he also knew the circumstances of Graham's previous encounter with the law. His job was to clear up the hideous doubt hanging over Cissie's death.

Melissa's thoughts turned to Jean Wilcox. She wondered if the poor bereaved mother was aware of police suspicions. The loss of a child — especially an only child — from whatever cause must be terrible; to know that he or she had been deliberately killed would surely make it a hundred times harder to bear. Melissa found herself thinking of her own son Simon, now a successful business-man living and working in the United States, and reliving some of her own maternal anxieties over the years. She felt a sudden urge to hear his voice, to know that he was safe and well. It was almost eight o'clock in the morning by New York time; he had probably already left for his office but . . . on impulse, she grabbed the phone and called the number of his apartment. Her heart surged with relief as he came on the line.

'Hi, Madre!' His voice was thick with sleep. 'Anything wrong? You don't usually call this early.' She heard faint grunts and rustlings and pictured him rolling over in bed, bleary-eyed, hair rumpled, heaving himself up on one elbow to squint at the clock.

'It's not that early. I was afraid you might already have gone to work.'

'It's Labor Day and I was having a lie in.' He gave a mighty yawn. 'It's nice to hear from you though. Anything special?'

'It just occurred to me that we haven't spoken for a week or so. How are things?'

'Fine. As a matter of fact, I was thinking of you only yesterday. It's time you came over for another visit. How about it? Come and do some early Christmas shopping.'

'Christmas! We're barely into September. Anyway, I'm struggling to finish a book.'

'When's your deadline?'

'End of this month.'

'Will you make it?'

'Provided there aren't any more traumas.'

'What do you mean?'

'The past few days have been a bit upsetting.' Skipping over her part in the discovery of Cissie's body, she gave him a brief outline of events since the previous Saturday, culminating in Graham Shipley's arrest.

'I do wish you'd try and keep clear of other people's problems.' His voice took on the familiar concerned tone that he had used in the past after learning — after the event — of previous brushes with murder and mayhem. 'It's terribly sad about the poor girl being drowned, but I don't like the sound of this Shipley guy. If they release him, do watch your step. Psychotics can turn nasty without warning — '

'Oh Simon, he's not psychotic, he's just desperately unhappy and under the most terrible stress. He's been teetering on the verge of a breakdown ever since it happened.'

'He's not your problem. Just keep out of it and get on with your book, okay? And when you've finished it, book yourself on a flight to New York and stay here for at least two weeks,' he went on, with the touch of bossiness that occasionally irritated her but which today she found reassuring. 'Think of it as an incentive to meet your deadline.'

'I will,' she promised. 'I'll really look forward to it. Is everything all right with you?'

'Yes, fine.' They spent a few more minutes chatting about things in general before hanging up. Feeling comforted, Melissa cleared away the remains of her lunch. She looked out of the window. It was another beautiful day; an hour or two in the open air would continue the calming process that the phone call to Simon had set in motion. She remembered the apples from yesterday's picking and considered the problem of how to dispose of them. Mrs Foster could probably sell a few in the shop . . . and perhaps old Tommy Judd would appreciate some. She found a cardboard carton and filled it with apples, put a few more in a plastic bag for Tommy, loaded up the car and set off.

'I don't want anything for these — just charge what you think and put the money in the charity box,' she said as she entered the shop with the carton of apples in her arms. 'After you've taken something for yourself, of course,' she added unnecessarily as she set it on the floor beside the carefully arranged display of other fruit and vegetables. Mrs Foster was an obliging soul in many ways, but she was not renowned for doing anything for nothing. Normally, she would have made some remark to drive home this point, but today there was something more important on her mind.

'Did you hear the *Cotswold Sound* news at one o'clock?' she asked, wildly fluttering eyelashes betraying her excitement. 'They've got the man who murdered Cissie — I'll bet it's that Mr Shipley!' she went on before Melissa had a chance to challenge the word 'murdered'. 'I always did think there was something dodgy about that man.'

'I don't think we should be assuming anything of the kind,' said Melissa, doing her best to conceal her annoyance at this blatant distortion of the facts. 'All it said was that a man is being questioned — '

' — and we know what that means, don't we? I wonder how soon they'll charge him.'

'So far as I know, there is no evidence at all that Cissie's death wasn't an accident,' Melissa pointed out.

'Then why don't they come out and say so?'

It was a question to which Melissa could think of no answer that would shake the woman's faith in her own opinion. All she could say was, 'I don't think it's fair to Mr Shipley to jump to conclusions.'

'I'm sure you're right,' said a gentle voice from behind Melissa. Alice Hamley had entered the shop unnoticed. 'It is upsetting, though. Poor Jean Wilcox is so distressed — she's not allowed to make the arrangements for Cissie's funeral until the police release her body — '

'Which they won't do until they've cleared things up,' Mrs Foster interposed. 'And isn't that exactly what I've been saying?' She shot a triumphant glance in Melissa's direction before asking Alice what it was she was wanting. 'And what news of Dr Thackray?' she asked as she cut and weighed a wedge of Double Gloucester cheese. 'Is his tummy-ache any better?'

'Oh, didn't you hear? He's had emergency surgery for appendicitis. Mrs Thackray phoned John just before I came out. He's getting on all right, but he'll be in hospital for several days.'

'Dear oh dear!' Mrs Foster shook her head in concern. 'Who's going to play the organ for the service on Sunday?'

'Oh, that's no problem, thank goodness. Mr Lane says he'll be pleased to do it.'

'Do you mean Mr Gideon Lane from Benbury Manor?' said Melissa in surprise. 'I didn't know he was a musician.'

'Oh yes, he was organist and choirmaster at a church in Somerset before he retired. He's promised to help out whenever there's a problem.'

'Well, that *is* fortunate.' Mrs Foster wrapped up the cheese and put it on the counter. 'Will there be anything else? How about some apples from Mrs Craig's garden. Only picked yesterday, so she tells me — '

' — and organically grown,' Melissa added. 'Do have some, Alice. The children will love them — and every pound sold puts something in the charity box,' she added with a mischievous glance in Mrs Foster's direction. 'Well, I must be on my way, I'm taking a few apples to Tommy Judd. Alice, do ask John to give my best wishes to Dr Thackray if he goes to visit him.'

★ ★ ★

The official postal address of the tumbledown dwelling where the old man had lived for as long as anyone could remember was Brookside Cottage, although it was never known locally as anything but Tommy Judd's. It was possible to reach it by car, but the ground was rutted, stony and inclined to be muddy in places in all but the driest weather. Melissa pulled off the road and parked the Golf on the verge, took out the bag of apples and set off to walk the half mile or so along the track. The air beneath the trees was close and humid after the previous day's rain; the overhanging branches cast a heavy shade for most of the way so that the pallid, spindly brambles that grew in profusion on either side bore only a meagre amount of fruit, too small to be worth the picking. Melissa, accustomed to the open aspect of her own home, found it slightly oppressive and she felt a sense of relief when she emerged into the clearing surrounding the cottage, which was bathed in dazzling sunlight.

She half expected to see Tommy working in his little vegetable plot which, despite his age and his arthritis, he tended regularly and kept in immaculate condition, raising crops of onions, potatoes, beans and carrots which would undoubtedly have won prizes at the annual horticultural show if he could have been persuaded to enter them. There was no sign of him outside, but the cottage door was ajar. Melissa tapped on it and called his name, but there was no reply. Remembering his deafness, she rapped more sharply and called again; this time, she heard a faint noise that sounded like someone stirring in their sleep. Thinking that he was probably having a nap and being reluctant to disturb him, she pushed the door open a fraction further and was in the act of putting the bag of apples on the floor when the sound came again, louder this time and sounding disturbingly like a groan. Raising her voice, she called, 'Mr Judd, are you all right?' before stepping inside.

The front door led straight into the kitchen. It took her eyes a couple of seconds to adjust from the brightness outside to the dim light within . . . and then she saw him, curled up in a foetal position under the window. He was clutching at his groin, his eyes were closed and his face was contorted in pain. There was blood running from his nose, one side of his mouth was split and bruised and there was an ugly gash on his forehead.

'Mr Judd, whatever's happened?' Melissa exclaimed in alarm. 'Have you been attacked — are you badly hurt?'

At the sound of her voice, the old man opened his eyes and hastily removed his hands from the region of his genitals. 'Beat me up . . . kicked me,' he mumbled through swollen lips.

'Who did?' He did not answer, but let out another groan and rolled on to one elbow. 'I don't think you should try to move just yet,' she warned, but he took no notice. Seeing that he was determined, she dragged a heavy, dilapidated armchair across the room and when he had managed to struggle to a half-sitting position she propped him against it. As she did so, her eye fell on a gaping hole in front of the fireplace from which the square section of floorboards that lay to one side had evidently been cut. *A hiding place for the old man's secret treasure board?* was the question that flashed into her head. She had often heard it remarked, mostly in jest, that Tommy Judd might have wealth hidden away. She stepped forward and glanced into the hole; it was empty. It looked as if robbery was the motive for the attack and the police would have to be informed, but first she must

182

get medical help. In the meantime, he needed to be kept warm; she found an old army blanket draped over the back of a shabby couch and spread it over him.

'I've left my mobile phone in my car,' she told him. 'Just stay there and don't try to move while I call an ambulance.'

'No!' A gnarled hand shot out from under the blanket and grabbed at her wrist. 'I don't want no ambulance. Just leave me be, I'll be all right.'

'But you need to be examined by a doctor. Those cuts on your face need seeing to, and you may have other injuries — '

'I don't want no ambulance and I don't want no doctor,' he insisted.

'But you've been beaten up . . . and robbed — '

'Robbed?' Seeing her gaze deflected towards the hearth, he turned his head and saw for himself. His face contorted again, but this time the cause appeared to be anger rather than pain. 'The bastard . . . the bleeding bastard!' he muttered through clenched teeth.

'Do you want me to inform the police?'

'No!' he shouted, even more emphatically than when he refused medical help. A strange, almost crafty expression crept over his damaged features. 'There weren't nothin' in there,' he said. 'Thank 'ee for your kindness, but I don't want no doctor nor no police. Just leave me here to rest for a while and I'll be all right.'

'At least let me bathe those cuts on your face,' urged Melissa, reluctant to leave the old man alone, but unwilling to go against his wishes. She noticed with relief that his breathing was more regular and his colour, apart from his injuries, appeared more normal. 'And perhaps you'd like a cup of tea,' she added.

Almost vehemently, Tommy shook his head. ''Tis kindly meant, I know, but I'm best left alone,' he insisted, and as there seemed to be nothing else she could do she put a cushion behind his shoulders, adjusted the blanket and got up to go. 'What brings you here, anyway?' he asked suddenly. She thought she detected a note of suspicion in his voice.

'I brought you a few apples from my garden.'

He grunted and closed his eyes. She took this as a sign of dismissal, and left. She was almost back to her car when she met Gideon Lane heading towards the cottage. He was carrying something in a plastic carrier and appeared slightly disconcerted on seeing her, but quickly recovered and greeted her with his usual charm, which changed to concern as she said, 'Oh, Mr Lane, I'm so glad to see you. Poor old Tommy Judd's been beaten up in his own cottage.'

'Good heavens! When?'

'Not long ago by the looks of it. I found him curled up on the floor in terrible pain.'

'Is he badly hurt?'

'It's hard to tell. He said he'd been kicked and his face is in a mess, but he wouldn't let me call an ambulance or inform the police. He even refused to let me clean up some of the blood.'

'Dear, dear!' Gideon winced at the mention of blood and his cherubic countenance registered acute anxiety. 'Have you any idea who did it?'

Melissa shook her head. 'He wouldn't say. I wonder if you could call in as you're going that way?' she suggested. 'He might be more willing to tell another man what happened.'

'Yes, yes, you're probably right. I was just on my way to see him, as it happens.' Gideon fiddled nervously with the handle of the plastic bag and cleared his throat. 'Was anything taken, do you know?'

'He says not, but there's a big hole in the floor in front of the hearth and as far as I could see it's empty.'

Gideon sucked air through pursed lips. 'Dear, dear!' he repeated. 'You're right, I'll see what I can do. At least, I'm forewarned, thank you.'

As he was about to walk on, Melissa said, 'Perhaps you can persuade him to see a doctor . . . and the police should be informed. It was a nasty, vicious attack, and even if nothing's missing — '

'Yes, yes, just leave it to me.' He raised the plastic carrier in a vague gesture of farewell and hurried away.

16

It was gone half past three when Melissa reached home. There was no sign of life at Elder Cottage; she tried the doorbell without success, went indoors and called Graham's number, and when there was no reply put down the phone with a sense of foreboding. The attack on Tommy Judd, following so soon after Cissie's death, seemed to intensify the cloud that was hanging over the village. On the face of it, there was no reason to suppose that there was a connection between the two, yet she could not avoid a sense of impending evil, as if some malignant force had set in train a monstrous domino effect that was heading unstoppably towards final disaster. Then she told herself that this was hysterical nonsense, that her imagination was running away with her. 'Pull yourself together, Mel Craig!' she told herself severely, and reached for the kettle. There was just time for a restorative cup of tea before Becky Tanner arrived for her weekly French lesson.

She could not help wondering, as she drank her tea, why Tommy had been so adamant in refusing both medical attention and a police investigation. She was quite sure that he knew his attacker and she was equally certain, despite his emphatic denial, that he had been robbed. Robbed of what? The obvious answer was money. Although he gave every appearance of having an income only marginally above subsistence level it was possible that — in common with other eccentric characters with similar life-styles whose stories featured from time to time in the newspapers — he had a considerable amount of cash hidden away. In most cases, such wealth came to light only after death, but perhaps in Tommy's case someone had already stumbled on his secret. It was one possible theory; he had lived and worked in the village for a long time and when he was younger and fitter he had doubtless done plenty of odd jobs around the village, in addition to his regular work for Benbury Estates, for which he would have been paid in cash. Over the years he might well have accumulated a considerable sum. Had he sustained his injuries while trying to defend it? If he recovered quickly it was unlikely that the question would ever be answered. But if he did not recover . . . Melissa's gloom deepened at the prospect of the village becoming the focus of what might then turn out to be a second murder enquiry.

She was diverted from further speculation by the arrival — several minutes after four o'clock — of an unusually subdued Becky Tanner. Her hair hung loose about her face and she kept her head half-turned away as she entered the cottage, trailing behind Melissa instead of making straight for the kitchen in her usual jaunty fashion and deliberately taking a seat with her back to the window. Even so, the make-up she was wearing — applied no doubt after she had left the house and was out of her father's sight — could not disguise the unnatural redness round her eyes.

Melissa gave her a keen glance. She could not remember the last time she had seen Becky otherwise than bursting with self-confidence and she felt a twinge of concern. Despite her precocious ways she was still a child, and motherless. Jake was a devoted father, but there must be times when, with the best will in the world, he failed to recognise his daughter's emotional needs.

'Becky,' she said gently, 'is anything wrong?'

The girl affected an air of defiance. 'No!' she declared, but she kept her face averted. 'Got shampoo in me eyes, didn't I?'

'You're sure there's nothing else?' Becky shook her head vigorously and dived floorwards to drag books and papers from her schoolbag. When she straightened up Melissa saw fresh tears spilling down her cheeks. 'There is something,' Melissa insisted as Becky sniffed and brushed them away with the back of her hand. She pushed a box of tissues across the table. 'Here, have one of these — and try not to smudge your mascara,' she said with a smile of encouragement.

Becky glanced up in surprise. 'You reckon it's okay for me to wear make-up?' she asked unexpectedly.

'I'd say you were old enough to wear a little — out of school of course, and so long as you don't overdo it.'

'You reckon I overdo it?' For the first time, Becky looked directly at Melissa.

'I think maybe you went OTT with the eye-shadow this time, but I guess that was to hide the redness.' Having, she felt, won the girl's confidence, she went on, 'Are you sure it wouldn't help to talk about what's upset you?'

'It's nothing really. There was a bit of a run-in at home — Gary told tales and then me Dad had a go at me.' Becky blew her nose, stuffed the used tissue into the pocket of her jeans and flipped back her hair. 'You know I've been helpin' out at the Manor?'

Melissa shook her head. 'No, I didn't. How did that come about?'

'I knew they'd be looking for someone to fill in until Cissie's Mum got over things a bit and I thought, if they found someone that suited, Mrs Wilcox might lose her job.' Becky assumed an aggrieved expression. 'I explained to me Dad that it's only for a week or so, but he kicked up no end of a fuss.'

'Why did he object?'

Becky shrugged. 'Search me. Anyway, in the end he said it was okay, but the minute I got home he picked on me. An' all I was doin' was try to help out Cissie's Mum,' she added virtuously.

'I think it was very kind of you, but I can see your Dad's point of view,' said Melissa diplomatically. 'After all, you'll be going back to school very soon and you'll have homework to do — he probably doesn't want you to get over-tired.' Gathering from the curl of Becky's lip that she did not accept this explanation, Melissa decided to let the matter drop. 'It's time we got on with your lesson,' she said

'Okay, I'll tell you how I got on at the Manor, shall I? — *en Français, naturellement,*' she added and, her self-possession now completely restored, launched into a surprisingly humorous, if halting, account of her morning's work under the fussy supervision of Mrs Judith Waghorne.

The lesson was practically over when there was a ring at the bell. Leaving Becky to write down some new vocabulary, Melissa went to answer. To her surprise, Gideon Lane was at the door.

'I just thought you'd like to know that Tommy — ' he began, breaking off as Melissa, glancing over her shoulder, put a finger to her lips.

'I've got Becky Tanner here — she's in the kitchen,' she whispered. 'How is he? Did you manage to get him to the doctor?'

Gideon shook his head. He appeared taken aback at the news of Becky's presence, but quickly grasped the implications and dropped his own voice as he replied, 'I've had a look at him and I don't think he's seriously hurt. That's really why I'm here, as it happens. Tommy is *most* anxious for this, er, unpleasantness not to go any further.'

Melissa was about to object that 'unpleasantness' was hardly an appropriate way to refer to a violent attack on an old man, but at that moment Becky emerged from the kitchen. 'I've written down all what I've to do for next time — ' she began, then broke off as she realised who was standing in the doorway. 'Ooh, Mr Lane, fancy seeing you again!' she exclaimed coyly. 'Did Mrs Waghorne tell you, she was so pleased with what I did this morning, she asked me to come again next Wednesday if Cissie's Mum still can't make it.'

Gideon beamed. 'I'm not at all surprised — I had no doubt that you'd do a splendid job for us,' he said with his customary hint of gallantry.

Becky treated him to a roguish smile as she slipped past him, hitching the strap of her bag over her shoulder and managing as she did so to expose a strip of tender young flesh between her jeans and her scanty T-shirt. 'Bye-bye, Mrs Craig,' she said, 'see you next week. Bye-bye, Mr Lane!' She set off at a brisk, purposeful walk, but Melissa noticed that she glanced with what seemed to be more than casual interest at Elder Cottage as she passed, as if she was hoping for a glimpse of Graham Shipley at one of the windows. *The last thing he needs is attention from that little baggage*, she thought to herself as she turned back to Gideon Lane and found that he too had his eyes on Becky's retreating form.

'Would you care to come in?' she suggested. 'I'm really very concerned about Tommy — are you sure it's right to leave things like this? I mean, don't you think the police should be informed? Anyone capable of doing that to an old man should be caught as soon as possible. He might easily do it again.'

Having declined the invitation with a shake of his head and a wave of one carefully manicured hand, Gideon gave every sign of being anxious to be gone. 'I think we have to leave that up to him,' he said.

'But he should at least see a doctor,' Melissa persisted. 'Suppose there are internal injuries? It could be very serious.'

'He's quite determined not to, and we can't force him against his will, can we? He made it very clear that he wants the whole thing forgotten. I for one will respect his wishes and I know he is hoping you will do the same. Now, I really must be going.' Without giving her a chance to say anything further, he swung round and hurried away, almost colliding with Gemma, the one female member of the Woodbridge brood, who had recently taken over delivery of the *Gloucester Gazette* from the youngest of her numerous elder brothers.

'Nearly 'ad me off me bike,' she said indignantly as she skidded to a halt. She handed over Melissa's paper, pulled out a second copy and then returned it to the bag suspended from her handlebars. 'Not much

194

point in leaving this, is there?' she said with a meaningful glance towards Elder Cottage. 'See the front page?'

Melissa unfolded the paper and stared in consternation at the sight of the stark black capitals proclaiming: MAN HELD OVER GIRL'S DEATH. She scanned the report in growing dismay; although no name was mentioned, it was obvious — even if Gloria had for once managed to keep her mouth shut — that local residents would have no hesitation in identifying Graham Shipley as the person referred to. It would be common gossip in no time.

'You reckon he did Cissie in?' Gemma asked.

'I don't think it's at all certain that anyone 'did her in' as you call it,' said Melissa reproachfully, thinking as she did so that she was wasting her breath, that despite the carefully non-committal wording of the report, few local people would now doubt that Cissie's death had not been accidental. 'But if anyone did, I don't think for a moment it was Mr Shipley,' she added in a decided voice and Gemma, looking disappointed, turned her wheel and cycled away.

Back indoors, Melissa studied the piece more closely. Nowhere was the word 'murder' used; in fact, the writer had been careful to avoid stating categorically that the police were treating Cissie's death as suspicious. Instead, he had quoted one of their spokeswomen as saying that there were 'certain aspects of the case for which satisfactory explanations had not yet been found' — an obvious reference, Melissa felt, to the fact that Cissie's body had apparently been removed from the water by a person or persons unknown. All in all, she thought as she turned to the next page, it added nothing of any significance to what she already knew.

She threw the paper aside and turned her mind to the problem of what she should cook for her evening meal. She was not particularly hungry; the disturbing events of the day had blunted her appetite and she settled for a couple of poached eggs on toast. When she had eaten them she put her plate and cutlery in the sink, ate an apple, brewed some coffee and tried to settle down with a book, but all the time the questions she had been asking herself ever since learning of Graham's arrest were fretting away at the back of her mind. Several new ones had now been added to the list: Who attacked Tommy Judd, and Why? Had he been robbed or not? Why was he so anxious to keep the episode secret? The thought of him alone in his desecrated cottage, possibly more seriously hurt than he would admit and almost certainly in pain, was disturbing. She could not help feeling that Gideon Lane might have done more to persuade him to have his injuries seen to, then told herself that she herself had done her best and had no right to interfere further. It occurred to her to wonder what had prompted Gideon to call on Tommy. On the face of it, they seemed to have little in common, but one never knew.

She put the book aside and turned on the television, surfed all the channels without finding a single programme to interest her and finally, realising that she was dog-tired, had a long soak in the bath and was in bed before ten o'clock. As she snuggled down under her duvet, the memory of a snatch of overheard conversation slipped into her mind. She spent several minutes trying to recall the details, then abandoned the effort, telling herself it could well be totally irrelevant anyway. On the other hand, it might just be worth following up. She would do it tomorrow. To make sure she remembered, she made a note on the pad she kept on her bedside table. Moments later she was fast asleep.

17

For Melissa, early to bed on Wednesday night meant early to rise on Thursday morning. By six o'clock she was showered, dressed and seated at her desk with a cup of coffee and a plate of buttered toast, preparing to begin work on the final chapter of her second attempt at so-called 'literary' fiction. Almost twenty years had passed since the publication of her first crime novel. It had enjoyed immediate success and was followed by a steady stream of titles featuring Nathan Latimer, a senior police detective who had caught the imagination of the mystery-reading public and featured in a long-running television series that had brought her fame and a comfortable income. A year ago, somewhat to the consternation of Joe Martin, her agent, she had announced her intention to change direction and within a matter of weeks produced a comparatively short but what one critic had described as 'an enthralling, by turns intensely moving, stimulating and slyly humorous tale of a woman's fight to establish an identity in the face of parental possessiveness and marital failure'. She was still somewhat bemused by the fact that, less than a month after publication, it had entered the bestseller list and her editor — who, until she read the script of *Driving Force*, had been highly sceptical about her decision — was now eagerly awaiting its successor.

It was an effort at first for Melissa to concentrate; her thoughts on waking had been of anxiety over the possible psychological damage his arrest and questioning by the police, followed by a night in custody, might be doing to Graham Shipley. This was swiftly followed by unease over the injuries suffered by Tommy Judd and a persistent feeling of guilt that she had not insisted that he at least have medical attention. It had taken a determined effort to thrust concern for the two victims to the back of her mind, but as her fingers moved over the keys of her word processor, at first slowly and with several false starts and then with increasing confidence, the climax of the drama she had created began to gather pace and within minutes she was completely absorbed in her imaginary world. When at length she sat back and waited for the first draft to emerge from the printer, she was astonished to realise that it was almost eleven o'clock, that the last slice of buttered toast had congealed on the plate and that she was both hungry and thirsty. She gathered up the printed sheets, took them downstairs and had just settled down with a fresh instalment of coffee and toast when the telephone rang.

'Mel, it's Joe. Thought I'd give you a call to find out how things are going as I haven't heard from you lately.'

'Joe! It's good to hear from you — but I thought it was editors who worry about missed deadlines and disruption to publication schedules, not agents.'

'Agents like to feel everything's under control as well.'

'I know — and to be reassured that they won't have to wait too long for their share of the advance.' Melissa was fond of teasing Joe about his supposed preoccupation with money matters.

'That's not nice,' he protested, but there was no rancour in his tone. It was a private joke that they had shared ever since her books had been the subject of the lucrative television contract.

'Just kidding,' she said. 'And you'll be pleased to know that the first draft of the last chapter is even now lying on the table before me, hot from the press . . . and covered with marmalade,' she added as a blob fell on to the first page from the slice of toast she was holding in her free hand.

'Are you pleased with it?'

'Reasonably.'

'When can I come and collect it?'

'Give me a couple of weeks — there's a bit of revision to do to some of the early chapters.'

'Right. Give me a date as soon as you can. I'll book in at the Queen's and we'll have a celebratory dinner.'

'That would be lovely.' The invitation conjured up a pleasant image of luxurious relaxation, in sharp contrast to the painful stiffness in her neck and shoulders. She became suddenly conscious that the stress of the past week and the intensity she had brought to the morning's work had combined to produce a feeling of utter weariness. To her consternation, she had to choke back tears. 'It'll be good to have something pleasant to look forward to,' she said shakily.

He must have detected the suppressed emotion in her voice, for his immediate response was, 'Is something wrong?'

'Several things are very wrong . . . not with me personally,' she added hastily as the sound of a sharply drawn breath sped along the wire. 'The one note of comfort is that so far the story hasn't hit the national press.'

'That sounds serious. Tell me.' He listened

intently and without interruption as, with an uncharacteristic lack of conciseness, she recounted the events surrounding the horrifying discovery of Cissie Wilcox's body. When she had finished, he said quietly, 'Who is this Shipley character?'

'I told you, he's a schoolteacher who's rented Iris's cottage.'

'And you've known him just a couple of weeks?'

'That's right. What's that got to do with it?'

'Only that you seem to have become quite involved with him in a very short time.'

'Oh Joe, I'm not *involved* with him — '

'You seem very exercised over his problems.'

'He's a human being, and a neighbour, and he's badly in need of help.'

'It doesn't have to be your help.'

'Joe, what are you suggesting?'

'You know what happens when you start poking your nose into other people's affairs. It's led to one or two quite narrow squeaks.'

'You've never objected in the past,' she pointed out. '*Au contraire*, when news has broken about 'Cotswold crime writer helps solve real-life mystery' you've rejoiced in the way my sales have shot up. I've been a nice little earner for you over the years.'

'Mel, I wish you wouldn't keep saying

things like that. You know you're more to me than just a brilliantly successful writer. I really care about you.'

'I know, I was only kidding,' she said, with a pang of remorse. It wasn't fair to tease him like this. He was a dear friend who would, she knew, like to be a great deal more; she would not hurt his feelings for the world. 'But I can assure you that Graham doesn't pose any kind of threat, to me or anyone else,' she insisted. 'He's a gentle soul and a dedicated teacher who's been landed in an appalling situation through no fault of his own.'

'How can you be sure of that? You've only known him five minutes.'

'I'm convinced he's been telling me the truth — '

'Are you sure there isn't more to it than that?'

'Whatever do you mean?' It suddenly dawned on Melissa that it was more than simple concern for her welfare that lay behind the probing. 'You aren't suggesting I've taken a shine to the bloke, are you? For goodness' sake, Joe, I'm not an impressionable teenager.'

'No, but you're a very attractive woman in a vulnerable situation.'

'Are you saying I can't take care of myself?'

'No, of course I'm not. I'm sorry, Mel, I

didn't mean any offence.'

'None taken. Look, I apologise for having burdened you with all this, but it's been on my mind and there hasn't been anyone else to talk it over with except young Bruce Ingram and Sergeant Waters. Bruce tends to see everything in terms of its news potential and to Matt it's a routine police enquiry, whereas to me it's a human tragedy in the making.'

'That's one of the things I love about you Mel — your humanity.' There was a tender note in his voice which brought an unexpected feeling of comfort. 'All I ask is that you don't allow yourself to become too deeply involved in other folks' troubles.'

'I'll do my best. It's been a great help talking to you, Joe, and I'm really looking forward to our date at the Queen's.'

'Likewise. See you soon. Take care.' And he was gone.

She put down the phone and went back to rereading her draft, but the conversation had stirred into life all the unanswered questions that she had been wrestling with over the past few days. And with them came the recollection of the reminder that she had written for herself shortly before falling asleep the previous night. She hurried up to her bedroom and checked the scribbled note, wrinkling her brow and reflecting that she must have been almost asleep when she wrote it. Only three words were legible: 'barbecue', 'tickets' and 'boys'.

Well, there had been boys in plenty at the barbecue; she had helped any number of them to salad, rolls, tomato sauce and mustard. She sat down on the edge of her bed, puzzling over the reference to tickets. Gradually, it came back: Becky Tanner wanting to know where her brother and his friends got the money for their tickets and being told in no uncertain terms to 'forget it'. But it wasn't just a simple matter of an older brother telling his kid sister to mind her own business; Becky had seemed to suspect that the ticket money might not have been come by strictly honestly and Gary had taken a strong, almost violent exception to her words. What exactly *were* those words? Try as she would, she could not recall them fully.

Something else came back to her. One of the boys had commented on Tommy Judd's absence and the others had seemed to find this amusing. That rang a bell. Boys short of money, suddenly able to find five pounds each for a ticket to the barbecue, and a joking reference to Tommy Judd, who yesterday had been violently attacked. Her mind went racing on. If the boys had, for whatever reason, been near Tommy's cottage around the time of the barbecue, they might have noticed something unusual, a stranger perhaps, not necessarily acting suspiciously, just someone who, if traced, could provide a new lead in the enquiry into Cissie's death. Despite Joe's misgivings, she believed Graham Shipley when he swore that he had had nothing to do with that. If she could only convince the police . . . It was worth a try. She dialled their number and asked to speak to Detective Sergeant Matt Waters. By good fortune, he was at his desk; he greeted her warmly enough, but his manner changed to one of patient resignation when she explained her idea.

'Do you suppose we hadn't thought of that?' he said, a trifle wearily. 'We know from our house-to-house enquiries that those three lads are in the habit of congregating near that spot, but none of them could remember seeing anything or anyone unusual, either on or shortly before the day of Cissie's death.'

'That's not what I meant. Were they asked if any of them had actually been inside Tommy's cottage? Or whether he ever gave them any money?'

'No — why should they? And what difference would it have made if he had? Maybe they did odd jobs for him, fetched his shopping or something like that.'

'He does his own shopping and what he needs in the way of odd jobs he does for himself. He's always been very proud and independent.'

'Mel this is getting us nowhere — '

'You're just shrugging off everything I say to you,' said Melissa angrily and then, before she could stop herself, she blurted out, 'Are you still holding Graham Shipley?'

'So that's what this is all about.' It was Matt's turn to sound irritable. 'You've got this bee in your bonnet about Shipley being an innocent victim.'

'But he is, I'm sure he is. And he's in a very fragile emotional state. I'm terrified to think what your interrogation is doing to him.'

'I don't care for the word 'interrogation'. I assure you our interviews have been conducted on perfectly correct lines and he is having legal advice. Now, if that's all you have to say to me — '

'No, wait,' she pleaded. 'There is something else — '

'All right, but make it quick. Hang on a minute,' he added as another phone buzzed in the background. She heard him barking a series of staccato monosyllables before he returned to her, saying, 'Look Mel, I've been called away on something urgent.

Whatever you want to say will have to keep.'

'All right, but please make it soon. It really is important.'

He heaved a sigh. 'Okay then, be in the Grey Goose at one o'clock. I'll try and join you there, but I can't promise.'

Melissa's stomach gave a faint lurch. Her first date with Ken Harris had been in the Grey Goose and despite the fact that the affair was over — and that she had been the one to end it — to meet anyone else there, even on business, seemed oddly like a betrayal. 'Does it have to be the Grey Goose?' she objected.

'It's the most convenient place for me. Is there a problem?'

There was none that she was prepared to divulge. 'No, not really,' she said lamely. 'One o'clock, you said? I'll be there.'

'And whatever it is make it short, there's a love. We're snowed under with work here.'

'I'll do my best — and thanks, Matt.' she hung up and glanced at the clock; it was a little after twelve. It wouldn't take long to change out of her working clothes and into something more presentable and the drive to Stowbridge would take no more than fifteen or twenty minutes. That left plenty of time to call on Tommy Judd and find out if he was all right.

★ ★ ★

Tommy's front door was locked, as Melissa discovered when, having hammered several times without success on its peeling paint-work, she turned the rusty handle and tried to open it. She went to the back door, but that too was firmly closed. In some concern, recalling the state she had left him in the previous day, she walked round the cottage and peered through the grimy ground-floor windows. There was no sign of him. Perhaps, she reflected, Gideon Lane had been right after all when he indicated that Tommy's injuries were less serious than she feared. He might have gone out to do some shopping, in which case he could be back at any time. Remembering his angry insistence that he was not in need of help, it occurred to her that her presence would be unwelcome, to say the least. She returned to her car and drove into Stowbridge to keep her appointment with Matt Waters.

Everything in the saloon bar of the Grey Goose was exactly as she remembered, from the polished mahogany bar fittings and the ceramic pump handles to the frosted glass on the windows, etched with the name of a long-defunct Victorian brewery. It was, as she expected, crowded; among the throng she spotted one or two familiar faces of personnel from the police station a hundred yards down the street, but there was no sign of Matt. As she looked around in search of him she met the eye of a young man standing at the bar with a pint tankard in his hand. He said something to a companion and came over to her.

'Mrs Craig?' She nodded. 'DC Danville. DS Waters asked me to give you this.' He took an envelope from his pocket and handed it to her.

'Thanks.' Conscious of the young detective's eye on her, she went over to an unoccupied table, put down her handbag and opened the envelope. It contained a single sheet torn from a police notebook, and read: *Mel, sorry I can't make it. You can leave a message with Bob Danville if you like, or get in touch later. Matt.*

The main reason for wanting to talk to DS Waters had been to let him know about the attack on Tommy Judd, even though it was fairly certain that the old man would refuse to co-operate with any police enquiry. Now that he was apparently recovering from his injuries, the matter had suddenly ceased to be urgent. Melissa stuffed the note into her pocket, signalled 'No reply' to DC Danville and went back to her car. It crossed her mind to wonder whether Matt's reason for being unable to keep their appointment had been genuine, then told herself that he was not the kind of man to make phoney excuses. She would say what she had to say at the first opportunity, although there was no guarantee that he would take it seriously. She considered what her next step should be, came to a decision and drove home.

There was still no sign of life in Elder Cottage. Knowing Graham's habit of standing at the window she scanned every one, but he was not visible at any of them. That meant he was probably still in custody, although there was always the slim outside chance that he was at home, but deliberately keeping out of sight. Once indoors, to satisfy herself that the cottage was genuinely empty, she dialled his number and allowed his phone to ring over twenty times before giving up. Next, she called the office of the *Gloucester Gazette* and asked for Bruce Ingram.

18

'I find this amusing,' Bruce remarked as he put a glass of white wine and a pint of beer on a corner table in the bar of the Lamb and Shearling and sat down opposite Melissa.

'Why?' she asked with the wine halfway to her mouth.

'Don't you remember, last Sunday, saying to me something like 'You aren't going to drag me into one of your off-the-record investigations'?' Bruce's blue eyes twinkled at her over his tankard. 'And here you are, enlisting my help in some sleuthing of your own.'

'All right, I did say that and I meant it at the time. Things have changed since then and if I'm on the right track there could be a scoop in it for you.'

'I take it this has something to do with your dodgy neighbour? The police have asked for an extra twenty-four hours to question him, by the way.'

'I was afraid of that. Poor Graham, he must be in a terrible state by now.'

'No worse than the girl's mother,' Bruce commented drily.

'I can't argue with that,' Melissa admitted, 'but I'm more and more convinced that he had nothing to do with Cissie's death. Only the police seem so certain he did that they don't want to listen to anything that might suggest otherwise.'

'And you believe in 'otherwise'?'

'I do. It all seems to hinge on the fact that he denies having pulled her body from the water and that they don't believe him.'

'And you do?'

'Yes. So far as I know, there's still no firm evidence that she was actually murdered, but whoever found her first must have something to hide, otherwise why keep quiet?'

'And you want my help in tracking down that person?'

'Yes, please.'

'The problem is,' said Bruce, 'I'm not half so sure as you are that such a person exists.' He took a pull from his beer before adding, 'Convince me.'

'I admit I haven't found any definite proof that he does — that's why Matt Waters gave me the brush-off — but there are some things that don't seem to me to add up.'

'Okay, I'm listening. What's your theory?'

'At the moment it's hardly a theory, more of a hypothesis. First of all, I'd better bring you up to date. There's been a rather nasty attack on old Tommy Judd which I have a feeling is in some way connected with Cissie's death.'

Bruce's slightly bantering manner vanished and he lifted his head in a sharp movement that made her think of a guard dog listening to an unfamiliar sound. 'Tell me,' he said.

She gave him a brief account of her discovery of the old man lying injured in his cottage, of his refusal to accept help of any kind and her conviction that, despite his denials, he had been robbed of something of value which had been concealed under the floorboards.

'I've been trying to figure out why he should be so secretive about it,' she said. 'It could have been money that he'd either stolen or earned without declaring it for tax, but I find it hard to believe he's a thief and I'd say that tax fiddles are way out of his league.'

'What about drugs?' Bruce suggested.

'He's never shown any sign of being a junkie, so far as I know.'

'He could be dealing.'

'Yes, I suppose he could.' Melissa wondered why that explanation had not occurred to her before. 'It seems unlikely, though,' she added on reflection. 'If there had been suspicious comings and goings to

214

his cottage, someone's bound to have noticed. You can't keep that sort of thing quiet in a village.'

'So what makes you think the attack's got anything to do with the girl's death?'

'That's where I start hypothesising. Let's assume for a moment that Cissie *was* murdered. Perhaps Tommy knows something, or the killer believes that he knows something?'

Bruce considered his half-empty glass with pursed lips. 'If that's the case, and your killer was feeling seriously threatened, surely he'd have gone the whole way and made sure the old boy was silenced for good. But if he's already well enough to go out — ' He shook his head and downed a long swallow of his drink before adding, 'No, it sounds like a straightforward case of aggravated burglary to me.'

'Then why refuse help? He must feel pretty strongly about it, because Gideon Lane got the same message when he called on him shortly after I did.'

'Who's Gideon Lane?'

'He's a recently-retired church organist from Somerset who's come to live with his two elderly sisters at Benbury Manor. Supposed to be early retirement on health grounds, but he looks as fit as a flea to me.'

'So does my auntie, and she's diabetic. One of her favourite sayings is, 'My looks never pity me'. Anyway, tell me about Mr Lane.'

Melissa recounted her meeting with Gideon and his subsequent call on her. 'That's something else I find puzzling,' she finished. 'He's what you'd call a gentleman of the old school, very polished manners, cultured accent and all that, whereas Tommy Judd's a decent enough old boy, but a bit of a rough diamond who to my knowledge hasn't set foot inside the church for years. It's hard to see what they can possibly have in common.'

'A mutual interest in wild flowers or collecting matchbox labels?' Bruce suggested with a grin. 'Two old boys can usually find something to rabbit about. Look, if this is all you have to go on, Mel, I can't see — '

'I haven't told you everything yet. I overheard some teenage kids talking at our village barbecue last Friday. I didn't pay much attention at the time and it had slipped my mind, but last night I remembered one or two things they said that set me thinking.' As accurately as she could, Melissa repeated the snatch of conversation she had overheard on the night of the barbecue. 'I spoke to DS Waters this morning, but he didn't seem all that interested.'

'Did you tell him about the attack on Tommy Judd?'

'No. I told him there was something else that might interest him, but it was off the record. He was called away so we made an arrangement to meet in a pub near the police station, but he sent a message to say he couldn't make it. That's when I decided to call you.'

'Hmm.' Bruce made some notes and considered them for a few moments. 'I take it you aren't suggesting that it was the kids — or one of them — who attacked Tommy?'

'No, but it occurred to me that they might somehow have stumbled on his secret — whatever it is — and perhaps persuaded him to part with a little hush-money. That could account for their being able to afford tickets to the barbecue when they were skint a couple of days earlier. I'm sure young Becky suspected them of being up to something and her brother turned quite nasty when she hinted as much.'

'Have you any idea when this attack on Tommy Judd took place?'

'Not really. It could have been several hours before I found him, I suppose. The blood on his face had dried, but the light was poor and anyway I'm not an expert — '

'No?' Bruce treated Melissa to a mischievous smirk. 'With all your crime writer's experience of blood and guts?' His smile faded as he went on, 'The Bill picked up Shipley while we were on the phone yesterday — about eleven o'clock, wasn't it?'

'I suppose so. Yes, Gloria was about to make the coffee.'

'And you found Judd a couple of hours later?'

'A bit more than that. Say two and a half. What are you driving at?'

Bruce fiddled with the handle of his beer tankard for a few moments before looking Melissa full in the eye and saying, 'You aren't going to like this, Mel, but it seems to me quite possible that it was Shipley who carried out the attack.'

'I don't believe it!' she exclaimed indignantly. 'I keep telling you, he's not the violent sort — '

'Don't give me that. He took a swipe at young Blake, don't forget. It could have injured the lad quite seriously if he'd connected.'

'He'd had a few drinks and he was under provocation,' Melissa protested, but without conviction. She put down her empty wineglass and covered her eyes with her hands, suddenly sickened and bewildered by the whole nasty business. 'How come I got myself involved in all this?' she groaned.

'It's your insatiable curiosity,' Bruce chuckled. 'If you take my advice, you'll go home and forget all about Shipley and his troubles. They're not your concern.'

'That's what everyone tells me.'

'There you are then.' Bruce picked up his empty glass and reached for hers. 'How about a refill?'

'No thanks, not for me. Bruce, I can't give up now. I *know* there's something important that hasn't come to light.'

Melissa felt her voice tremble slightly with the intensity of her conviction and she saw Bruce's expression become serious again. For a few moments he sat turning the glass between his hands, apparently deep in thought. Then he said, 'This Gideon bloke, you reckon he's been in the habit of visiting Tommy Judd?'

'I can't be sure, but I do have that impression. I only saw him there once, just after I'd found Tommy injured, but he could well have been before . . . yes, on reflection, I'm sure he had.'

'I wonder if he went there the day Cissie died?'

'I've never heard anything to suggest that

219

he did.' Melissa felt a twinge of excitement as the significance of the question sank in. It died down again as she heard herself saying, 'Still, I imagine he and his sisters were interviewed in the course of the house-to-house enquiries. If he had seen anything relevant it would have come out then.'

'Yes, probably. Just a thought.' Bruce glanced at his wrist-watch. 'Look Mel, I really should be getting back to work. Someone's been peddling porno magazines to kids from Stowbridge Comprehensive and my editor wants me to get the story.'

'Oh well, I suppose that's more important than helping an innocent man with a murder charge hanging over him,' said Melissa sarcastically.

'Only doing my job. Mel, if you manage to turn up one concrete piece of evidence — '

'I'll give it to the police. Bruce, there have been times in the past when we've acted on your hunches and they've paid off. I've got a very strong hunch, but I can't get you to help me.' With a resigned sigh, she got to her feet. 'All right, go and look for dirty books. I'm not giving up.'

'Knowing you, I wouldn't expect anything else.'

They were about to go their separate ways when Bruce said, 'By the way, whereabouts in

Somerset was old Lane choirmaster?'

'I've no idea. Why?'

'Just curiosity. My auntie — the one I told you about — lives near Clevedon, on the Somerset coast.' He raised a hand in farewell. 'So long, keep in touch.'

★ ★ ★

Melissa was in low spirits as she drove home. She longed to be able to detach herself from the situation, give her whole mind to completing her novel, hand it over to Joe and then arrange the trip to New York that Simon had proposed. Yet all the time her brain persisted in reviewing all the impressions and odd scraps of information she had gathered and the questions they gave rise to, arranging them this way and that in an attempt to detect some new pattern, pinpoint some new indicator that would lead her to the truth.

The most promising source of such an indicator — if promising was the right word to describe something so elusive — would seem to be Gideon Lane. Her way back into Upper Benbury took her past the end of the road leading to the Manor; on impulse, she turned into it and found herself a couple of minutes later approaching the entrance to the gravelled, tree-lined drive. The wrought-iron gates mounted on tall pillars of Cotswold stone stood wide open and after a brief moment of hesitation she drove up to the house, parked outside the studded oak front door and pressed the huge brass bell-push. The sound echoed from somewhere deep within and several seconds passed before she heard movement. At last there was a rattling sound, the door opened a few inches and the somewhat forbidding countenance of Esther Lane appeared in the narrow opening. Her expression registered recognition but was far from welcoming as she released the chain.

'Mrs Craig,' she said as — with some reluctance, Melissa felt — she held the door open, mutely inviting the unexpected visitor inside. 'What brings you here?'

'I was wondering if I could possibly have a word with your brother?'

Esther raised an eyebrow as if she disapproved of the request, but all she said was, 'I suppose so. We're in the kitchen — this way.'

Feeling rather like the second Mrs de Winter trailing nervously in the wake of Mrs Danvers, Melissa followed Esther's stiffly upright figure along a passage leading to a large, well-appointed kitchen where Judith Waghorne and Gideon Lane were seated at a pine-topped table laid for afternoon tea. The minute he spotted Melissa, Gideon leapt to his feet with a beaming smile and pulled out a fourth chair.

'Mrs Craig!' he exclaimed. 'This is an unexpected treat. You will join us for a cup of tea, won't you — and one of Judith's delicious scones with home-made jam?'

'No, really,' Melissa protested in some embarrassment. 'I don't want to intrude, I only popped in to — '

'Oh, please do stay!' Judith too was on her feet and reaching into a cupboard for an additional cup, saucer and plate. The next minute, Melissa found herself seated next to Gideon with a buttered scone on her plate, cream and jam in silver dishes placed conveniently to hand and a cup of fragrant Lapsang Souchong tea steaming invitingly at her elbow.

'This is really very kind of you,' she said.

'It's our pleasure,' Gideon assured her. 'We don't receive many visitors.' He raised his cup in salute and Judith, her round pink face alight with pleasure, did the same. Only Esther, sitting erect and unsmiling between her brother and sister, made it clear by her body-language that she disassociated herself from their expressions of welcome.

After she had eaten her scone, drunk some of her tea and praised the quality of the plum jam — 'made with fruit from our own tree,' Judith was at pains to assure her — Melissa said casually, 'The reason I dropped in was to say that I called on Tommy Judd this afternoon, but he was out so presumably he's feeling better.'

At the mention of Tommy Judd's name, Gideon gave her a sharp, anxious glance which turned to relief on the final words. 'I'm so glad to hear it,' he said.

'I didn't know Mr Judd had been unwell,' said Judith. 'Has he seen a doctor?'

'I tried to persuade him, but he's a stubborn old fellow,' said Gideon. 'Mrs Craig, do have another scone. They're at their best when they're eaten fresh.' He pushed the dish towards her and she had the impression that it was an attempt to switch the conversation away from Tommy before any details emerged. 'And how about some more tea?'

'No more, thank you. It was all absolutely delicious.'

Esther, who had hardly uttered a word since Melissa's arrival, suddenly said, 'Gideon, I can't understand why you take such an interest in that odious old man.'

'Oh Essie!' Judith turned to her sister, her mobile features registering gentle reproach. 'Giddy's told us several times — he's trying to reach out to Mr Judd, get him back into the church — '

'That's a job for the rector — not that I've noticed *him* making any pastoral visits,' Esther sniffed.

'He's terribly busy looking after four parishes,' Melissa pointed out. 'And I hardly think he'd get much of a welcome from Tommy if he did call. By the way, I expect you know that Graham Shipley is being questioned by the police about Cissie Wilcox's death?'

'We do indeed.' Esther's face registered grim disapproval. 'We also know that various unsavoury stories are circulating about the gentleman's previous behaviour.'

'They're unsubstantiated rumours,' said Melissa hotly. 'I have it from Graham himself that whatever happened before he came here was due to a terrible misunderstanding — '

'That's what he would say, isn't it?' Esther inspected the teapot, found it empty and stood up. 'I assume you've all had enough —?' The unfinished question was a clear hint that so far as she was concerned, their guest had outstayed her welcome.

Melissa, who had noticed Gideon looking distinctly uncomfortable at the mention of Cissie, had no intention of leaving until she had probed a little more deeply. 'I was wondering,' she said, looking him straight in the eye, 'knowing that you call on Tommy from time to time, whether you have ever seen anyone else — either someone from the village or even a total stranger — hanging around near his cottage. You see,' she went on as Gideon opened his mouth with, she was sure, the intention of issuing an immediate denial, 'Somehow I find it hard to believe it was Graham Shipley who pulled that poor child's body from the water and then walked away without getting help, but so far there's absolutely nothing to indicate who else it might have been.'

'And what gives you the authority to go round asking that sort of question?' Esther said angrily. 'The police called on us, as I imagine they did everyone else in the village. We answered their questions fully and frankly, and so far as we're concerned it's the end of the matter.'

'I'm sure you did.' Melissa did her best to sound conciliatory. 'It's only that I imagine their questions were all about what any of you saw on the actual day Cissie died?'

'Of course — what else?'

'But that's just the point I'm trying to make. There may have been someone hanging around at some time beforehand. Not many people use that path and it's possible that no one noticed anything unusual. I just thought that as Mr Lane — '

'I'm sure if my brother had noticed anything like that, he would have informed the police at the time,' said Esther in a tone of finality. She went over to the sink, turned on the cold tap and rinsed out the teapot.

It was unmistakably a dismissal. Judith, looking extremely ill at ease, got to her feet and began clearing the table while Gideon made a great show of helping Melissa on with her jacket, which she had slipped off and hung over the back of her chair. As the three of them escorted her to the front door, with Esther bringing up the rear — almost, as she recalled it later, like a shepherd driving a flock of sheep — her attention was caught by a framed photograph hanging on the wall of the passage and she paused to take a closer look. It was of Gideon surrounded by a mixed choir, all fully robed, assembled outside the door of an ancient church. Under the photo was printed, 'Gideon Lane, MA, Organist and Director of Music, with the members of the choir after the service to commemorate the 500th anniversary of the dedication of the church of St Laurence, Warefield, Somerset'. It was dated 31 May 1998.

'How interesting,' Melissa commented. She

turned to Gideon. 'You must have retired very shortly after that was taken.'

'He was already unwell, but he stayed until the celebrations ended,' Judith said. 'He'd worked so hard to make them a success.' She put out a hand and caressed the picture with trembling fingers. To Melissa's astonishment, the old woman's eyes were full of tears.

'Had you been there long?'

Melissa's question was addressed to Gideon, but it was Esther who answered with an abrupt, 'Long enough.'

'Well, Warefield's loss is our gain,' said Melissa as Gideon opened the door for her. 'I hear you're standing in for Dr Thackray until he's recovered from his operation.'

'It will be a pleasure and a privilege,' he said with an ingratiating smile. 'Goodbye Mrs Craig, and thank you so much for calling.'

'Yes, indeed,' said Judith. Esther said nothing at all.

Later on that evening, Melissa called Bruce at home and told him about her visit. 'I used my call on Tommy Judd and finding he wasn't at home as an excuse. Gideon looked very nervous when I mentioned his name, and then relaxed visibly when I gave the good news.' She went on to describe the rest of the visit, ending by saying, 'There's no doubt they all became quite uncomfortable the moment I mentioned Cissie. Esther — she's the unmarried sister, Judith's a widow — got quite snotty and more or less told me to mind my own business. She couldn't edge me out of the house quickly enough.'

'It does sound as if they know more than they're admitting,' Bruce agreed, 'but — '

'I know what you're going to say,' Melissa broke in. 'I still haven't learned anything concrete.'

'It doesn't seem like it, I'm afraid.'

'Oh, one thing I did find out — not that it's in the least relevant but your auntie might be interested. Gideon was organist at St Laurence's church, Warefield.'

'That's not far from Clevedon,' said Bruce. For the first time during the conversation, his voice showed positive interest. 'She might know him, she knows lots of church people. I'll tell her when I call her this evening to thank her for Kirsty's birthday present. Ciao!'

An hour later he rang back. Even before he gave his reason, Melissa could tell from his up-beat tone of voice that he had something interesting to tell her.

'I spoke to Auntie Edie,' he said. 'I asked her if she knew Gideon Lane and she said, rather guardedly, 'I know *of* a Gideon Lane — why do you ask?' I explained that he was now living in the Cotswolds and that I'd learned through a friend of mine that he used to be director of music at a church near where she lives.'

'And?'

'She confirmed that it must be the Gideon Lane that she knew, but when I asked if she could tell me anything about him, she became quite mysterious. 'I could tell you quite a lot,' she said, 'but not on the phone. You never know who might be listening'.'

'That sounds intriguing, but it's a pity she wouldn't be more specific.'

'It gets better. She wanted to know what my interest was, of course, and I said a friend of mine was writing a book in which a church organist was murdered. This friend — that's you, of course, although I didn't mention your name at first — had asked him for help with background information, but had been given the brush-off by both Lane and his family. I told Auntie Edie that this had aroused my professional curiosity and I wondered if she could suggest a reason for their being so cagey.'

'Clever old you! What did she say?'

'For a good Christian woman, her comments were somewhat surprising. She said that if your church organist is anything like Lane he deserves to be bumped off and that in her opinion people like him should be

230

locked up and the key thrown down a well. She ended up by saying, 'A friend of mine who lives in the parish told me that it was all hushed up to avoid scandal, but a lot of people thought he should have been charged'.'

'Good heavens!' Melissa exclaimed. For the first time since she began her probing, she sensed that she was getting somewhere. 'You know, I had a feeling Gideon might have what is generally known as 'a past' but it never entered my head that it might be anything criminal.' Her brain was working furiously. 'Bruce is there any chance that if I went to see your Auntie Edie, she'd be willing to tell me what it's all about?'

'I thought of that. I asked her that very question and she was a bit hesitant at first, and then I mentioned your name and guess what, she's one of your biggest fans and she'll be absolutely thrilled to talk to you. She sang in her own church choir for years, by the way, so she'll be able to give you all the dirt about what goes on behind the scenes.'

'It's dirt about Gideon Lane that I'm interested in.'

'Yes, I know, but remember not to blow the cover I've set up for you.'

'I won't. Bruce, that's marvellous. I can't thank you enough.'

'Glad to help.'

'How did your investigation into the porno market go, by the way?' she asked as she jotted down Auntie Edie's address.

'Very interesting. The police have suspected for some time that there's a distribution network in the county, but so far they haven't been able to pinpoint any of the suppliers. This is the first time the stuff has turned up on the street and they feel it's a break-through, although all the lad they caught trying to flog it to some other kids would say is that he got it from a man hanging around outside the school gates. The description he's given is pretty vague. He lives near you, by the way. Name of Dave Potter.'

Melissa's pulse, which had been gradually accelerating during the conversation, sud-denly went into overdrive. 'Dave Potter is one of the kids I told you about — the ones I overheard at the barbecue,' she said excitedly.

'There you are then, two brand-new leads to follow up,' said Bruce with an air of great magnanimity. 'Who says I never give you any help?'

19

Melissa spent the remainder of Thursday evening concocting the outlines of a plot which would convince Bruce's aunt that a new Nathan Latimer mystery was in the making and at the same time give her a valid excuse to touch on the reasons for the departure of Gideon Lane from his post as musical director of St Laurence's church in the village of Warefield in the county of Somerset. That there had been more behind his early retirement than the glib phrase 'on the grounds of ill-health' suggested seemed reasonably certain. Whether a knowledge of the full circumstances would shed any light on the death of Cissie Wilcox was much less so. She could find herself up another blind alley, but it was worth a try.

She lay awake for some time that night pondering the other lead that Bruce had so fortuitously given her. Dave Potter, one of the group of youngsters she had overheard talking at the barbecue, had been caught with a pornographic magazine. Knowing the attitude of the Potters to the police, his explanation of where it had come from could quite well have been deliberately misleading. Members of the family featured regularly in accounts of court proceedings in the *Gloucester Gazette*, but their offences were generally limited to the run-of-the-mill variety such as burglary, shoplifting or sundry breaches of the peace. Handling stolen property had also been known to feature in the list of charges, but somehow dealing in pornography did not sound like their style. Melissa was sorely tempted to try to have a quiet word with Dave, mention the conversation she had overheard and see if she could get more out of him than he had told the police. To do that without seeking his parents' permission, however, was not without risk. If it reached their ears, she might easily become the target of angry accusations of trying to stitch up their son, or possibly of actual threats. A mental picture of Charlie Potter, a man with a temper as ugly as his face, made her dismiss the idea out of hand. While she was trying to think of some other approach to the problem she fell asleep.

She awoke on Friday to a fine day with a hint of autumn in the air — ideal conditions for a drive to the coast. At nine o'clock she called the number that Bruce had given her. It was immediately obvious, from the cordial way Miss Edith Ingram received a request to be allowed to 'pick her brains' on the subject of church music and musicians, that she had been keenly anticipating the opportunity of meeting one of her favourite writers. 'I shall be delighted and honoured to help you in any way I can,' she said, adding with obvious sincerity, 'and I hope there may be time to talk about your other books. I do so enjoy them.'

By half past nine Melissa was backing the car out of the garage. As she drove passed Elder Cottage she scanned the front windows for signs of movement, but yet again found none. For a moment, it crossed her mind that she might have been wrong about Graham Shipley all along. Perhaps he had finally cracked under the strain of relentless police probing and confessed to Cissie's murder. If so, cold reason told her she was embarking on a pointless journey. She dismissed the thought; she had made up her mind that Graham was innocent and cold reason was no match for that inner conviction.

The traffic on the M5 was moving freely and shortly before eleven o'clock Melissa pulled up outside a neat brick-built bungalow standing at the top of a rise in a quiet road overlooking the sea on the outskirts of Clevedon. The small, symmetrically laid out front garden had a tiny patch of lawn on either side of the concrete path, each with a rose tree in the middle and bordered by carefully tended beds bright with dahlias and geraniums. Edith Ingram had evidently been watching out for her; as she opened the gate and approached the front door it opened to reveal a short, rather stout figure with cropped grey hair that looked as if it had been cut with blunt scissors. Keen blue eyes sparkled behind tortoiseshell-framed glasses and a stubby-fingered hand took hers in a strong, welcoming clasp.

'Mrs Craig, I am so happy to meet you,' she said. Her voice was low-pitched with a warm, vibrant quality that made Melissa take to her on sight.

'I'm delighted to meet you,' she replied, 'and please, do call me Melissa.'

'Thank you, Melissa, and of course you must call me Edith. Do come in.' She led the way along the narrow hall and showed her visitor into a snug sitting-room with a picture window looking out over the sea. 'I expect you'd like a cup of coffee and I thought perhaps we'd have it out on the patio. As you can see, it's quite a little sun-trap at this time of day.'

'That would be lovely — and what a gorgeous view!' Melissa exclaimed as she stepped outside and sat down in one of two

236

garden chairs placed at a table spread with a floral cloth to match the cushions.

'It is nice, isn't it? I never tire of looking out at the sea, no matter what the weather. Excuse me one moment while I fetch the coffee.' Edith disappeared indoors, returning within minutes carrying a laden tray. 'I can't tell you what a pleasure it is to meet you,' she said as she poured coffee and offered biscuits before sitting down. 'When my nephew mentioned that you wanted some help in researching your new novel, I told him I'd be delighted, but somehow I wondered whether it would actually happen.' She beamed at Melissa as she raised her cup in salute, displaying a set of beautifully white, even teeth.

'It's very kind of you to offer to help. I do appreciate this kind of opportunity to talk to people about their jobs and experiences. It enables me to create an authentic background to my books.'

'It shows.' Edith drank some of her coffee and put down her cup. She fumbled in the pocket of her faded cotton skirt, worn with a baggy T-shirt and canvas slippers that had seen better days, and pulled out a small notebook. 'I've jotted down a few things that I think would be of interest, and also one or two points I'd like to talk to you about — if there's time after I've answered your questions, of course.'

'I'm sure there'll be time,' Melissa assured her.

'So, your next Nathan Latimer mystery concerns the death of a choirmaster and you want a bit of local colour, is that right?'

'Please.'

The time flew while Melissa sat spellbound, almost forgetting to take notes, as Edith Ingram recounted her experiences as a chorister in the local church where — although her voice was, as she put it, no longer up to snuff — she still played an active rôle. She was, Melissa judged, in her middle to late sixties, with the slightly weather-beaten appearance that comes from years spent largely out of doors in a coastal environment. Yet her skin was firm and clear and the lines round her eyes and mouth owed as much to laughter as to age. Those lines had plenty of exercise as she recalled one episode after another, some moving, some hilarious or mildly shocking, and others — mostly in relation to funerals — containing elements of black humour which occasionally reduced both women to helpless giggles.

'This is wonderful stuff,' Melissa said when they paused for breath, giving her an opportunity to jot down a few of the choicest items. After a minute or two Edith went to recharge the coffee pot, leaving Melissa to refer to her own list of prepared questions which had somehow been entirely overlooked as her hostess came out with revelation after revelation.

'Well, you've given me a terrific insight into the choristers' point of view,' she said as Edith refilled her cup, 'I'm wondering, though, whether you can help me with some details about the actual work of the choirmaster. Ideally, of course,' she went on, 'I should talk directly to one. A local doctor plays the organ for our family services but our parish is too small to support a choir.'

'What a pity. I always think choral music in a church is so uplifting.'

'I think so too. It so happens,' — at this point, Melissa adopted the casual tone of someone about to throw in an unimportant aside — 'that there is a retired choirmaster and organist living in our village, but for some reason or other he didn't want to talk about his work. I don't think he approves of the kind of books I write,' she finished with a deprecating smile.

Edith picked up the plate of biscuits and offered them, saying, 'Do have another one of these — I made them especially for you. I'm not allowed sugary things with my diabetes.'

She put the plate down and looked directly at Melissa with the hint of a twinkle in her bright blue eyes. 'You're speaking of Gideon Lane, from St Laurence's, Warefield, of course. I was wondering when you'd get around to mentioning him. He's the real reason for your being here, isn't he?'

Melissa felt her own eyes stretching on hearing her cover so confidently blown. 'What makes you think that?' she asked feebly.

'Several reasons. One, I know my nephew and I can always tell when there's some ulterior motive behind something he wants from me.'

Melissa chuckled, once more at her ease. 'I've noticed that myself from time to time,' she acknowledged with a certain glee. 'It's the journalist's mind at work.'

'Quite so. And yours, if I may say so, is the mystery writer's mind — which I find eternally fascinating,' Edith hastened to add as if afraid she might have given offence. 'You see, Melissa, I have read and reread all your crime novels and I find you reveal as much of yourself in your writing as you do about your characters.'

'Gosh, that's a bit scarey.'

'Oh, I don't mean to be.'

'You mentioned several reasons.'

'Another one is that it's taken you over an

hour to come out with something I'd have expected you to mention at the outset. And a third,' — at this point, Edith bent down and took a magazine from a ledge under the table — 'is this piece from *Crime and Mystery Monthly*.' She flipped it open at a page where a report headed 'Passing of a Sleuth' had been marked in red. 'According to this, Mel Craig has 'finally and irrevocably' decided to forswear crime fiction, pension off her famous detective, Nathan Latimer, and concentrate exclusively in the future on a more literary genre. 'I was going to arrange for Nathan to die in the line of duty,' you are quoted as saying before going on to admit that you couldn't actually bring yourself to 'bump the old boy off'. So, when Bruce told me this yarn about setting a new Nathan Latimer mystery in an organ loft, having already asked me ever so casually whether I knew a recently retired church organist from Warefield, I was pretty sure that was just a pretext for probing into Gideon Lane's past.' She handed over the magazine and waited for Melissa's comments; when none came she asked, 'So, what's the old pervert been up to now?'

Melissa gaped at her. 'Is he a pervert?' she asked in astonishment. 'Is that what's behind his early retirement on the grounds of ill-health?'

'Of course. I hinted as much to Bruce, although I wouldn't talk about it on the phone. Conversations on these portable things can be so easily picked up by other people — remember the man who found himself listening in to some rather salacious details concerning a member of the aristocracy? Not that I imagine the misdeeds of a country choirmaster to be of national interest, but locally it would attract more readers than a dead donkey story. And I know from a friend who lives in the parish how desperate the PCC at St Laurence's were to hush up the whole sordid little episode.'

'Are you going to tell me about it now?'

'I'd like you to tell me your interest first.'

'It's nothing to do with perversion on Mr Lane's part, so far as I know.' Melissa referred to her list. 'But on second thoughts,' she added, conscious of a twinge of excitement as the idea took hold, 'it's always possible, I suppose. It started with the death by drowning in a stream of a young village girl.'

Edith listened with mounting bewilderment while Melissa read out the brief account she had prepared of Cissie's death and the unresolved mystery surrounding its cause, followed by the apparently unrelated attack on Tommy Judd and his determination not to have it reported. 'Are you suggesting that Gideon Lane has some responsibility for the girl's death, or that he attacked that poor old man?' she exclaimed. 'I find that hard to believe. He's been guilty of very grave misdemeanours, I know, but it has never been suggested that he's capable of anything so dreadful. But of course, one never knows.'

'I'm not suggesting anything of the kind,' Melissa assured her, 'but when I found out that Lane is in the habit of calling on Tommy Judd from time to time, it occurred to me that he might have noticed someone behaving suspiciously, not necessarily on the day Cissie died but perhaps a short time beforehand. It seemed a harmless enough thing to ask, but when he and his sisters were so obviously disturbed by my questions I began to think they must be hiding something. So when Bruce mentioned that you live in the area he came from, and offered to put me in touch with you, it seemed a Heaven-sent opportunity to find out a bit more about him. The story about researching a new novel was his idea, by the way.'

'It sounds just like him.' The blue eyes twinkled more brightly than ever. 'One thing bothers me, though. Why have you come to me, and not the police?'

'Good question. The fact is, they think

they've got their man, and I'm convinced they're mistaken.'

'I see.' Edith's expression became serious. 'Does this mean you suspect someone else of causing that girl's death?'

'To be honest, I'm not convinced anyone is directly responsible, but the fact remains that someone pulled her body out of the water and then left it for others to find. I'm trying to find out who that person is.'

'And you're convinced that it wasn't — what's the man's name?'

'Graham Shipley. Yes, I really believe his story. So if you'd be good enough to tell me a little more about Mr Lane's 'misdemeanours' and what caused him to leave his post in such a hurry — ?'

'Yes, indeed. Well, according to my friend, it was generally known that he had, how shall I put it, an eye for the ladies, particularly the young and nubile members of his choir, but it always seemed pretty innocent and people used to joke about it, call him a naughty old man — but only in fun, no one ever believed there was any real harm in him. He always took what he himself described as a fatherly interest in the girls' welfare. They loved him and he trained them to sing so beautifully — the choir was quite renowned in this part of the world. And then one day — they can't think what got into him, maybe he'd had a drop to drink or something — he was helping one of the girls to adjust her surplice and he suddenly bent down and put his hand right up her cassock and squeezed her bottom. She let out a yell, right there in the vestry with the congregation already assembling for morning worship.'

'He did that in front of the rest of the choir?'

'No, it seems there's a small room off the vestry — well, hardly a room, more a partitioned-off corner, my friend said — where the choir hang their cassocks and surplices. They were in there.'

'So what happened next?'

'There was a great kerfuffle, of course, and the vicar rushed over to see what it was all about and then hurried into the church and got the girl's mother. They managed to quieten her down and the service went ahead, but of course everyone in the church was wondering what on earth had happened.'

'So how did they account for the screaming?'

'Oh, they concocted some story of how she'd somehow tripped and wrenched her ankle.'

'But the other members of the choir must have known . . . or guessed?'

'Oh yes . . . and then I suppose they got talking among themselves and other stories began to come out. It was the first time he'd done anything quite so shocking, but several of the girls told their parents of suggestive remarks he used to make and how now and then he'd patted their bottoms, or brushed his hand against their breasts while pretending to flick specks of dust off their clothes, that kind of thing.'

'But none of them had said anything before?'

'Apparently not. And for all we know, there were other cases that never came to light at all. He was very popular, you see, and so he got away with it, until he . . . well, as I said, no one could understand what got into him.'

'I take it he was never charged with indecent assault?'

'No, and in my view that was a very grave mistake.' Edith Ingram's voice took on a steely edge and her expression hardened. 'Apparently everyone — the vicar, the other members of the choir, the PCC — were much more concerned to avoid a scandal than to make sure the dirty beast got his just desserts. They managed to talk the girl's parents into agreeing that she might suffer psychological and emotional harm from a lot of publicity — such a load of psychobabble.'

Her lip curled in disgust at what she evidently considered a chicken-hearted attitude all round. 'So it was all hushed up on condition he left the village quietly and never showed his face there again. The story about 'early retirement for health reasons' was concocted as a cover, of course.'

'And he fetched up in our village, where there are a number of vulnerable young girls,' said Melissa grimly. 'And now one of them is dead.'

'You think there's a connection?'

Melissa put down her notebook and sat back in her chair. She stared out at the wide expanse of blue sea, its surface glittering in the autumn sunshine and dotted here and there with sailing boats skimming along before a steady but moderate breeze. So peaceful, so innocent, so harmless — yet with the latent power to hurt and even destroy. She thought of the choir of St Laurence's church, singing their hearts out at the Sunday services, giving of their best under the direction of a man they and the congregation held in such high regard, whose benign and charming exterior nevertheless hid a dreadful weakness.

'I don't know what to think,' she said at last. 'I really don't know.'

20

It was nearly half past three when Melissa joined the M5 on her journey home. Edith Ingram had left her alone for a short time on the pretext of 'having to see to something in the kitchen' and she had been very grateful for the opportunity to write up her notes and put her thoughts into some kind of order.

The revelations concerning Gideon Lane certainly explained his and his sisters' refusal to admit the possibility of his being able to help the police enquiry into the death of Cissie Wilcox. Anything that might lead to his name being mentioned in the press carried a risk of recognition by someone with knowledge of his recent disgrace, someone who had kept quiet so far in the interest of avoiding scandal but who might — given the fact that the death of a young girl had been involved — consider it their duty to pass on that knowledge. Esther Lane and Judith Waghorne were proud women; whether or not their brother had anything significant to contribute to the investigation might carry little weight with them when compared with their desire to protect their good name. They would be aware that further visits from the police would inevitably give rise to speculation in the village. Mrs Foster in particular, who had many times voiced her resentment of Esther Lane's haughty, overbearing attitude, — 'Tells everyone what to do as if she owned the place' was an oft-repeated grumble — would not hesitate to seize on the opportunity to suggest, with many a nod and wink, that for all their airs and graces they were no more perfect than anyone else.

Melissa's mind went back to the light-hearted comment in her recent letter to Iris about Gideon Lane's 'mischievous twinkle' and the possibility that he might have 'an interesting past.' The old adage about many a true word being spoken — or, in this case, written — in jest took on a new and sinister meaning. That the man had unpleasant predilections which made him a menace to young women and girls was beyond doubt — but a potential killer? From what little she knew of him it seemed unlikely, but having once narrowly escaped public disgrace, who could tell to what lengths he would go to avoid exposure? His sisters obviously knew about his record — why else would they be so cagey? — but how far had he confided in them over his movements on the day of Cissie's death? And now that she, Melissa, had learned their secret, would she be justified in putting pressure on them to reveal what they knew? Most importantly of all, would such a revelation help to remove suspicion from Graham Shipley?

Her thoughts had been interrupted by the reappearance of Edith carrying a laden tray and saying rather shyly, 'I do hope you can stay a little longer so that we can have a chat about your books. I've made a little something for our lunch.' The 'little something' had turned out to be smoked salmon sandwiches made with home-made bread, followed by a dish of raspberries and cream, and the chat had developed into a stimulating and wide-ranging conversation that provided a welcome distraction from Gideon's sordid past. Edith's observations had been shrewd and stimulating and to her surprise Melissa found her mind actively considering a mystery plot based on the mock-up she had concocted as a pretext for her visit. By the time she left the motorway and was approaching the outskirts of Stowbridge she had almost decided to bring Nathan Latimer out of retirement once the current 'literary' novel, of which Joe and her editor had such high expectations, was completed and handed over. Poor Joe, she thought as she negotiated the final roundabout before entering the town, it's as well you don't know about this latest twist in my campaign to clear Graham Shipley.

She forced herself to consider more practical matters. It was Friday, the weekend was approaching and she was running short of cash. She found an empty space in one of the town's car parks and walked along the High Street to her bank; she was waiting in the queue at the cash dispenser when the bank's door swung open and Becky Tanner emerged. In one hand was a plastic shopping bag; the other held a deposit account book, the open pages of which she was studying with an air of considerable satisfaction. On hearing Melissa's greeting she hastily closed the book and stuffed it into her shoulder bag.

'Oh, er, hello Mrs Craig,' she said. 'Fancy seeing you here.'

'Fancy seeing *you*,' Melissa responded with a smile. 'I'm glad to see you're taking good care of your money.'

It was obvious that Becky was embarrassed by this lighthearted reference to her financial affairs; her colour rose and she avoided meeting Melissa's eye. 'Well, actually . . . I just opened the account . . . it's a secret,' she said jerkily. 'I'm saving up for Dad's Christmas present, see . . . it's to be a surprise . . . you won't tell, will you?'

251

'Of course not.' The story did not ring true, but Melissa let it pass. 'You look different,' she went on, giving Becky an appraising glance. 'I know what it is, you've had your hair done differently.'

'My friend Dorrie cut it for me.' Rather self-consciously, Becky patted the smooth, glossy style that replaced the former abundant and at times unruly mane. 'D'you like it?'

'Very much, it really suits you.' *And makes you look older as well*, Melissa added mentally. *Whoever would believe this is a fourteen-year-old?* Aloud, she observed, with a glance at the plastic carrier that sported in impressive gold lettering the name of Stowbridge's most up-market boutique, 'Shopping at Jane's, too. You *have* been splashing out!'

Becky's air of confusion deepened. 'N-no, I haven't . . . I mean, I haven't bought anything there . . . this is an old carrier. Dorrie's Mum bought something at Jane's a while back . . . Dorrie and I take it in turns to use it 'cos we reckon it looks kinda posh.' This hastily gabbled explanation was — given the pristine nature of the article in question — such a blatant lie that Melissa was on the point of challenging it, but at that moment she found herself at the head of the queue for the cash

252

machine. By the time she finished her transaction, Becky had disappeared into the crowd of Friday afternoon shoppers.

Melissa found the encounter vaguely disturbing. Prices at Jane's boutique were notoriously high and the hair-do — which looked far too professional to have been done by an amateur — would have cost many times the amount a girl of Becky's age and background could be reasonably expected to receive as pocket-money. Of course, she picked up the occasional stint as a baby-sitter . . . and within the past couple of days she had put in a few hours doing housework at Benbury Manor, but even so . . . An ugly suspicion began to form in Melissa's mind; she tried to thrust it away, telling herself that there were several ways in which the girl could have come by an unexpected windfall. From a lottery scratch card, perhaps? She was too young to buy her own, but she might easily have prevailed upon a sixteen-year-old acquaintance to buy one for her.

Yet, if that was the case, why not say so? Why the shiftiness and the lies? The more she thought about it, the more uneasy Melissa became. She recalled that only a couple of days ago Becky had described how her father had 'had a go at her' and wondered if there was any connection. Perhaps she should have a word with Jake? But what could she say that would not give offence to a man notorious for his protective attitude towards his daughter? On second thoughts, it would be better to leave well alone; it was really no concern of hers and she had more pressing matters on her mind.

She went back to her car and set off for home feeling deflated and depressed. All the buoyancy, optimism and interest in a possible new Nathan Latimer mystery that her discussion with Edith Ingram had aroused were swept away, leaving her with the problem of what to do with her new-found knowledge of Gideon Lane's past. She toyed with the idea of talking it over with Bruce and had decided to call him as soon as she reached home when, as she turned off the main road, she spotted the brake lights of another car in the lane a short distance ahead. It pulled up and a slight figure jumped out, slammed the door and scurried away without a backward glance.

The other car moved forward a few yards, braked again and turned right, heading for Benbury Manor. Acting on impulse for the second time in twenty-four hours, Melissa followed.

★ ★ ★

'Gideon's late for tea,' said Esther with a frown as she surveyed the table laid, as usual, with china cups, saucers and plates and a selection of home-made cakes. 'He knows we have it at half past four and here it is almost ten to five.'

'Perhaps he met a friend in Stowbridge and they got talking,' Judith suggested. 'You know how Giddy loves to chat — and he's got the car today so he's not dependent on the bus.'

'He's hardly had time to make any friends there. He's certainly never mentioned anyone particular.'

'Do we really have a right to know about everyone he meets?' Judith fiddled with the silver teaspoons that she had placed in each of the three saucers before adding, 'He is a grown man, after all. He's entitled to choose his own friends.'

'Of course he is, provided they're suitable,' said Esther pointedly.

Judith was quick to take her meaning. 'Oh Essie, you don't really think . . . I mean, he gave us his word — '

'I know he did, but to be honest, I'm not sure we can trust him. You know how he lied to us about being in the woods the day young Cissie drowned. We had quite a job to get the truth out of him.'

'It was only because he was frightened — '

'Frightened of what?'

'Of being questioned by the police and getting his name in the papers, of course. You were just as worried, and so was I.'

'That's true.'

'And we were both satisfied with his explanation, weren't we?'

'At the time — yes.'

'What do you mean by 'at the time'?' Judith's mild features puckered in a frown. 'What's happened to change your mind?'

Esther took a teapot from a cupboard above her head and poured hot water into it before saying, with apparent reluctance, 'It's that nosey Mrs Craig and her questions. Suppose she finds someone who actually saw Gideon there that day? Colin, the frozen food man, for example. Gideon said the van passed him in the lane.'

'If Colin had reported seeing him, we'd surely have heard by now.'

'I suppose so. Just the same, that woman had no right to come here and poke her nose in.'

'I suppose it was rather impertinent of her,' Judith agreed, 'but I'm sure her intentions were of the best. She was only trying to help poor Mr Shipley, after all.'

'She should mind her own business.' Esther tipped out the hot water and spooned tea into the pot. 'Just because she's had a few trumpery crime books published I suppose she thinks she's some kind of a detective.'

'Oh, her novels aren't trumpery,' said Judith earnestly. 'They've been on television,' she added, as if that conferred some kind of classic status on any book so treated.

'I'm not going to argue with you,' said Esther grumpily. 'And I'm not going to wait for Gideon any longer. We'll have our tea. If it's stewed by the time he comes in it'll be his own fault.'

'I think I hear him now.' Judith opened the kitchen door and popped her head out. 'Yes, that's his key in the lock. There you are at last, Giddy!' she called, 'we've been quite worried about you . . . oh dear!' She hastily closed the door and turned to her sister with a look of dismay.

'What's the matter now?' Esther demanded.

'It's that Mrs Craig . . . she's here again.' Judith's voice sank to a shaky whisper. 'Whatever can she want this time?'

*　　*　　*

Melissa's second visit to Benbury Manor was in several respects a retake of the first. She was escorted — with a similar degree of

257

reluctance, but by Gideon this time instead of Esther — into the large, lavishly-equipped kitchen where once again the table was laid for tea. Here the resemblance ended; there were no cordial smiles of welcome or an invitation to sit down. Instead, the three siblings drew together in a silent group on the opposite side of the table, one sister on either side of Gideon with an arm linked with his, their gaze not merely defensive but — at least in Esther's case — actively malevolent. Melissa had been prepared for anger and bitter resentment, had been steeling herself for it from the moment when she recognised the Lanes' car and decided to have it out with them there and then, but the force of their combined hostility was like an electric shock.

'I'll be completely honest, this isn't a social visit,' she informed them. 'I called in to tell you that I have had a long conversation today with a lady who has a friend in Warefield. She remembers you very well, Mr Lane. Very well indeed,' she added for an extra touch of dramatic effect.

For a moment, no one spoke. Judith let out a little sigh that was almost a moan and put her hand to her mouth. Gideon shuffled his feet and stared down at the table, his face scarlet. Esther was the first to respond. 'I suppose you think you're very clever,' she snarled. 'A man sins, repents and tries to build a new life, and you take it upon yourself to expose and punish him — '

'Please, don't misunderstand me,' Melissa cut in hastily. It occurred to her that Esther's words could apply equally to Graham's own situation. 'I'm not concerned with retribution. All I want is to get at the truth.'

'And what gives you the right to come here questioning us?' Esther's eyes blazed and her attitude became for a moment so threatening that Melissa was relieved that the heavy table stood between them. 'Did you expect us to betray our brother, have everyone pointing the finger at him, at all of us?'

'No, of course not, and there would have been no need for his past, er, indiscretion to come out if only he had been a little more forthcoming about what happened the day that Cissie died.'

'I don't know what you're talking about,' Esther snapped.

'When I asked him if he had seen anything or anyone unusual around the time of the tragedy, he refused to answer and you backed him up, but you see I happen to know,' — here she took a wild, unpremeditated gamble — 'that he was in the neighbourhood of Brookside Cottage the day that poor girl died.'

'Who told you that?' Judith blurted out. From the looks of alarm that passed between the three, Melissa knew her random shot had hit the target.

'Colin,' Gideon muttered. 'I told you he drove past me. He must have recognised me after all.'

'Wouldn't it have been better if you'd said so at the time?' said Melissa gently. In spite of herself, she felt a twinge of pity for the old rogue. 'The police tend to be suspicious of people who withhold information.'

'You're not going to tell the police? But that's not fair!' Judith turned wide, beseeching eyes on Melissa and clutched her brother's arm more tightly. 'Giddy had nothing to do with Cissie's death.'

'I'm not suggesting that he had, but don't you see, he might have noticed something that could help with their enquiries. Surely, your duty as citizens should have told you that, yet he — all three of you in fact — said nothing about his being there around the crucial time. I couldn't help wondering why.'

'So you began poking and prying into things that are none of your business. You meddling bitch! Get out of this house!' Esther released her brother's arm and took a step forward as if to move round the table. For a moment, Melissa thought she was going to be physically attacked, but Gideon restrained her.

'Please go, Mrs Craig,' he pleaded.

'Of course. I'll leave you to think things over,' she said, backing towards the door. 'If it's any comfort,' she added with her hand on the doorknob, 'the police won't release your name to the press if you specifically ask them not to.'

'We'll bear that in mind,' said Gideon. Suddenly, he appeared to remember his manners. 'I'll see you out,' he added with a pathetic flash of gallantry.

At the front door, Melissa said in a low voice, 'If you take my advice, you'll keep away from Becky Tanner. Her father has a very nasty temper.' She went back to her car without waiting for a response.

If her mind had been in a whirl after her visit to Edith Ingram, it was almost in a frenzy by the time she arrived home. Once indoors she sat down with her notebook and scribbled furiously for half an hour before reaching for the telephone and calling Bruce's office number. A couple of minutes later she put the phone down in frustration; a colleague at the *Gazette* had informed her that he had gone out earlier and not returned, his mobile number was unavailable and he was not at home. She left messages that she had something interesting to report before taking off her jacket, kicking off her shoes and brewing the cup of tea for which she had been thirsting ever since leaving Stowbridge and which her unwilling hosts had — not unnaturally in the circumstances — failed to offer. She smiled a shade grimly at the thought of the consternation she had caused, especially to Gideon, whose expression when he realised who had followed him down the lane had been an almost comical study of guilty dismay. 'Well,' she said aloud as she waited for the kettle to boil. 'I've certainly set the cat among the pigeons there. I wonder what their next move will be.'

She went back into the hall and picked up the morning's post, which she had barely glanced at in her haste to put on paper an account of her second visit to the Manor. At the bottom of the half-dozen or so items was an envelope addressed simply 'Melissa'. The note inside was from Graham Shipley and read, 'They've let me go and I desperately need someone to talk to. Please can you spare me a little time?'

21

'I'm on police bail. You know what that means? It means,' Graham went on without waiting for a reply, 'that I have to report to them every day as if I was a criminal. It's monstrous, I've done nothing wrong and they can't prove that I have. I told them the truth and I wouldn't let them bully me into changing it — ' His agitation increased visibly and his voice became progressively more querulous as he spoke.

'And that's why they've had to let you go,' said Melissa. 'It must have been a dreadful ordeal for you — I'm so sorry I wasn't here when you got home.'

'It was worse this time than last,' Graham went on as if she had not spoken. 'At least, I wasn't arrested then, just subjected to endless questions — '

'The difference is that this time a girl is dead,' Melissa pointed out gently. 'And you have to admit that you didn't tell them the whole truth straight away.'

'Yes, I know,' he said tonelessly. 'I kept saying, over and over, that I'd help if I could, how much I wished I hadn't run away instead of stopping to see if she needed help . . . I even admitted I felt some moral responsibility for what happened to her . . . my solicitor wasn't very pleased about that,' he finished with an ironic twist of the lips that was meant to be a smile.

'No, I don't suppose he was.' Melissa smiled back, but inwardly she was appalled at the change in the man's appearance. His features were drawn and haggard, his skin had a greyish tinge and his eyes were dull and staring like those of a sleepwalker. He lapsed into a moody silence while she waited for him to speak again, sensing that there was more behind his urgent invitation than the need for sympathetic company.

They were sitting in the kitchen of Elder Cottage where, in the old days, Melissa had enjoyed many a chat with Iris over cups of herbal tea or glasses of home-made wine. Although, as caretaker and keyholder, she regularly entered the cottage between lets to check on the condition of the place, she had never been there as the guest of the current tenant. Almost for the first time since her friend moved out she became aware of the absence of the personal touches that had given the room so much character: the herbs growing in hand-thrown pots on the window-sill: the collection of *santons,* traditional pottery figures from Provence, ranged alongside the vegetarian cookery books on the shelves: the wicker basket by the Aga where Binkie, Iris's beloved cat, used to sleep.

'And just to make my day,' Graham said suddenly, 'I come home to this.' He pulled an envelope from his pocket and put it on the table between them, rather, it seemed to Melissa, in the manner of an investigating officer showing an exhibit to a witness. 'Read it,' he said. His voice was almost a growl. 'Here,' he picked up the envelope, took out the single sheet of paper, unfolded it and almost thrust it into her hand.

The letter, dated the previous day, was handwritten on good-quality watermarked paper headed 'St Monica's Preparatory School for Boys and Girls'. It read:

Dear Mr Shipley
In view of your involvement in the ongoing police enquiry into the recent death of a young girl, apparently in suspicious circumstances, I felt it prudent to make some further enquiries into your background. What I have learned has brought me, regretfully, to the conclusion that I have no choice but to withdraw my

offer of a teaching post at this school.
Yours truly
Millicent Monroe, Principal.

'How cruel.' Melissa handed back the letter and watched with a lump in her throat as Graham pushed it back into the envelope and tossed it aside. She could think of nothing else to say; the despair in his eyes very nearly brought tears to her own.

'But inevitable. You can see her point of view, can't you? It's the Jazzy Dixon affair all over again. I'm innocent of any wrongdoing, but the doubt will always be there because I can't prove it.' He gave a sharp, bitter laugh. 'Who said lightning never strikes in the same place twice?' He got up and began prowling around the little kitchen, adjusting lids on saucepans and fiddling with the controls on the cooker with an almost feverish intensity. Then, without warning, he swung round to face her, smiling as if nothing untoward had happened. 'I do apologise, I'm being very inhospitable,' he said. 'May I offer you a drink? I've got the usual things . . . sherry, gin — '

'A small dry sherry would be nice,' she said, not sure whether to be relieved or disturbed at his sudden change of mood.

He fetched a decanter and glasses, poured

the drinks, opened a packet of crisps and shook them into one of Iris's ceramic dishes. 'Cheers!' he said as he sat down opposite Melissa and raised his glass. As she took the first sip from hers, he tossed down his own drink in one gulp, reached for the bottle and poured another. 'First drink in two days,' he explained with a touch of bravado. 'Have to start making up for lost time.'

'I hope you've had something to eat.'

'Had a cheese sandwich for lunch. Couldn't be bothered to cook.'

'But you'll have something more substantial this evening?'

'Probably.'

'You have to look after yourself.'

'What for?' His temporary, unnatural cheerfulness waned as suddenly as it had dawned; he sat hunched over the refilled glass but made no further move to drink from it. 'What have I got to look forward to now? I've got no job, no future, no contact with my child — '

The deadness in his expression, the hopelessness in his voice, sent a chill through Melissa — a chill that swiftly gave way to a surge of anger at the injustice of it all. On impulse, she put out a hand and touched his; it was as cold as ice. 'You mustn't give up hope,' she said. 'The truth will come out soon, I'm sure of it.'

'What truth? I've told the truth. Someone else pulled that poor child from the water and then left her lying there, but no one's making the slightest effort to find him because — '

'That's where you're wrong,' Melissa interrupted. 'I've been doing a little sleuthing on your account.'

'That's very kind of you.' His look of gratitude was almost childlike, but there was little hope or expectation in his voice as he asked, 'What have you found out?'

The minute she had spoken, Melissa wondered whether she had been wise. Athough her efforts during the day had uncovered some interesting information and suggested further lines of enquiry, she was quick to recognise that none of it amounted to anything concrete. She would have to tread very carefully and not raise false hopes. Aware of Graham's eyes on her, she said, 'All I can tell you at the moment is that I have identified someone who might have information which could help the police to discover the truth about Cissie's death, but who has a very strong personal motive for remaining silent.'

'Who is it? Give me his name and I'll shake it out of him!' A feverish light flared in Graham's eyes. He tossed back his second sherry and slammed the glass down on the table with such force that the stem broke. At the sight of a thin line of blood trickling from his finger, the momentary spasm of rage evaporated. He gathered up the broken pieces and put them in a bin under the sink before running cold water over the cut. 'You were saying?' he prompted over his shoulder.

'That's all I can tell you at the moment,' Melissa repeated firmly. 'There are several more people I want to talk to. As soon as I learn anything definite I'll inform the police . . . and of course, I'll let you know as well. In fact,' she went on, getting to her feet, 'I'm expecting to hear soon from someone who may be able to help, so I'd better be going.'

'It was very kind of you to call.' He dried his hand carefully and wrapped his handkerchief round the injured finger. His manner was perfectly composed as he escorted her to the front door. 'Goodbye,' he said with a smile that was almost, but not quite natural. 'Thank you so much for everything.'

'Goodbye. I'll pop round in the morning to see how you are. And do have something to eat soon.'

'I will, I promise.' His eagerness to please her was touching.

Bruce telephoned almost as soon as Melissa got back indoors. 'Sorry I couldn't get back to you before,' he said. 'Today's been a bit hectic. What news? Oh, by the way, Graham Shipley's been released on police bail.'

'I know. I've just been talking to him, and I'm very concerned. On top of his other problems, he's lost the job at St Monica's and he's taken it badly. He's in a pretty volatile condition and he's been hitting the sherry bottle.'

'It's probably just as well — about the job, that is. The parents would soon start complaining once they heard about his arrest and he'd have had to leave anyway.'

'It seems so unfair.'

'It's not a fair world, is it? Anyway, what's your news? Was Gideon's crime embezzling parish funds — or did he seduce the vicar's wife?'

'Not funny. Indecent assault on choir girls.'

Bruce whistled. 'That puts a different face on things, doesn't it?' He listened without interruption while Melissa recounted her visit to his aunt and her subsequent call on the residents of Benbury Manor. He gave a dry chuckle when she explained how she had trapped them into a virtual admission that they had withheld information from the police. 'You're getting as devious as you're always accusing me of being,' he said slyly.

'Maybe that's where I've learned it. Anyway, their line was that the fact that he just happened to be nearby, but saw nothing, couldn't possibly have contributed anything useful to the investigation so there was no point in coming forward and risking his past coming out,' Melissa explained. 'At least, that was what the women were saying — ' She broke off as a new thought struck her. 'Come to think of it, they did almost all the talking. In effect, it was as if they were repeating assurances that their brother had given them.'

'You're saying, he might not have told them the whole truth?'

'It's possible, isn't it? He's almost certainly an inveterate liar, but his sisters are just the opposite — high-principled, staunch church-goers, real pillars of society. My guess is they'd go to hell and back to protect him, but they'd draw the line at telling barefaced porkies. And there's something else.' She went on to describe her encounter with Becky Tanner and her subsequent sighting of the girl jumping out of a car driven by Gideon Lane. 'She may be only fourteen, but she's a sexy little baggage and just the sort that dirty old men go for. Is he up to his old games again, I wonder? I warned him off, by the way — hinted that her father would half kill anyone who laid a finger on her.'

'That sounds really serious. Have you passed any of this on to the police?'

'Not yet, but I think I made it clear that I would if they didn't.'

'You amaze me. I'd have expected you to blow the whistle right away.'

'I thought of it, but it's the old problem. I've got no evidence — the Benbury Manor crowd could simply deny everything and I'd get another raspberry from Matt Waters for my pains. And as far as the indecent assault is concerned, he's got no record — as you know, the Warefield people never reported him. I was going to tell Matt about the attack on Tommy Judd, only he didn't have time to listen to me, and then when it seemed that Tommy was okay there didn't seem much point.'

'Hmm. Let's give this a bit of thought.' After a moment, Bruce said, 'What about that Scottish chap — the frozen food merchant? If Gideon was around at the crucial time, he might have spotted him but never thought to mention it in all the excitement of nearly running Graham Shipley down.'

'Colin? Yes, I could speak to him — I've got his mobile phone number.'

'It's worth a try. Ask him if he did see anyone else and if he did, get him to contact the police and say he's just remembered something else. That should start things moving.'

'I'll get on to him right away. Thanks for your help. Your Auntie Edie's a lovely lady, by the way.'

'Knew you'd like her. Ciao!'

Melissa had hardly put the phone down when her front doorbell rang. Gemma Woodbridge stood there with that evening's edition of the *Gazette* in one hand and the other extended, grubby palm upwards. 'One pound eighty please, and sorry it's a bit late,' she said with a bright smile. 'Heard the latest?' she went on as she checked the money and put it into her pocket. 'Old Mr Judd's in hospital.'

'Good gracious! When did this happen?'

'Dunno exactly. Nurse called by to dress his leg or something and found him half dead on the floor. Saw him through the window,' Gemma went on with some relish. 'The ambulance people had to break in.'

'How dreadful!' Melissa exclaimed. 'I do hope he'll be all right.'

'Yeah, hope so.' Having collected her money and delivered her titbit of news, Gemma hopped on her bicycle and pedalled away, leaving Melissa reflecting in horror on her visit to the cottage the previous morning and her conclusion, on finding it locked and with no sign of Tommy, that he was out and about and therefore not too seriously injured. He must have been in there all along, his condition steadily worsening. Supposing he were to die without saying anything about the attack on him? His killer would get away with it — and she would be partly responsible.

Putting her decision to call Colin on hold, she rushed to the phone and dialled Matt Waters' home number. This time he would have to listen to her.

22

'Matt, it's so good of you to come,' said Melissa as she opened the door to him. 'I'm sure when you hear what I've got to tell you, you'll agree I'm not wasting your time. Come in the sitting room and I'll pour you a drink — what shall it be?'

'A small Scotch and water, please. Coming to see you is never a waste of time, Mel — and how nice to see a log fire.'

'It's the first time I've lit it this autumn — it hasn't been cold enough up to now.'

He sank into one of her comfortable armchairs, leaned back and stretched his legs towards the blaze while uttering little grunts of contentment. 'This is an unexpected pleasure after a pretty gruelling day,' he said. 'It's so much easier to unwind in company than alone.'

'I find that too. It's at times like these that I miss Iris even more than usual.' She handed him his drink and sat down with her own. 'Cheers!'

'Cheers!' He took a mouthful and sat nursing the glass, his eyes appraising her. 'You look all in,' he said in sudden concern.

'I feel it.' For the first time that day she had time to reflect on her own state of mind and it came as a shock to realise that she felt physically and mentally drained.

'How's the book going?'

'Finished, except for a final read-through and tidy up before I print it off. It's taken quite a lot out of me — I'm seriously considering abandoning this 'literary' lark and going back to good old-fashioned whodunnits.'

'Mightn't be a bad idea. I've always enjoyed your books.'

'Thanks. Ken Harris never bothered to read them.'

He gave her a sharp look at the mention of the ex-DCI's name, but all he said was, 'Have you heard from him lately?'

'Not for a couple of months.' She hadn't intended to mention Ken. In fact, she had hardly given him a thought for some time — until the abortive visit to the Grey Goose brought it all back. But it was a relief to find that it was hurting less and less. 'Does he keep in touch with you?' she asked, trying to sound casual and matter-of-fact.

'Now and again. He seems to be enjoying life as a New York PI.'

'Yes, I think he's found his niche. Anyway, don't let's talk about him. Here,' Melissa picked up her sheaf of notes and handed it over. 'I've been keeping a sort of diary ever since Graham Shipley was arrested and this evening I brought it up to date.'

Matt reached out and took the notes, but did not immediately start reading them. 'What is it about this bloke Shipley?' he asked curiously. 'He doesn't seem your type at all — why are you so interested in him?'

'I'm not interested in him — not in the way you're suggesting — but I think it's diabolical the way your people have been hounding him after all he's been through in the past.'

'It's not fair to accuse us of hounding him. We're trying to get at the truth about Cissie Wilcox's death and we had good reason to believe he could help us, that's all. If he'd come clean in the first place about his movements — '

'You know perfectly well why he felt he couldn't do that — '

'Mel, if that's the reason why you've asked me over, to bang on about how badly we've treated Shipley — '

'No, that isn't the main reason, but I do feel strongly about it. He's in a pretty bad way at the moment, especially as he's lost his new job through all this.'

'I'm really sorry to hear that.'

'Yes, well — ' Melissa stood up and

reached for Matt's half-empty glass. 'Let me top that up while you read the notes.'

'No more booze, thanks, but I wouldn't mind a coffee.'

'Right.'

When she returned with the coffee he was sitting with the notes on his lap, gazing reflectively into the fire. She put down the tray, filled two china mugs and handed him one. 'Well?' she said.

'Mel, I have to hand it to you — you never give up, do you? You should have joined the force and gone in for real-life detection instead of just writing about it. It wouldn't have paid so well, of course,' he added with a chuckle.

'So what do you think?'

'I have to be honest — until I came to the last sheet there didn't seem to be a great deal that would help us over the Wilcox kid's death. The fact that this Gideon Lane seems to have been in the neighbourhood at the crucial time and that he has a secret weakness for groping young girls is certainly interesting, although by itself it's not much to go on. The attack on Judd is much more serious and I'll certainly make sure an officer goes to have a chat with him when he's well enough, but if he won't co-operate there's not much we can do. You've really no idea what might have been stolen — if anything?'

'None at all, I'm afraid — but something's just occurred to me. You'll see I've mentioned the fact Gideon has been in the habit of calling on Tommy, which has always struck me as a bit odd, considering what different people they are.'

' 'Pastoral visits', with a query, it says here,' grinned Matt with a glance at the notes.

'That's a bit of guesswork on my part. The entire family has a very strong church background and they must know that Tommy never sets foot in the place. Maybe they see him as a soul worth saving. Anyway, the two men must have chatted about something and you never know what might have come out in conversation that could give a lead.'

'And Lane was at great pains to endorse Judd's refusal to have the attack reported.' Matt referred back to the notes and rubbed his chin reflectively. 'Well, now that Judd is in hospital and we've been informed about it, we have a perfectly valid reason to go and have a word with both of them.'

'You'll do that?'

'Have to report back to the DCI first, but yes, I'm sure he'll agree. May I take your notes?'

'Of course, I'll get you an envelope.'

'Thanks.' He put down his empty coffee

mug and got to his feet. 'I'd better be going now. You look as if you need a good night's sleep.'

'You can say that again.'

At the door, he took her hand and said quietly, 'You've always been something of a crusader, Mel, and I respect you for it — even when I've felt like shaking you for getting under our feet.' He gave her hand a squeeze before adding, 'You know, I'm beginning to hope that Shipley's in the clear after all — for your sake as much as his.'

'Thanks Matt. Goodnight.'

She stepped outside as he drove away and glanced at the windows of Elder Cottage. It was only a little after ten o'clock, but they were in darkness. 'He's probably as shattered as I am, or more so,' she told herself as she went back inside and locked the door.

A short while later, as she put out her bedside light and waited for sleep to close in on her, she remembered something she had forgotten to draw to Matt's attention. Tomorrow, she resolved, she would do a little more sleuthing of her own.

It was after eight o'clock when she awoke. Her normal routine in the morning was to get up around six and work in her study for a couple of hours before getting showered and dressed. This morning there was no question of working; after a good night's rest her mind was clear, sharp and focused on the day's objective, and she was impatient to be up and doing.

Her first task was to fetch the morning papers. She walked briskly into the village, enjoying the sharp sweetness of the morning air with its hint of colder days to come. In the shop, Mrs Foster was regaling Miss Brightwell with such details as she had been able to persuade the District Nurse to reveal about the Tommy Judd affair. 'She reckoned he might've fallen downstairs and knocked himself out — said his face was all bruised. Not surprising if he did fall, the state that cottage is in it's a wonder it hasn't all collapsed on top of him before now.'

'It's a wonder he didn't kill himself,' said Miss Brightwell as she handed over the money for her *Daily Mail*. 'The Benbury Park people have a lot to answer for, letting one of their properties get in that state. He ought to sue them.'

'He might have died too, if Nurse hadn't called round. In agony, all by himself, poor old man.' There was a certain macabre relish in Mrs Foster's voice as she put forward this worst-possible scenario.

'Has anyone heard how he is?' asked Melissa, who had made a snap decision not to mention the attack on Tommy in front of the two old gossips. Her suspicion that they were quite capable of attributing it to Graham Shipley was confirmed a moment later.

'Afraid not,' said Miss Brightwell. 'I hear the police have released that Mr Shipley,' she added frostily. 'It seems all wrong to me — supposing he were to attack another young girl?'

Melissa was on the point of angrily pointing out that the reason for Graham's release was the absence of evidence that he had attacked anyone at all, but she held her tongue. As it was her turn to be served, she took the copy of *The Times* that Mrs Foster handed her and said, in a defiantly audible voice, 'I'll take Mr Shipley's *Independent* as well, please.' She was conscious of two pairs of appraising eyes on her as she marched out of the shop, almost bumping into Gary Tanner.

'Good morning Gary, you're just the lad I want to speak to!' she said. 'Can you spare a moment?'

Gary returned her greeting politely enough, but he appeared less than overjoyed at her request. 'Got to get me Dad's paper — he likes to read it over his breakfast,' he said, edging away from her.

'This'll only take a second. I expect you've heard that old Mr Judd's in hospital?'

'Yes.' Gary eyed Melissa warily. 'Did hear something about it. What's wrong with him?'

'He doesn't want this spread around,' she said, having satisfied herself that there was no one else within earshot, 'but someone beat him up and he sustained some quite serious injuries.' She waited for a moment, fixing Gary with the kind of direct stare that policemen use when questioning a witness. It might have been her imagination, but she had the impression that he was uncomfortable with the direction the conversation was taking. 'You and your friends often hang around near his cottage, don't you?'

'What of it?'

'Have any of you noticed anyone else hanging about there lately — anyone strange, I mean?'

'No.'

The lad appeared to relax a little, but his unease returned with a rush at Melissa's next question. 'Have you or any of your friends ever been inside Mr Judd's cottage?'

'No!' He almost shouted the word. 'No, I never! I don't know nothing about it!' He turned away from her and dashed into the shop, emerging a couple of moments later with a newspaper under his arm.

283

'Gary, just a moment,' said Melissa. She moved in front of him, blocking his way. 'What is it that you don't know anything about?'

'Don't know what you're talking about.' He dodged round her, grabbed his bicycle, mounted it and rode away at a furious pace. She stood watching him for a moment before setting off for home, having already decided what her next move would be.

Meanwhile, there was Graham's paper to deliver and her promise to 'pop round to see that he was okay' to fulfil. Detecting a movement at an upstairs window as she approached Elder Cottage, she gave a short ring on the bell. There was no response and after a moment she lifted the flap of the letter-box and called, 'Graham, it's Melissa. I've brought your paper.'

'Thank you.' The voice came from a distance, as though he was standing at the head of the stairs. 'Will you put it through the door, please?'

'Of course. How are you this morning?'

'All right, thank you.'

'Good. It's a lovely day, I hope you enjoy it.'

'Thank you.'

His voice had the same dead quality that she had noticed the previous evening. Poor chap, she thought as she went indoors and began to prepare her breakfast. She tried to think of some way of cheering him up. He really needed another man to talk to; suddenly, she thought of Sam Rogers, a down-to-earth, sympathetic character, an experienced and dedicated teacher himself who would surely understand what he was going through. From one point of view he was hardly the ideal person, being the deputy of the woman who had so cruelly put an end to Graham's hopes for the future, but he might be able to help him come to terms with his situation and even suggest some other avenue he might explore when he had recovered from the trauma. She checked Sam's number and was relieved to find him at home.

'Just getting myself organised for school — term starts on Wednesday but we poor staff have to go in a day early to get ready for the little darlings,' he said breezily. 'What can I do for you, Melissa?'

'Not for me.' Briefly, Melissa explained her mission. To her surprise, Sam knew nothing of Graham Shipley's arrest, or of the letter withdrawing the offer of a post at his school.

'We've been on holiday in Turkey, only got back last night,' he explained. 'There's probably a copy of Millie's letter in the post, but I haven't had a chance to go through it. You know,' he went on, 'I find this hard to believe — Shipley seems such a decent sort. A bit down-beat at times, but he's had a rough time by all accounts. Are you saying that Millie sacked him just because he's been questioned by the police?'

'I'm afraid there's more to it than that. He had a bad experience a couple of years ago with a randy little teenager who set out to ruin him . . . and it seems she's succeeded,' she added bitterly.

Sam clicked his tongue in sympathy, but said, 'Look, there isn't a lot I can do. I mean, Millie may have appeared a bit brutal, but she's got the kids to think about, and the parents — '

'I know, and I'm not suggesting you can do anything to make her change her mind. I just thought it might help if you were to call round and have a chat with him, try and cheer him up a little. At the moment I think he feels utterly desolate and without any hope for the future. Having another man to talk to might help.'

'Well, I suppose I could do that. I'll drop by later on.'

'I wish you would. I'm really very concerned about him. I hope you don't think I'm interfering.'

'Not a bit, I'm glad you told me. I'll have to be thinking about arranging cover for him while we look for someone else.'

Greatly relieved, Melissa finished her breakfast and made a few notes about her encounter with Gary Tanner before setting off to call on the Daniels family.

23

The door of the neat, brick-built semi in Lower Benbury was opened by Billy's mother, a thin, anxious-looking woman in her forties, prematurely lined and grey-haired. She peered at Melissa with an expression of vague enquiry on her face.

'Yes?' For a moment she did not recognise her caller. Then she said, 'Oh, it's you, Mrs Craig. Good morning.'

'Good morning Mrs Daniels. Is your Billy in?'

'He's still in bed. I've been trying to get him to come down for his breakfast.' Mrs Daniels jerked her head round and shouted over her shoulder. 'Bill-ee! A lady to see you!' She stood aside and held the door wide open. 'You'd better come in, I'll go up and rout him out. He's not been in any trouble, has he?'

'Not that I know of. I just wanted to ask him something.'

'Come in the kitchen, d'you mind? The front room's a bit of a pigsty.' Mrs Daniels led the way along a short passage into a small, square room fitted with shabby but clean units and work surfaces. A frying pan containing rashers of raw bacon and slices of tomato stood on the top of a gas stove, evidently awaiting Billy's appearance; the remains of other breakfasts, presumably those of his parents, were stacked on the draining board. Four wooden chairs were ranged round a table covered with a plastic cloth and laid for one. Mrs Daniels pulled out one of the chairs, saying, 'Sit down, Mrs Craig. I'll give him another call.' Her footsteps went thumping up the stairs, accompanied by repeated shouts of 'Bill-ee!'

After an interval, during which the sounds of scolding from the mother and surly grumbles from her son came floating down through an open door, Mrs Daniels reappeared with Billy trailing in her wake. He was not an appealing sight; his hair, normally tied in a pony-tail, hung in greasy wisps round his unhealthily pale face and his shirt and jeans were rumpled and stained. He directed an unfriendly stare at Melissa before going to a teapot standing beside the stove and peering inside. He helped himself to some of its contents, added milk and sugar and stirred the mixture as if he was trying to bore a hole in the bottom of the mug with the spoon. He brought it to the table, slumped into a chair and took a couple of noisy gulps.

'Where's your manners? Aren't you going

to say good morning to the lady?' scolded his mother with the weary air of one pursuing a hopeless cause.

'Morning,' Billy grunted without raising his eyes.

'Good morning, Billy,' Melissa replied briskly. 'I just wanted to ask you one or two questions about old Mr Judd. You know he's in hospital, I expect?'

At the mention of the name, Billy started. Mrs Daniels looked at Melissa in surprise. 'No, we didn't know, did we Billy?' There was no response from her son, who ran the back of one hand across his nose and then continued drinking his tea. 'What's wrong with the old gentleman?'

''Gentleman', that's a good one!' sniggered Billy. 'He ain't no gentleman.'

'What's that supposed to mean?' his mother demanded. A crafty gleam appeared in Billy's pale eyes, but he ignored the question. She turned back to Melissa with a frown. 'Is that why you're here, Mrs Craig? I don't see what Mr Judd being ill has got to do with us — we're very sorry to hear it, of course — '

'He isn't ill, he's in hospital because on Thursday morning he was beaten up in his own cottage,' said Melissa.

'Beaten up! That's terrible — but I still

don't see . . . here, you aren't suggesting that my Billy had anything to do with it, are you?' Mrs Daniel's attitude underwent a subtle change and she gave Melissa a defiant look as if to say, *He might be an ill-mannered layabout, but he's my boy and I'm not having him accused of that sort of thing.*

'I'm not saying that for a moment,' Melissa assured her. 'I'm sure Billy wouldn't hurt anyone, but I think he might know a little more about Mr Judd than you might think. That's true, isn't it Billy?' she said. 'Isn't it?' she repeated, and this time he reluctantly met her eye. His face had turned a dull red and for the second time in two days she knew that a random shot had found a home.

'Sort of,' he muttered.

His mother gave him a sharp poke in the ribs with a forefinger. 'What's that supposed to mean?' she snapped for a second time. 'Come on, out with it!'

The lad's colour deepened. 'He's a right dirty old sod,' he said after a pause.

'Billy Daniels, just you watch your language!' She aimed a slap at his head, but he anticipated the blow and took it on his arm.

'She asked me and I told her,' he protested.

'That's all right,' Melissa assured her. 'Just let him tell me in his own words.' She turned back to Billy. 'How do you know this?' she asked gently.

'Saw him, didn't we?'

'Who's we?'

'Me and Gary Tanner and Dave Potter.'

'You saw him doing what?'

There was another pause before Billy, by this time scarlet to the ears, answered, 'Looking at a dirty book while he was — ' He broke off, too embarrassed to go on, but it was not difficult to guess what he left unsaid.

'When was this?' she asked.

Bit by bit the story came out. The boys, finding themselves hard up and wanting five pounds each for their tickets to the barbecue, conceived the notion — planted in their heads by Dave Potter — that Tommy Judd might have money concealed under his floorboards. The three of them had managed to get a look through the window of Tommy's cottage while the old man was in there and had actually seen the rolled-back rug in front of the grate, which convinced them that they had guessed correctly. They had also witnessed Tommy Judd performing the sordid act at which Billy had hinted, but it had not occurred to them that there was a connection between the two. Their sole interest was in the money they were convinced lay concealed in a hiding-place under the rug.

The following day Dave, who had obviously masterminded the whole enterprise, summoned the others and told them that Tommy had caught the ten o'clock bus into Stowbridge and his cottage would therefore be empty until it returned at two. Thinking that there would be no one around in the middle of the day, they had gone there at twelve o'clock, got in through an unfastened window and quickly discovered Tommy's secret hoard. To their disgust, it did not consist of money. Instead, piled up between the floor joists, were a number of magazines containing pornographic photographs, many of them featuring young girls. Disappointed at failing to find cash, the lads nevertheless spent some time sniggering over their find when, to their dismay, Tommy Judd appeared and caught them red-handed.

Mrs Daniels, who had sat in open-mouthed horror at this catalogue of misdemeanours, could contain her indignation no longer. 'Serves you right!' she exclaimed. 'I suppose you forgot the time while you were reading that filth!'

'It weren't like that, he came home early,' said Billy. 'Someone must've given him a lift.'

'What's the difference? You got caught breaking and entering, didn't you? I'm surprised he didn't hand you over to the police.' Mrs Daniels seemed unaware of the penalty attached to the possession of pornography, especially of a paedophile nature, but her son was better informed.

'Then he'd have been in dead trouble himself, wouldn't he?' Billy gave a smirk. 'Our Dave knew how to handle it. He said, 'Give us a fiver each and we won't tell on you'. And it worked, didn't it? We got our ticket money.'

Mrs Daniels threw up her hands in despair. 'Blackmail as well! Just you wait till I tell your father!' she wailed. 'Mrs Craig, I don't know what to say, I'm that ashamed. We've tried to bring him up decent — '

'I know you have,' said Melissa gently. 'You can't be behind your kids all the time.' She turned back to Billy. 'Just a couple more questions. Did you or either of the others take any of those magazines away?'

Billy shook his head. 'I never. Don't know about the others.'

'Did you know that Dave Potter's been caught with some pornographic material? Dirty books,' she explained as Billy gave her a puzzled look.

'Yeah, did hear something,' he admitted. 'Dunno where he got it.'

'Could it have been from Tommy's cottage?'

'Suppose so.'

'Billy, look at me.' Reluctantly, he complied. 'Have *you* ever been back to the cottage, or taken any of Mr Judd's magazines?'

'No.' He looked at her beseechingly. 'Truly, Mrs Craig.'

'All right Billy, I believe you.'

'You goin' to tell the Old Bill?'

'I'm afraid I'll have to, but if Mr Judd hasn't complained they won't be arresting you.' To Mrs Daniels, Melissa said, 'They'll want to talk to him, of course, but I'll tell them how helpful he's been and I don't think they'll be too hard on him.'

'I hope not. I don't know what his Dad's going to say.'

'Try not to worry.'

Some hopes. I wouldn't care to be in Billy's shoes, thought Melissa as she headed for home, eager to write up her notes on the interview and to consider how the information she had just acquired fitted into the puzzle. The picture was not yet completely clear, but it was beginning to take shape.

★ ★ ★

At about the same time that Melissa rang the doorbell of the Daniels' house in Lower Benbury, DCI Holloway and one of his detective constables were being admitted to Benbury Manor by a startled and flustered Judith Waghorne. She led the way to a small sitting-room, invited them to take a seat and fled to the kitchen, where Esther was loading the breakfast things into the dishwasher.

'Essie, the police are here again. They want to talk to Giddy.'

'What about?'

'How do I know? Oh Essie, what can he have been doing?'

'Let's hope it's just a routine enquiry. I'll go and call him. You continue with this.' Esther handed her sister the cereal bowl she had been rinsing at the sink and left the kitchen. Upstairs, she knocked on her brother's bedroom door, but did not wait for him to respond before bursting in. He was at the window with his back to her; as she entered, he gave a start and thrust something into his pocket before turning round to face her with a childlike expression of guilt on his face.

'It's usual to wait until you hear someone say, 'Come in',' he said in an attempt to regain his dignity.

'Never mind the social niceties. There are two policemen here to see you.'

'What?' Gideon's expression registered acute anxiety. 'What do they want?'

'They didn't say, they just asked to speak to you. They're waiting in the blue room.'

'Well, I suppose I'd better go and see what they want. I'm sure it can't be anything too awful.' He assumed a jaunty air and made for the door, but Esther blocked his way.

'What was that you put in your pocket?' she demanded.

'I didn't put anything in my pocket,' he protested, but he refused to meet her eye.

'I saw you hiding something. Show it to me!'

'I tell you, it's nothing — '

'If it's nothing, why the fuss? Come on, let me see it.' She stretched out a hand and, as had been the case almost from birth, he found himself powerless to defy her. Scarlet with embarrassment, he pulled a photograph from his pocket and gave it to her.

'Where in God's name did you get this?' she demanded, her tone a mixture of censure and amazement.

'She gave it to me.'

'Don't lie to me.'

'It's true, I swear it.'

'Why?' He did not answer. He was a pitiable spectacle, like a schoolboy awaiting a whipping, his head bent and his face burning. 'We'll discuss this later,' Esther declared. 'You'd better pull yourself together before you talk to the police. I'll tell them you'll be down in a minute . . . and I'll take care of this.'

Half an hour later, after the police had gone, Gideon found himself seated at the kitchen table facing his sibling inquisitors.

'Why did they come here?' Esther demanded. 'Exactly what did they want?'

'They said that I'd been seen in the lane round about the time they thought that girl died, and asked me why I hadn't mentioned it.'

'And what did you tell them?'

'I didn't deny it, of course, but I explained that when they questioned me before, I thought they meant actually in the woods near the brook, and that's why I didn't say anything.'

'What else did they want to know?'

'That was all, really. I suppose they have to tie up all the loose ends, as they say in mystery novels.' From appearing uneasy and apprehensive before them, Gideon looked both his sisters almost defiantly in the eye. 'I can't for the life of me think what all the fuss was about,' he finished sniffily.

'It took half an hour for them to ask one question?' Esther's tone was sceptical.

'Well, they put it several times in different ways — you know how it is.'

'Not having been questioned by the police, I don't know how it is. Are you sure they didn't ask you about anything else? What happened at Warefield, for example?'

'Essie, how on earth would they know about that?' Judith protested. 'Even the Warefield police never questioned him — and that's all behind him anyway. He never really hurt anyone and he's given us his word he's turned over a new leaf.' She linked one arm through Gideon's and gave it an affectionate shake.

'Turned over a new leaf, has he? Then how does he account for this?' Esther pulled open a drawer in the table and took out an envelope. She extracted the photograph she had confiscated earlier and showed it to her sister. 'I caught him sneaking it into his pocket.'

Judith gave a horrified gasp and rounded on her brother. 'Giddy, whatever were you doing with this? How did you come by it?' Without waiting for a reply, she turned a bewildered face to Esther. 'Essie, what on earth shall we do?' she wailed. 'We've done everything we possibly could for him . . . we've given him all our love and support . . . we've prayed for him . . . Giddy, how could you do this to us when we trusted you?'

He looked beseechingly from one to the

other, his mouth working and his eyes moist. 'You aren't going to tell the police?' he whined. 'Essie, Judy, it was just a solitary lapse. I promise not to do anything like this again.'

'I'm beginning to understand just how much faith we can place in your promises,' Esther said coldly. She replaced the photograph in the envelope, got to her feet and took the car keys from a peg near the back door.

'Essie, where are you going?' cried Judith. 'Please, not to the police — let's give him one more chance!'

'I'm not going to the police, but there is something else that has to be done.'

'What do you mean?'

'I'll tell you when I return — I shouldn't be very long,' said Esther. With a contemptuous glance at Gideon, she added, 'Keep an eye on him, make sure he doesn't get into any more mischief.'

Left on their own, Gideon and Judith sat in silence as the slam of the front door closing behind Esther echoed through the house, followed by the crash as she flung open the garage doors and drove out. When the sound of the car's engine had died away Gideon said, his voice full of apprehension, 'Where do you think she's gone?'

Judith's normally placid face distorted in a spasm of uncharacteristic anger.

'Use your imagination, you fool!' she almost screamed at him. 'Who do you think has the most right to know what you've been up to?'

'She said she wasn't going to the police.'

'Think a bit nearer home.'

His face turned ashen and he started to his feet. 'I must get out of here,' he muttered. 'That Mrs Craig . . . she warned me — ' He rushed out of the room, then rushed back saying, 'Phone for a taxi! Say it's urgent!'

'But why — ?'

'Just do it!'

Blinded with tears, she obeyed. Then she went upstairs, following the sound of drawers and cupboards being violently opened and shut. She stood in the doorway of her brother's room, helplessly wringing her hands while tears dribbled down her cheeks as she watched him flinging clothes into a suitcase. 'I've got everything I need for the moment,' he muttered as he checked the contents of his wallet and stuffed it into his back pocket. 'I'll send for the rest of my stuff later.'

'Giddy, don't run away,' Judith pleaded. 'Stay here with us, we'll look after you — '

'Sorry, got to go.' He dropped a kiss on his

sister's forehead, then rushed to the window at the sound of an approaching car. 'Here's my taxi. So long, Judy.' And he was gone, leaving her sobbing hysterically on her knees beside his bed.

24

Melissa had acquired the habit of glancing up at the windows of Elder Cottage every time she passed and she automatically did so on returning from her call at the Daniels' home. In the absence of any movement, plus the fact that an upstairs window that had been half-open first thing was closed, she concluded that he must have gone out. That appeared promising; at least, it was better than sitting around moping. Making a mental resolve to contact him again later in the day, she put away her car and went indoors to write up her notes.

One fact which the information elicited from Billy had established beyond reasonable doubt was that what Tommy Judd and Gideon Lane had in common was an unhealthy interest in young girls. That would account for the latter's visits to Brookside Cottage. It did not, of course, explain how they had discovered their shared weakness — that was something the police would have to investigate — but one possible explanation was that they obtained their supplies of pornographic material from the same source.

That should be a very useful lead for the Vice Squad.

It seemed likely that it was from Tommy Judd that Dave Potter had obtained the magazines he had been caught trying to sell, especially in the light of the robbery which the old man had been at such pains to deny. But there seemed no reason for the violence; Dave could easily have used blackmail to obtain further supplies by repeating the threat to expose him. Had he perhaps become greedy, broken into the cottage yet again with the intention of stealing the entire stock of magazines, been caught in the act and turned on the old man in a panic? The latter scenario was difficult to visualise as Dave was a somewhat puny specimen and Judd, although elderly, was by no means frail. Potter senior, however, was a very different animal; he was built like a tank and had a reputation for keeping his brains in his fists. Had he muscled in on his son's sordid little scam?

There remained the over-riding question of exactly how Cissie Wilcox had died. It seemed reasonably certain that something or someone had frightened her, causing her to leave the track, plunge down the bank and fall into the brook. But had she drowned as a result of that fall, or was there a more sinister explanation? She had been sent on an errand to deliver eggs to Tommy Judd and since the eggs were found in his cottage she had evidently carried it out, but according to the old man's testimony it had been without his knowledge; he claimed not to have realised that he had not brought them home himself. That would indicate that he had not seen her bring them. But had he been telling the truth? Or had he, perhaps, been otherwise engaged? Had Cissie witnessed him in the act of masturbating, possibly with the aid of one of his sex magazines, and fled from the cottage in disgust? And had Tommy, realising that the girl would almost certainly run home and tell her mother, and being terrified of the shame of having his secret revealed, pursued her with the intention of persuading or — should that attempt fail — of forcing her to keep silent? In either event it would not have been long before he realised he had no chance of catching her, and since Graham Shipley had not seen him it was reasonable to assume that he had very quickly given up the chase. That made it unlikely that he had caused or witnessed her fall.

There remained the possibility of Gideon Lane's involvement. He had denied being anywhere near the scene until forced by the testimony of a witness to change his story. She tried to visualise the probable sequence of events: Gideon on his way to visit Tommy and being spotted by — presumably — Colin somewhere between the point where the turning from Benbury Manor joined the road to Upper Benbury and the end of the track leading to Brookside Cottage. It could have taken him up to ten minutes to reach the cottage from the junction, in which case he would not have seen Tommy chasing Cissie — if indeed the old man had done so. But perhaps he had found Tommy in a state of agitation and had learned from him what had happened. In that case, the pair of them would almost certainly have been ready to lie through their teeth rather than risk the true reason for their association becoming known.

With Tommy in hospital and known to be unwilling to testify even if he was fit to do so — Melissa made a note to enquire about him later on — Gideon's evidence could prove vital. She experienced a grim satisfaction at the thought of his receiving yet another visit from the police, possibly the Vice Squad. This time, they would be asking some very searching questions indeed. 'Looks like you're going to get your comeuppance at last, you old humbug!' she said gleefully to herself as she put down her pencil and read over what she had written.

Her momentary satisfaction was short-lived as she reminded herself that Graham Shipley was still under suspicion of having brought about Cissie's death and subsequently, out of sheer horror at what he had done, dragging her from the water — perhaps in the desperate hope that he had not killed her after all — before fleeing the scene, only to return later and claim to have discovered the girl's body. She had uncovered nothing in the way of evidence to support Graham's version of what had happened. Nothing to point at any alternative to the police theory. Nothing. Unless . . . supposing . . . ?

At this point there was a ring at her doorbell, accompanied by a thunderous knocking as if someone was trying to break in. Somewhat alarmed, she went to her bedroom window and saw Sam Rogers' Jeep parked outside Elder Cottage and Sam himself in her front porch, pounding on the door. With a premonition that something was seriously amiss, she hurried downstairs.

'Can you help? Something's wrong next door,' said Sam. He was plainly alarmed; his voice was hoarse with apprehension. 'Shipley isn't answering his bell and there's a car in the garage with the engine running . . . it's locked . . . have you got a chopper, or a crowbar or something — ?'

307

'I've got a key — hang on!' She dashed to fetch it.

'Let's hope he hasn't bolted the door from inside!' Sam muttered as he shoved it into the lock and turned it.

Graham had not bolted the door, neither had he thought it necessary to lock himself in his car. Coughing and choking in the fumes that filled the small garage, Sam wrenched open the driver's door and switched off the ignition, then reached across the unconscious man and released the handbrake. He staggered back outside, fighting for breath. 'Help ... me ... pull ... the ... car ... out!' he gasped, but Melissa had already grabbed the rear bumper and was tugging for all she was worth.

Between them they got the car outside and Sam took Graham by the shoulders and dragged the upper part of his body clear. 'There's a rug on the back seat,' he said. 'Get it out and spread it on the ground, and then give me a hand lifting him out.'

Thankful that Sam was there to take charge, Melissa helped him to lower Graham onto the rug. His mouth hung open and his face was a bright cherry red. '*Dear God!*' she prayed silently as they worked. '*Don't let it be too late! Help us to save him!*'

'Okay,' said Sam crisply. 'Leave him to me

while you call for an ambulance.'

'Right.' Once again she hurried to obey. When she returned from making the call she found Sam squatting over Graham, arranging him in the recovery position with the calm competence of one who knew exactly what he was doing. 'He's still breathing and there's a slow pulse,' he said over his shoulder. 'I think we got to him in time. Find another rug to put over him, will you?'

The fifteen minutes that it took the ambulance to arrive were some of the slowest that Melissa had ever known. For the sake of something to do, she brewed some strong coffee and they drank it standing in the open beside the still form at their feet. From time to time Sam handed his mug to Melissa while he checked Graham's pulse against his wristwatch. Each time she held her breath as she waited for him to report, mutely repeating her prayer, *Help us to save him!*

'It's picking up,' he said at last, 'and I think the colour's beginning to improve.'

'Thank God!' she said fervently. 'I didn't even hear the engine running, and I'd never have been able to get him out by myself. It was providential that you arrived when you did.' At that moment they heard the ambulance approaching and she sprinted to the end of the track to wave it down. Within minutes it was on its way to Stowbridge hospital with life-giving oxygen driving the poison from the patient's lungs. The two rescuers listened in silence as the wail of the siren faded into the distance.

'Shall I make some fresh coffee?' said Melissa after a moment. 'You've hardly drunk any of yours and it must be cold.'

'Thanks, that'd be nice.'

'I daresay you'd like to clean up as well.'

'When I've put the car away.' He started the engine, drove into the garage and relocked the door.

They both felt too on edge to sit down and they drank their coffee standing at the kitchen window. 'Millie Monroe will be devastated when she hears about this,' Sam remarked. 'She'll blame herself for writing that letter.'

'That was probably what tipped him over the edge,' Melissa said sombrely, 'but it's only part of the story.' She gave him a brief outline of Graham's tragic history. 'Finding Cissie's body was bad enough, but to be arrested on suspicion of her murder must have been a nightmare. I don't know . . . I feel I should have done more to help him . . . in fact, I told him yesterday that I've been doing a bit of sleuthing on his behalf in the hope of cheering him up. It doesn't seem to have worked, does it?'

'You've been sleuthing?' Sam's eyebrows lifted in surprise. 'Have you made any progress?'

'Until this morning, not very much, but now I think I might have come up with something significant. I was just figuring it out when you came banging on the door. Ironic, isn't it? If you hadn't turned up it might have been all for nothing.'

'Well, that was partly your doing — my coming to call on him, I mean. You asked me to, remember?'

'So I did.'

Sam went over to the sink and rinsed out his mug. 'I must be going. I've got some business in Stowbridge so I'll call at the hospital and find out how he is.'

'That's good of you. If you see him, tell him from me not to give up hope and say I'll try and visit him later on.'

'Will do.'

After Sam had driven away, Melissa took her scribbled notes up to her study, transferred them to the word processor and ran off a copy. She put the sheets into an envelope, addressed it to Detective Sergeant Waters and marked it 'Urgent'. She glanced at her watch, saw that it was twelve o'clock and decided to have an early lunch before taking her report to the police station. With luck, she would be able to hand it to Matt personally.

'What a morning!' she said aloud as she prepared her scrambled eggs. 'Let's hope the rest of the day will be quieter.'

★ ★ ★

Melissa set off for Stowbridge in brilliant weather, but the small valley town which in bygone times had been the centre of a flourishing wool trade lay smothered in a downy white mist which soon blotted out the sun. She found a space in a car park and walked the short distance to the police station, where she managed to catch a word with Matt Waters as he was on the point of leaving with a colleague.

'Can you spare five minutes?' she asked. 'I really think I've hit on something significant. I've made these notes — '

'Leave them with reception, will you? I'll read them when I come back.'

'We're talking paedophile porn at Stowbridge Comprehensive,' she said and was gratified to see an abrupt change of demeanour.

'Okay, five minutes.' Instructing his colleague to wait for him in the car, Matt opened the door of an interview room and beckoned her inside. 'Right, let's have it,' he said briskly without offering her a chair.

She had rehearsed what she was going to say on the drive into town and was able to give a rapid, clear and concise account of the results of her morning's investigations and of the startling theory concerning the association between Gideon Lane and Tommy Judd that had occurred to her just before Sam Rogers had come banging on her door for help. Matt listened attentively without comment until she ended with a brief reference to Graham Shipley's abortive suicide attempt.

'Poor chap!' he exclaimed. 'I'd no idea he'd come to that.'

'I did warn you.'

'Yes, I know, but we never realised he was that desperate. Is he going to be all right?'

'Sam Rogers seemed to think so, and I had the impression he knew what he was on about. I'll call at the hospital to inquire after I leave here.'

'Good. Now about this information you've just given me . . . I'm really grateful. It should provide us with a very useful lead.'

'I suppose it would be unfair to remind you that if you'd given those three lads a more thorough questioning — '

He gave a rueful grin. 'Not unfair at all,

except that we were looking for a possible murderer, not a peddler in porn.' His face became serious again. 'You may well be right in your theory on that count as well,' he admitted. 'It's a pity old Judd is still too ill to be questioned. He might not be such a glib liar as our friend Gideon Lane.'

'Been telling more porkies, has he?'

'Only by pretending he misunderstood our earlier questions. Mr Holloway wasn't fooled, of course, but even he couldn't trip him up.'

'He must have had plenty of practice,' she said wryly. 'Thanks for your time, Matt.'

'Thank you for your efforts, Mel. You ought to enrol as a Special. We could use your analytical mind.'

'Bruce Ingram thinks my mind is devious, but I much prefer analytical,' she chuckled. 'Cheers, Matt. Keep me posted, won't you?'

The hospital was some ten minutes' walk from the police station. It took almost another ten to track Graham Shipley down, but eventually she found herself looking at him through the open door of a side ward. He was lying back on a mountain of pillows with his eyes closed and his colour reassuringly normal.

'How is he?' she asked a nurse who was checking his pulse.

'He's doing all right. We're keeping him in

overnight for observation, but he should be able to go home tomorrow.'

'Is it all right if I have a word with him?'

'Of course. See if you can cheer him up a bit.'

Melissa walked to the bedside and said, 'Hullo, Graham. How are you feeling?'

His eyelids fluttered for a second, then lifted. He stared at her, at first blankly, then with a faint smile of recognition. 'Nice of you to call,' he said weakly. 'Sorry I've been such a trouble.'

'We'll let you off if you promise not to do it again.' She fished in her handbag and brought out a letter. 'The postman came late today and he brought this for you. It looks as if it might be important.'

He took the envelope she handed him and turned it over. Suddenly animated, he ripped it open. 'It's from my solicitor,' he said. She watched as he unfolded the letter and read it with growing delight. 'It's wonderful news!' he exclaimed. 'They've tracked down my ex-wife to an address in Swindon and they're taking steps to arrange for me to have access to Patsy.'

'How lovely! I'm so happy for you. It could hardly be more convenient — Swindon's only twenty miles from Upper Benbury.'

'So long as the court doesn't hear about all

this.' His face clouded and he made a vague gesture with one hand. 'It could all fall apart if it comes out that I've been involved in another case with a teenage girl — '

'Now stop thinking all those negative thoughts. I'm really hopeful that you'll soon be cleared of suspicion and then you can start planning your future. Patsy might even be able to come and stay with you for a weekend, or during the holidays.'

'I doubt if Sheila would agree to that. And I haven't even got a job now.' He shook his head sadly, then lifted his chin as if in response to Melissa's encouraging words. 'Still, it has to be one step at a time, doesn't it?'

'That's exactly right!' she said warmly. 'You hang on to that thought and let's have no more melodrama — promise?'

'I promise. Thank you so much for coming.'

'No problem. See you tomorrow, then.' She gave him a cheerful wave as she left, thinking how nice it was to have some really good news for a change. Perhaps, once DCI Holloway had followed up the information she had passed to Matt Waters, there would be more to come.

She was about to leave the hospital when she remembered her intention of asking after Tommy Judd. Matt had indicated that he was too ill to be interviewed, but there might have been some overnight improvement. She turned and went back to the reception desk.

25

Tommy Judd's bed was in a cubicle off a corridor in the intensive therapy unit. At first, Melissa hardly recognised him; his hair had been neatly trimmed, his face — which habitually sported two or three days' growth of stubble — had been freshly shaved and his hands, lying still and relaxed on top of the covers, had an almost manicured appearance. His colour was healthy, the monitor at his side showed a steady pulse and, apart from the drip attached to one arm, the swollen lip and the fading bruise on the side of his face, he showed little sign of his ordeal.

A young man was sitting in a chair beside the bed and when Melissa appeared he got up and approached her with a smile, saying, 'Good afternoon, Mrs Craig. Remember me? DC Bob Danville — we met in the Grey Goose a few days ago.'

'So we did. I take it you're here to question Mr Judd when he wakes up?'

'He's awake, has been since six o'clock this morning so they say. I've been here since midday, trying to get him to talk.'

'Has he said anything at all?'

318

The constable gave a rueful grin. 'Only to repeat that he hurt himself falling over, which according to the medics is totally inconsistent with his injuries.'

'It's inconsistent with what he said when I found him,' said Melissa. 'He quite definitely said he'd been kicked and beaten.'

'Well, that's his story now and he's sticking to it. He's had plenty to say about the people who brought him here, though. Been telling everyone in no uncertain terms that he wants to go home. Let's go outside a minute,' Danville added with a glance over his shoulder. They moved out of earshot and he pulled out his notebook. 'Before he came round properly he was heard mumbling to himself. Half of it was unintelligible, but he did say something that sounded like 'yellow shoe in the lane', and then, 'spotted it too late'. Does that mean anything to you?'

'Yes, I think it does,' said Melissa eagerly. 'Cissie Wilcox was wearing yellow shoes the day she died, and one of them had come off. It wasn't in the lane, though — it was lying beside her body when she was found. 'Spotted it too late',' she mused. 'I wonder what he meant by that. Have you asked him?'

Danville shook his head. 'Never thought to — it didn't seem to be relevant.'

'I take it you haven't been working on the

Cissie Wilcox case?'

'I was on leave when it happened. I know a bit about it, of course. Do you think there might be a connection with the attack on old Judd?'

'It occurred to me once that there might be, but — ' Melissa closed her eyes for a moment, trying to re-enact in her memory the rapid sequence of events from the moment she first saw a distraught Graham Shipley at the scene of the tragedy. The spot where Cissie's body lay was a good fifty yards from the lane at the bottom of a steep bank and, so far as she could remember, completely out of sight from both the lane and the track leading to Brookside Cottage. How could Tommy Judd, in the normal course of events, have seen Cissie's shoe? Unless it had been lying somewhere else, somewhere visible from the path he normally took — which would indicate that someone had moved it. And then another possibility occurred to her, one that at first thought seemed so far-fetched as to be unthinkable and yet, if it were true, could explain almost everything. She opened her eyes and found Danville regarding her with a puzzled expression.

'You okay?' he asked.

'I'm fine, I was thinking. Look, could you

leave me alone with him for a minute or two? There's something I'd like to ask him — nothing to do with the attack on him. It'd be a waste of time trying to get him to talk about that.'

'Sure, no problem. I'll go and find myself a cup of tea.'

Melissa approached the bed and pulled up the chair the detective had been sitting on. 'Hullo Mr Judd, how are you feeling?' she asked.

The old man's eyes half-opened. 'Who're you?' he mumbled, peering vaguely in her direction. He appeared to have difficulty in focusing.

'I'm Mrs Craig. I've come to see how you are. Everyone in the village has been very worried about you.'

At the sound of her name, his eyes opened fully and he glared at her. 'I told you to keep quiet!' he said and his voice, though weak, held an angry rasp. 'Why d'you have to interfere? I'd have been all right — '

'It wasn't me who called the ambulance, it was Nurse Simonds. You were in a bad way when she found you and you'd have been dead by now if she hadn't got you to hospital.'

His jaw set in a stubborn line. 'I'm not saying nothing,' he insisted. 'I told that interfering young copper I weren't saying nothing.'

'You're talking about . . . your fall?' Just in time, Melissa checked herself from saying 'the attack.'

'Kept on about someone beating me up. Told him it were a load of rubbish. Fell down the stairs, that's all.'

'That's all right. I just wanted you to answer one question about something else.'

On learning that she was not going to press him on the cause of his injuries, he appeared to relax and even showed a mild interest. 'What's that then?' he asked.

'You remember the day Cissie Wilcox fell in the brook and drowned?'

'What of it?' At the mention of Cissie's name, his expression became once more wary and suspicious.

Convinced that she was on the verge of a breakthrough, Melissa had some difficulty in keeping her voice calm and casual as she put her question. From the way his hands clenched, she knew she had scored yet another bulls-eye.

'Get out of here. You're talking crap!' he snarled.

'All right, I'm going now,' she said soothingly. 'I hope you'll soon be better.'

He gave a surly grunt and closed his eyes.

A glance at the monitor showed an increase in the pulse rate and she hastily got up and went outside. A nurse hovering nearby came over. 'He's getting a little excited. I hope I haven't tired him,' she said.

The nurse nodded knowingly. 'It doesn't take much to get him going,' she said as she went to the bedside. 'He's doing okay, though.'

'That's good.'

Melissa found DC Danville alone in the day room, clutching a polystyrene cup of tea and watching a football match on the television in the company of a somnolent gentleman in a wheelchair. 'Any joy?' he asked.

'Plenty. Can you get an urgent message to DS Waters for me?'

'No problem.'

She sat down, scribbled a few lines on a sheet torn from the notebook she invariably carried with her, and handed it to him. He glanced at it and whistled. 'Are you sure about this? Did he admit it?'

'Only by looking guilty and ordering me out, but I'm positive I'm on the right track.'

'Let's hope you're right.'

After a brief visit to a supermarket for a few items that Mrs Foster did not stock, Melissa set off for home with a sense of achievement, at the same time conscious that her nerves had been stretched to somewhere near their limit by the events of the day. As soon as she got indoors, she told herself, she would unwind with a nice quiet cup of tea.

The weather had steadily deteriorated during the afternoon and by the time she reached home soon after four o'clock sheets of rain were being driven across the Cotswolds by a blustery gale. She stopped the car outside the front door of Hawthorn Cottage and hurried indoors with her shopping; she would put the car in the garage later, when — as promised on the local weather forecast — the rain would ease. She put away her purchases, filled the kettle for the longed-for cup of tea and while waiting for it to boil went to her study to check her answering machine.

There were two messages, the first from Bruce. 'I've just heard from a contact in the ambulance service that they picked up an attempted suicide from your village,' he said. 'I was wondering whether there's any tie-in with your case. Give me a bell when you've got a moment.'

'Not now I won't,' she muttered as she noted the call on her pad. 'There's no way I'm going to go over that lot again just yet.'

The second message, from the Reverend

John Hamley, was more disturbing. 'Melissa, I'm sorry to trouble you,' he apologised. 'I have Becky Tanner here and the poor child is in very great distress. She's run away from home because she claims her father will, to use her words, 'half-kill her when he finds out'. Knowing that you see her regularly for her French lessons, Alice and I are wondering whether you might have some idea what it's about.'

So much for my peaceful afternoon, Melissa thought as, having called back to check that Becky was still taking refuge with the Hamleys, she went downstairs, switched off the kettle, put on her coat, collected her keys, turned the car round and set off for the rectory.

'It's so good of you to turn out in this awful weather,' said Alice as she opened the door. 'Becky's in the playroom with the children and she seems a lot calmer, but we're really very concerned about her. Go in the study for a moment and talk to John while I make a cup of tea.'

'I do apologise for troubling you,' the rector repeated as he offered Melissa a chair in his cosy, book-lined den. 'We feel Becky's father should know where she is and that she's safe, but every time I suggest speaking to him she becomes almost hysterical.'

'Hasn't she given you any idea at all what it's about?'

'Not the slightest. All she would say is what I told you on the phone — she daren't go home because she's terrified her father will get violent. We can't understand it — we know he's an irascible sort, but Becky's always been the apple of his eye and it seems unthinkable that he'd hurt her.'

'It depends on how much he's found out about what she gets up to behind his back,' said Melissa drily.

The rector gave her a searching glance. 'Whatever do you mean?'

'I've thought for a long time that Becky is — potentially at least — sexually active, and I know for a fact that she's attracted to older men, partly because she once told me so and partly because I've actually seen her flaunting her charms at Graham Shipley. I expect you heard about what happened this morning, by the way?'

'Yes, Sam Rogers told me. I understand that he's out of danger.'

'That's right. I saw him this afternoon and he's had some good news about his daughter so he's more cheerful than I've seen him since he came to the village.'

'Excellent. Now, about Becky — you were saying?'

'I'm convinced she's in serious moral danger. I actually saw her yesterday, coming out of a bank in Stowbridge looking very pleased with herself.'

At this point Alice entered with a tray. While she poured tea and offered biscuits, she and her husband listened in a shocked silence as Melissa explained her anxiety over an apparent association between Becky Tanner and Gideon Lane. 'I had absolutely no idea of all this,' John exclaimed when she had finished. 'Do you suppose Mr Lane's sisters are aware of what went on at Warefield?'

'Oh, I'm perfectly certain they are, and so far they have been protecting him.'

'Perhaps they suspect him of having bad intentions towards Becky and threatened to have a word with her father,' Alice suggested. 'But surely, knowing Jake, he'd be more likely to go storming round to have it out with their brother than take it out on Becky.'

'Unless there was some reason for him to be equally angry with her,' said John, frowning. 'What do you think, Melissa?'

Melissa gave a start, realising that she had completely missed the last remark. Her mind had been racing off at a tangent as one more piece of the puzzle seemed to be falling into place. 'I'm sorry?' she said in embarrassment.

'I was thinking that perhaps, in the light of

what you were saying a moment ago, Becky isn't entirely innocent of blame. Perhaps that's why she refuses to say anything.'

'Well, she can't stay here indefinitely,' said Alice as she inspected the contents of the teapot. 'Would anyone like a refill?'

Melissa shook her head. 'Not for me, thank you, that was lovely.' She got to her feet and the others did the same. 'Shall I have a word with her now?'

'We'd be very grateful,' said John. 'If she continues to refuse to go home, I shall have to contact the social services.'

'Knowing Becky, she'd probably prefer to face her father's wrath than be taken into care,' said Melissa.

'I'll go and get her. You can talk to her in here.'

It was obvious when the rector returned with the runaway that she had not expected to see Melissa. A startled look crossed her face and she glanced nervously from one to the other. 'I'll leave you two to have a little chat,' he said and left them alone. The moment the door closed, the girl burst into tears.

'Don't let them send me home to Dad, he'll kill me!' she begged through her sobs.

Melissa put an arm round her shoulders, eased her into a chair and sat down beside her. 'Don't cry, just tell me all about it,' she coaxed. She found a clean handkerchief in her pocket and pushed it into Becky's hand. 'Was it something that happened after you got out of Mr Lane's car yesterday?'

Abruptly, Becky stopped crying. 'How d'you know about that?' she asked suspiciously. 'You been spying on me?'

'Of course I haven't. I just happened to be behind his car in the lane. And I saw you earlier yesterday in Stowbridge,' Melissa reminded her. 'Coming out of the bank, remember? I think you had some money to pay in.'

The girl's expression turned sullen. 'What if I did?'

'Did Mr Lane give it to you?'

'Might have done.'

'What was it for?' The girl's cheeks turned a dull red and she stared at her feet while twisting the soaked handkerchief between her fingers, but she ignored the question. 'Old men like Mr Lane don't usually give money to pretty girls without wanting something in return,' Melissa persisted. 'What did you do for him?'

'Nothing much,' Becky muttered.

'What does that mean?' No reply. 'Look, Becky, I have to tell you something about Mr Lane. He's been in trouble in the past for indecent assault on young girls. You know what that means, don't you?' Becky nodded, her eyes still lowered. 'Did he want to do anything like that to you?'

'Just a little. I let him,' the girl added with a flash of defiance.

'You let him?' Melissa felt her stomach turn over. This, she thought in horror, is worse than I thought.

'Why not?' Becky gave a little smirk, as if the experience had not been unpleasant. 'There weren't no harm — it isn't as if he wanted to go the whole way.'

'I see.' Determined not to betray how shocked she felt, Melissa asked quietly, 'And I suppose your father knows about it and is very angry with you — is that it?'

Mention of her father produced a startling change in the girl's demeanour. From being crestfallen and defensive, she flew into a rage. 'He'd never have found out if it hadn't been for that interfering old cow Miss Lane coming to the house. Dad were out, but she said, 'Don't you think you're getting away with your wickedness, my girl. I'll see him and show him this as soon as he gets back'.' She primped up her mouth as she gave a typical adolescent girl's contemptuous impression of an elderly spinster. 'Bloody dried-up old hag,

330

she meant it, too. That was when I took off.'

Melissa listened in a stunned silence as Becky, her reticence blasted away by fury, blurted out the rest of the story.

26

'It's such good news about Mr Shipley being able to see his daughter, isn't it?' said Alice Hamley. 'I'm sure it will make all the difference to him.'

'I'm sure it will,' agreed her husband. 'He has been constantly in my thoughts — I would have visited him myself this evening if young Becky hadn't turned up on the doorstep begging for sanctuary.' John Hamley's face was troubled. 'I was so shocked when Sam Rogers phoned to tell me what had happened. The poor chap must have been carrying a far heavier burden than we ever imagined.'

'It has been pretty ghastly for him,' Melissa agreed.

'The shock of finding Cissie's body must have been dreadful. I tried to have a word with him after morning service the following Sunday, but he slipped away before I had a chance and I had a feeling he didn't want to talk about it. I really feel I should have given him more support.'

'You can't force people to confide in you if they don't want to, dear,' said Alice gently.

'How about you, Melissa? You were with him on that awful day and I know you've done your best to scotch the rumours that have been flying about.'

'He did confide in me quite a lot and I suggested he think about having some counselling, but he didn't seem very receptive to the idea. Maybe I should have pushed it a bit harder.' As she spoke Melissa found herself sharing John Hamley's doubts about the extent of her own support. 'He had a breakdown some time ago because of the failure of his marriage and there were other problems as well. He was pinning everything on starting a new life in a new environment. Losing the job at St Monica's on account of his involvement with the police was the last straw.'

The rector nodded. 'Sam told me about that — it must have been a devastating blow. As you know, Alice and I were away with the children for a few days, but somehow I feel I could have done more for him. I'll check with the hospital and visit him either there or at home tomorrow.'

'I'm sure he'd be delighted to see you, dear,' said Alice. 'Such a nice man, I'll never believe he did anything to harm Cissie.'

'I'm glad to hear you say that,' said Melissa with a grateful smile. 'I was beginning to think I was the only one convinced of his innocence. As a matter of fact, I've been ferreting around a little on his behalf and I really think . . . no, perhaps I'd better not say any more for the moment,' she finished, aware of two pairs of interested and questioning eyes turned towards her. 'All I can tell you is that if my theory is right, it should be cleared up very quickly.'

The three of them were sitting at the table in the rectory dining-room. A social worker had duly arrived to take charge of a somewhat mutinous Becky, who had agreed to be taken to a hostel only after extracting a solemn promise that her whereabouts be kept a secret from her father. Alice had whisked the children into bed and she and her husband had insisted that Melissa stay to share their evening meal. Part of her had longed to go home and unwind in peace, but having given in to their pressing invitation she realised that it had been the right decision. In their friendly and sympathetic company she was already aware of the tension slipping away. When, after a simple but delicious supper that Alice seemed to have conjured up out of nowhere, she got into her car to drive home, she felt more relaxed than she had done for days. With any luck, the mystery surrounding Cissie's death and the attack on

Tommy Judd would be cleared up within twenty-four hours without the need for any further contribution on her part.

Her optimism received a jolt when she arrived home and found a message from Matt Waters. 'We sent a couple of officers round to interview Gideon Lane,' he said, and even before she heard the rest of the message the frustration in the detective's voice warned her that there had been a hitch. 'And what do you know?' the detective continued. 'The old buzzard's done a runner. We'll catch up with him soon enough, though. I'll keep you posted.'

As she reset the machine and plodded upstairs to bed, Melissa speculated with a certain relish as to precisely what had prompted Gideon's hasty departure. Had it been the possibility of a further call from the police, or — as seemed to her more likely to be the case — fear of a more direct form of retribution? Either way, she told herself as she put out her bedside light, I'm not losing any sleep over that old sinner. He deserves all that's coming to him.

She slept soundly for over eight hours, awoke refreshed and was eating her breakfast prior to making a start on printing the final version of her novel when the telephone rang. Remembering that she had not yet responded to Bruce's call of the previous day, she half expected to hear a reproachful reminder. Instead, a rather hesitant male voice that she did not immediately recognise said tentatively, 'Is that Mrs Craig?'

'Speaking.'

'This is Gideon Lane.'

Melissa almost dropped her slice of toast and marmalade in her astonishment, but managed to answer calmly enough, 'Good morning, Mr Lane. What can I do for you?'

'I've just been listening to the local news on the radio.' The voice shook slightly, betraying considerable agitation. 'Something about an attempted suicide in Upper Benbury. They didn't give a name — do you know who it was?'

'Yes, as it happens I do. I was one of the people who found the victim.'

'Aah!' The drawn-out sigh seemed to come from a great distance. 'Would you be kind enough to tell me — ?'

'I understand the police aren't revealing the victim's name, so I don't think I should either,' Melissa interrupted, deliberately making her voice brisk and businesslike. 'If you have a particular interest in knowing, you can always call them.'

'Yes, er, well — ' There was a silence for a moment before Lane said, 'I just wanted to know — will the poor man be all right?'

'What makes you think it's a man?'

To Melissa's glee, Lane walked straight into the trap. 'You mean — it wasn't Mr Shipley? Oh, thank God!' There was a click and the line went dead.

'I wonder,' Melissa mused as she tapped out the code for checking the source of the call, 'why you were so concerned about the fate of Graham Shipley? Guilty conscience, perhaps? We'll soon find out.' She reached for a pencil and a scrap of paper to jot down the number dictated by a precise, android-like female voice. She called it and found herself speaking to the receptionist at a small private hotel in Reading.

'Gotcha!' she exclaimed in triumph as she put down the telephone.

★   ★   ★

'Apart from the fact that Graham Shipley has been completely exonerated,' said Melissa thoughtfully, 'there are a few small crumbs of comfort in all this.'

'Oh?' Joe Martin took the cup of black coffee she handed him with a question in his dark, deep-set eyes.

'One is the fact that Cissie's death turned out to have been accidental.' She sat down in the armchair opposite him and began sipping her own coffee. 'Her mother was half out of her mind at the thought that she might have been murdered. Now she knows that isn't the case, the healing process can start.'

'Yes, I can understand that. It must have been a nightmare for the poor woman. What about the other crumbs?'

'Gary Tanner was very upset when he heard that Jean held him in some way responsible for Cissie's death, and he went to see her to explain that he felt badly because he never offered to walk her home that day. Somehow a kind of bond has sprung up between them and I think that has helped Jean with her grieving as well.'

The two of them fell silent for a minute or two, each busy with their own thoughts. They were in the sitting-room of Hawthorn Cottage after the promised celebratory dinner at the Queen's Hotel in Cheltenham. A fat envelope containing the typescript of the completed novel lay on the table, ready — once it had received Joe's blessing — to be handed to her publisher. A disc of Beethoven bagatelles played softly in the background. For the first time in nearly a fortnight, Melissa felt a sense of fulfilment which was not entirely due to the completion of another book.

'You know,' said Joe as he helped himself to sugar, 'I'm still not entirely clear as to exactly what happened. You've told me bits on the phone, but there are lots of gaps that need filling. Those two old men — Tommy Judd and the randy old choirmaster — just what did the two of them get up to, and how did it bring about the death of that poor girl?'

'They discovered a mutual interest in paedophilia by obtaining their supplies from the same dodgy newsagent in Stowbridge, and it seems they had regular sessions in Tommy's cottage where they indulged in what Matt euphemistically called 'unnatural practices'. Cissie blundered in on one of Tommy's solo performances and fled; he ran after her — not with any intention of hurting her, he insisted, he just wanted to reassure her that he meant no harm and there was no need to tell anyone — but of course she panicked. Then she saw Graham Shipley approaching from the opposite direction and fled from him as well. We know what happened after that.'

'Dreadful.' After a moment's reflection, Joe asked, 'So exactly how did the truth come out?'

'Gideon Lane finally spilled the beans, once the police picked him up. He'd taken off because he guessed that his sister Esther was going to show Becky's father the photo that she had confiscated from her brother — incidentally, that must have been how Becky got the money for her shopping spree the day I caught her coming out of the bank. Knowing Jake's temper he was scared stiff he was going to get the same treatment as Tommy.'

'Ah, so it was Jake who roughed up Tommy?'

'That's right. It seems that when the lads broke into the cottage and found the stock of porno mags, there was a nude photo of Becky at the bottom of the hole. Her brother was reaching for it when Tommy turned up unexpectedly and he left it there rather than risk the others seeing it. He returned a few nights later and stole it — incidentally, Dave Potter was there shortly afterwards to nick more supplies so Tommy had two burglars that night. Unfortunately for Gary — and for Becky — Jake caught him with the photo and shook the whole story out of him. Then he gave Tommy a going-over, took the rest of the mags and burned them.'

'Did he give Becky a going-over as well? It sounds as if the little monkey deserved it.'

'I think she got a dressing-down for allowing the photo to be taken, but she managed to convince him that she'd been doing a favour for a friend of hers, a girl doing a Media Studies course who was putting a portfolio together for an assignment she was working on. Becky claimed she must have dropped it near Tommy's cottage on her way home through the woods one day. The first part of the story was probably true, but the rest was complete baloney — Tommy admitted latter that he'd given her money for it. Jake believed it because he couldn't bear to think of the alternative. He's completely disillusioned now, of course, having found out that she's been fooling around with Gideon Lane as well. He's having to face the fact that she's a thorough little whore in the making — he's a broken man.'

'Poor blighter.' For a while they sat quietly listening to the music. Then Joe said, 'I understand it was Gideon Lane who actually found the body?'

'That's right. He was on his way to see Tommy a short time after Cissie's fatal visit and by chance he spotted one of her bright yellow shoes that she lost as she went plunging down the bank towards the brook. He didn't think to do anything about it at the time, but when he found Tommy in a state of great agitation and heard what had happened, bells rang and he went back to investigate. Knowing how steep and slippery the bank is, he was worried she might have fallen and hurt herself. He was horrified when he found her body and claimed to have done everything he could to revive her after hauling her out of the water, but it was too late.'

'It's dreadful to think how a comparatively simple chain of events could have led to such a tragedy,' said Joe. 'If only Shipley hadn't turned up at the crucial moment — '

'Oh, don't blame poor Graham. He feels in some way responsible for what happened to Cissie because he just ran away and left her to it.'

'What do you suppose he'll do now? I doubt if he'll want to go back to teaching.'

'Ah, that's one more bit of good news I learned yesterday. Sam Rogers has a friend who's curator of the Stowbridge Museum and has been looking for an assistant to organise educational courses in local history. He's persuaded Graham to send off for the application from — it sounds just his cup of tea. He's got a project he calls 'History on the Hoof' which according to Sam is tailor-made for the job.'

'Well, good luck to him. He deserves a decent break.'

'You're dead right. What makes me so angry is the way that nasty little toad Gideon Lane allowed him to remain under suspicion

342

for so long, just to preserve his own lily-white reputation. It was only when he heard about the suicide attempt and suspected it might be Graham that his miserable conscience pricked him. When I planted the idea that it wasn't Graham at all, he couldn't back off quickly enough. He really thought he was in the clear — but my final bit of detective work tracked him down.'

'Ah yes, speaking of detective work — what was the question you asked Tommy Judd that rattled him so much it made you sure you were on the right track?'

'Oh that!' Melissa chuckled at the recollection. 'I merely asked him whether he and Gideon Lane got their girlie magazines from the same shop.'

'Brilliant! I can't think how Gloucestershire Constabulary would manage to solve a single case without you!' The earnestness in Joe's voice was totally belied by the mischievous glint in his eyes.

'No need to be sarky,' Melissa reproached him. 'I'd have you know there have been times when they've been most appreciative of my help — '

' — and even more times when they've told you to keep your nose out of their cases, I'll bet.' This time Joe made no attempt to hide his amusement. Suddenly, he grew more serious. 'You know,' he said, 'in spite of all he's done I can't help feeling some sympathy for that poor wretch Lane. From what you've told me about his gorgon of an elder sister, he can't have had much chance of establishing a normal relationship with a woman. And he must have brought joy to a lot of people with his music.'

Melissa gave his shoulder an affectionate squeeze as she passed his chair after putting on a fresh disc. He grasped her hand and smiled up at her.

'Dear Joe,' she said softly as she returned the pressure, 'you manage to find good in everyone, don't you?'

'There's usually something, if you look for it hard enough,' he said.

'It's a comforting thought,' she agreed.

Their eyes met and he moved his chair a little closer to hers as the magic of Schubert filled the room.